W9-ADX-593

TALES OF
BEATNIK GLORY

TALES OF
BEATNIK GLORY

by Ed Sanders

STONEHILL PUBLISHING COMPANY
New York

MIDDLEBURY COLLEGE LIBRARY

PS
3569
A49
T3

11/1977
Genl

The events and people described herein are fictitious.

Copyright © 1975 by Ed Sanders.
Published by the Stonehill Publishing Company,
A division of Stonehill Communications, Inc.,
38 East 57 Street, New York, N.Y. 10022.

No part of this publication may be reproduced or
transmitted in any form or by any means without
permission from the publisher except by a reviewer
who wishes to quote brief passages in connection
with a review written for inclusion in a magazine,
newspaper or broadcast.

ISBN: 0-88373-029-4

Book design by Esther Mitgang

First Printing

Printed in the U.S.A.

*Most of this book is set in
New York City in the late 1950s and early 1960s.
It focuses on artists, musicians, filmmakers, and writers,
and speaks in the language and modes
of culture of the time.*

TALES OF
BEATNIK GLORY

The Poetry Reading

CUTHBERT'S SISTER, AGATHA, was tepidly torturing him over the phone for the fifth time that day. Why won't she leave me alone? "Look, Agatha, I will never agree to selling the house. My decision is final."

Cuthbert lived in a gloomy room at the Hotel Colburne on Washington Place just off Washington Square, scattered with forty or fifty dried orange peels. "Those orange peels will attract copperheads, you know"—his sister had warned him.

"Here in Greenwich Village?"

"You never can tell. I bet there's at least *one* pet copperhead in your neighborhood, with the kind of queer denizens it attracts."

Cuthbert's hair was white and almost shiny. His eyelids were pink most of the time as were his cheeks which had almost sharply defined ovals of pinkness. His upper lip lifted up and out when he read poetry. He was sixty-one. And he had been writing poetry slowly and quietly for forty years. His room at the hotel was jammed floor to ceiling with memorabilia of the literary life of the Village from the twenties on.

"Agatha, I have to click off. I'm going to a poetry reading in a few minutes at the Gaslight Café."

"Are you going to be reading?"

"Yes. Everyone will be about forty-five years younger than I—you see it's an open reading—so it should be quite an evening; either terrifying or terribly exciting. And, please, leave me alone for a few days, all right?"

Cuthbert stood naked in the center of his room, eating a cucumber, trying to remember what pile he had worn yesterday. The poet had devised a clothing system whereby he had thrown everything away except for seven complete sets of attire and had placed a complete clothing bundle every few feet around the perimeter of his room. To select his clothes of the day, he merely spotted the pile he had worn the day before, moved his eyes one pile-notch counterclockwise, and put on the bundle. In this way he found that he only had to do his laundry every forty-nine days.

The Gaslight was packed. Several newspaper cameramen were pushing people aside to get better shots. Someone whispered to the woman selling dollar admission tickets, "Is Ginsberg here?" Cuthbert had scant admiration for the beats but he certainly respected the attention—hostile, friendly, and otherwise—generated for modern poets and poetry by Ginsberg, Burroughs, Corso, Kerouac, and company. Student beat-fever was running high. Poetry readings were suddenly s.r.o. The N.Y. *Daily News* for instance had featured last week's reading in their centerfold. The New York–based newsmagazines had published several articles on the beats which, however, salivated with cynicism and deprecation, such as the article titled "Zen Hur," which ap-

2

peared in *Time*. Such garbage-jobs by the middle-class/mid-brow publications helped spew energy into the movement. For it was Cuthbert's belief that if you piss off the cultural frontal lobes of *Time Mag*, you must be doing something right. And Cuthbert, who had missed out on the Lost Generation in Paris after World War I, was not about to miss out on another successful literary generation—especially one that seemed to be such an unstoppable and interesting phenomenon. So he decided to join in, to take a shower in the same energy as the beats. What could he lose?

The reading had been advertised as an open reading of "beat poets" but as it turned out, none of the stars of beatdom showed up. About forty other poets did, however, nineteen of whom signed up to read at the sacred table of the list-mistress.

One woman was irate at the fifty-cent minimum. "We should at least get a free cup of coffee for our coming all the way down here to read," she protested.

The manager had an answer all ready. "There is some argument possible that you should pay *us* to let you read."

The poets were requested to read only three poems each, or five minutes, though most managed to eat up at least seven minutes before the nervous poets in the audience began to stare balefully and to twitch with displeasure. The owner of the café announced that there could be no applause because of neighborhood complaints about the noise. By an arrangement worked out with the police, the form of applause would be fingersnaps.

The woman leaned down close to a stenopad and jotted each reader's name upon the list which was supposed to be maintained democratically; first to sign first to read. The man in front of Cuthbert had an imperious voice: "Please

3

place me at the head of the first set"—wearing a fur-trimmed cape, silver-headed walking stick—"for I intend to read a short verse play, *Theseus and The Time Machine* and I seek an advantageous moment for its presentation, for it is a work of genius"—bowing his head, clicking the heels of his spit-shined riding boots.

As for Cuthbert, he found himself scheduled for the second slot in the third set, meaning that his ears would be long assailed with verse blizzards, not that he minded it at all for he loved to listen to poets. But he didn't want to get burned for his slot either, so throughout the reading he monitored the list-table, alert for hanky-panky. Indeed, he occasionally would observe a human approach the table, bend down, maybe smile and whisper at the lister; and lo! she sometimes would scratch out a name here, write in another there. Cuthbert did not care about the others as long as Set 3, Slot 2 remained "Cuthbert Mayerson."

Fingersnaps were somewhat inadequate to satisfy the approval-hungry needs of some poets. For a very few, when they had completed their poems, and the audience was enthused, there was a flurry of snaps like someone crashing through twiggy underbrush. But after a poet who was not well received or not understood (not humorous) there were a pitiful four or five snaps then a dissolving silence. For the fingersnaps to end even before the poet made a move to return to its table, this was painful. And especially painful to Cuthbert, who thought along this line: If the previous reader was given a mere five fingersnaps, what am I to receive, three?

Cuthbert noted that there were several poets present who wrote frantically when anyone was on the podium reciting, stopping only when there was no urging voice, as if the flowing words unleashed their own goat-pen of babble.

Other poets came fortified with an honor guard of close friends who sat at the same table protectively and when the poet rose to utter its verse, the entire table would turn their chairs to face the poet directly, would smile appreciatively and laugh heartily, and at the end would snap their fingers calisthenically and with great duration.

Set 1, Reader A: The screamer. This jarred the reading to a start. Carl Rothstein, just released from the madhouse, pointing to his shock burns, with a flat long face and wire-rimmed spectacles, his hair pulled up and back for that Aldous Huxley look, beginning with a deep voice (a feigned deepness it would seem because of the poet's extreme youth): "I have just been disgorged from the alimentary ward of Shreveport Psychiatric." At once he ripped open his shirt, the buttons popping upon the floor, and pointed to his T-shirt upon which was crudely painted: I WAS BUDDHA. Then he read:

> *My mother offered me*
> *a bobsled saying*
> *"There is the Hill."*
>
> *"What Hill?" I replied. "You mean*
> *that Mountain over there*
> *with cliffs and gorges?"*
>
> *"Go on down the Hill*
> *my son!" said she and*
> *gave me a quick,*
> *may I say rude, shove*
> *of her boot*

This was immediately followed by a piercing scream, ap-

5

parently to indicate the nature of the down-mountain bob-sled ride, which lasted, with pauses for breath, at least five minutes. Man, could he scream.

After his voice gave out, the audience was almost silent as Rothstein walked back to his table, about four fingersnaps punctuating the displeasure.

There was a jazz fingersnapper in the audience in a beret and sun glasses and a black silk scarf knotted on his neck above his Oberlin sweatshirt. He had begun to snap vigorously in abstract patterns about halfway through the scream, nodding and weaving, eyes closed, shaking his wrists like a maracas player, whispering "dig it" and "Groo-oovy!"—"solid"—"existence"—"Dhammapada, man."

After the scream, jazz fingersnapper pulled out a bottle of wine. There was a man and woman and two children, apparently a family of tourists, who sat next to the snapper. He took a swig and passed the wine to the boy of the family who hesitated, looked at his father, shrugged, took a swig, offered it to his mother and father, who said not a word, then handed it back to the snapper. The boy's mother looked like a case of hydrophobia as her eyewhites flared and mouth fell open. She shook her fist at her son, "I'll see you about this later."

Set 1, Reader B: This particular reader looked unlikely to offend, dressed as he was in a business suit with a blue polkadot bow tie knotted crookedly. The poet began, nervously holding a trembling fist of crinkled white pages. "This is titled *Nocturne Number 467*"—followed by a long pause then a deep hissing sucking of air,

> *Cloistered in the convents of our minds*
> *we pull down our pants*
> *and show our behinds . . .*

6

A titter tattered the silence. The woman from Des Moines grabbed her husband, son, and her daughter and pulled them away, "C'mon, this is filth."

> . . . *while lemon aardvarks from Jersey City*
> *invade the white*
> *undergarments of fate*

Another titter. And the poet continued. The father knocked over his metal-backed ice cream parlor chair. The sight of the family splitting upset the reader so much that he began to stammer. He regained his composure by lighting a cigarette in the middle of his poem with a metallic click-clack of his Zippo lighter followed by a fierce intonation of a doublet of religious sonnets after which he sat down.

Set 1, Reader C: This reader was popular with the throng, for he was the first obvious real-life beat poet. Poverty was written upon his face as was Zen fanaticism and the ravages of compulsive hitch-hiking. He insisted on standing on a chair to read, and doing so he bumped his head on the low cellar ceiling, but remained there nevertheless, his head having to lie upon its right side to fit beneath the ceiling. His sandals were homemade, of rope and soles cut from leather luggage. He was funny, at least the packed coffee house thought so. At this point, early in the reading, people were standing in line fifty feet up MacDougal Street waiting to get in. The police were on the scene and the manager of the Gaslight made an announcement that people could not block the exits or the aisles and that the police had threatened to call the fire department. Spectators were forced to squat along the side wall or to sit on the stairway leading up to the toilets for each table was

7

hopelessly packed. The manager sneaked all the fives and tens out of the cash register into the safety of the thick wad in his pocket, thinking "Money! I'm making money!"—urging his waitress on with an occasional goad, sell more! lean over the table! unbutton a blouse button maybe, touch the customer, anything, sell!

"This poem is called *Ten Thousand Statues of Walt Whitman on Roller Skates Hitch-hike Across America*." The title alone got the biggest laugh of the evening. He read with a moan-drone, the tone dropping at the end of each line like a passing truck.

America! *we cannot grasp the walnut.*
America! *robots with shoes made out of living gophers*
          climb from the TV dinner plates to eat your teeth!
America! *you are trying to treat me like a sewer!*
          A new Spartacus is going to grow from the mutant garbage dump at the Mum Deodorant factory and then you're gonna be in trouble, America
                    (the first laugh)
America! *your hucksters of Madison Avenue with ice-cube armpits. . . .*
          (*laughter drowned out the rest of the*
          line so that Cuthbert could not hear it.)
America! *your hulahoops form a mandorla above the Final Sausage Factory!*
          Porky Pig and Donald Duck have stomachs full of broken lightbulbs, America
America! *the A-bomb is trying to read us a bedtime story*
                    (big laugh)
Fuck Fuck Fuck,
          America
                    (bigger laugh)

8

The poet paused scrupulously at all laughs. Sometimes he'd join in and laugh also. Then he waited not only till the laughter faded but also till the smiles faded, before resuming. He was a great success, the fingersnaps were like a great bonfire.

Set 1, Reader D: The shy mumbler. This man read in a near whisper so that gradually the audience grew quiet: it became almost like a game as they leaned across their tables positioning their ears for maximum data. But it was impossible to hear; the reader was sitting on a stool and had turned almost away from the listeners. "Louder!" someone rudely yelled, which brought about a temporary rise then a long fade. The poems were like papyrus fragments:

> *. . . . . love . . . .*
> *ratchet wrench . . . . .*
> *. . . . . goodbye . . . .*
> *. . . . . unguent!.*

This was good for those who wrote their own poetry while listening to the readers, for the whisperer's lines were phantom inspirations—and his words, half heard, were permutated wonderfully in their minds.

Was it: "In spite of the late moon"?

Or was it: "Spade of the lagoon"?

Or: "Supplicated tortillas of the bent spoon"?

Set 1, Reader E: The angry witch. This poet possessed a cutting voice with overtones of shrill. By the end of her first poem her voice had risen maybe half an octave, glasses sliding down her nose because of the way she trembled.

"This poem is dedicated to my husband Roger, who is a skull by now: *Sick Bard In The Lonely Cave.*" The poem opened with notification that a kettle of tapir eyes was

9

slowly simmering and that "even the Sybil" was banned from The Cave of The Bard. The next quatrain asserted the existence of a catacombs beneath Washington Square Park where the "covening minstrels" of Washington Square North were wont to meet.

To appease the "hungry ghost" of her husband Roger, she had buried his (hopefully symbolic) teeth in The Cave of The Bard, the entrance to which was a hidden door at the base of Washington Arch, guarded by a silver baboon and six owls.

This particular poem was causing the jazz fingersnapper to beat on his table with a coffee spoon, he was so excited. The poem mentioned the Gnostic Pleroma where "broomsticks are toothpicks." "Sick Ghosts muttering Neck! Neck!" were to sprout from the teeth. Cuthbert shuddered at this line, and wound his scarf around his neck, reminding himself of his long distaste and distrust regarding the possibility of the reality of vampires, a fact that had caused him to wake up many a morning with a crick of the neck due to having wrapped his head in a protective towel during the night. Cuthbert was quite relieved when the next two poems were translations from Ovid. "Thank God for Ovid," he muttered to himself.

Set 1, Reader F: An experimental versifier who had flown in from Toronto, he happily announced, just for this august reading. His first poem was entitled *Sixty-nine Drips*. To effect the poem, he brandished a maroon gym sock filled with pea soup into which had been affixed a cocktail straw so that the soup dripped slowly from the sock through the straw into a teacup. As each drip dripped, the reader shouted, "Drip one!" then "Drip two!" and so on until sixty-nine had been reached.

The next and last poem he called *2X2 Infinity* and slowly

began to stagger forward, "Two ....Four ....Eight ....Sixteen ....Thirty-two"—varying the time-lengths between numbers. He made it to 2,097,152 before the M.C. hooked him off the stage. This concluded the first set.

Intermission involved a rapid-delivery sell of lukewarm coffee crowned with questionable whipped cream, tea, and cider with cinnamon sticks; and for Cuthbert Mayerson, the rising of the fear.

The second set seemed interminable. Everyone seemed bent upon translating into elegiac couplets their versions of the Babylonian Creation Epic. Cuthbert, nervous, ceased to pay much attention to the tonal blasts. Rather, he concentrated on the all-important final selecting and sequencing of what he was to read.

Cuthbert looked intently at what he proposed to read. All at once, right in front of his eyes, he saw at least four lines that had to be changed immediately. "Neatly, neatly"—he told himself, for he did not want to be unable to read his own stuff. Next he shuffled the order of the poems to achieve that perfect rhapsody.

But angst afflicted him: I have not read for years, for years! Am I sweating? Are my eyes red? Why is that person reading forever? Maybe I should recite instead some Shelley from memory. I wore the wrong clothes.

Certain readers interrupted his fear. A man who ran a candy store in the Bronx intoned his Image Trouvé Manifesto, based on certain poetic principles learned while stocking his candy jars prior to noontime klepto invasion of schoolchildren. There was a schoolteacher who began a poem: "Carpathian horsemen joust inside the rotating triangle"—Cuthbert thought that was the funniest he had heard, and giggled so, and was sneeringly stared at by the teacher's table of henchmen. There was another poet who

11

read at least a three-hundred-line poem called *The Philosophy of Thales The Milesian,* although Cuthbert knew, and snickered accordingly, that Thales had left not *one* extant line of work from which to draw such a fierce and lengthy poem.

There were a couple of diverting sex maniacs, one in particular who read a series of haiku relative to experiments with mayonnaise and the Bayonne, New Jersey telephone book for 1959. But it did little to allay the fears of Cuthbert Mayerson who, at that moment, would have bet the family mansion that he was to be booed from the reader's chair.

During the second intermission Cuthbert walked over again to check the reading list. Had one or two perchance moved up above him? He scowled appropriately at the list-keeper who assured him, no, no, nothing could ever alter the ordained array for Set 3. Yet, even as she was protesting her innocence, a wan poet with a W. B. Yeats/Bill Haley haircut strode up, checked the list and uttered an angry wail. "Hey, you moved my name down the list!"

The keeper was really caught this time. "Oh! Well? I looked for you and I didn't see you—I thought maybe you'd split. Sorry."

"A pitiful excuse"—the man replied, stalking back to his chair.

As the assembly was hushed for the beginning of the set, Cuthbert suddenly became aware of a painful fact. Whereas the Gaslight had been packed for Set 1, the several hours intervening had seen the place become half-empty. And more were oozing toward the door each minute. To make things worse, the first reader had left his table to approach the podium carrying an armload of work that had to consist

12

of at least a thousand pages. "I'll never get to read!" Cuthbert exclaimed.

The man commenced. "The work I shall read tonight is a section from my life-long endeavor, *Voyage of the Sun God, To Brooklyn.* It is rather lengthy, so I shall read only the final and culminating six hundred lines. The sentences in Gaelic will be numerous and represent the Seventy-eight Commandments from the Sun God to the people of Brooklyn. I shall translate the Seventy-eight Commandments at the end of the poem."

The introduction alone caused about ten patrons to lunge for the exits. A shudder passed among the remaining poets, stomachs churning, fearful, eager, taut fingers on black springbinders.

The man read like a tent revivalist, raising his fist, moaning. Even his frantic performance could not stanch the flow of fleeing feet. Cuthbert was caught, helpless; wanting really to leave, yet tied to his chair with desire to read.

At last it was Set 3, Slot 2. Cuthbert Mayerson read slowly, his coin-shaped pinknesses of cheek aflame. His upper lip jutting out pointedly; sonorous was his voice chanting his short, subdued, and symbolic poems of paidopygophilia. The audience was very appreciative of his work and afforded him the only actual handclapping of the night, a temporary violation of rules that sent the manager rushing to the front door to see if any police were outside.

At last it was over. A woman approached Cuthbert, "Say, I liked your poem."

"You did? Which one do you mean?" Cuthbert was all smiles.

The woman paused, a cheek-muscle twitching. "Uh, the one, uh, about America."

"You mean the last one I read, *The Barefoot Moth?*"

13

"I guess that was the one. It was the one that received all the applause."

Cuthbert walked happily up MacDougal Street toward his hotel, where, depositing his poetry, he decided to reward himself for bravery; so he proceded to Sheridan Square, grabbing the IRT Uptown to 42nd Street and a refreshing saunter.

The Mother-In-Law

WHEN SHE MARRIED the dirty beatnik, the calamity of it spiraled upward and outward though the extant family tree. That a girl of impeccable family, destined to marry well and wealthily, beautiful, conversant in three languages, with nine years of piano study behind her, should stoop to wed a mumbling, shabby, poetry-writing person with an unknown family from an unknown place, perhaps Nebraska, was a profound shock that sent the parents into a numbed period of consulting the police, lawyers, private investigators, and laws involving insane asylums.

As for the beat poet, he didn't care. The parents were just another couple of notches on the stick of squares. This was his attitude: They do not exist. And if they try to exist, I will travel with their daughter, my love, where they do not. And this was the message he once bothered to convey, after which there was no message from the accused beatnik to the parents, only silence.

The bazooka-spews of hostility, however, began years before the wedding. They met in a café on MacDougal Street in late summer of 1959. He was more or less the resident balladeer at the coffee house and was busily occupied that summer organizing a series of Sunday afternoon poetry readings at the café attended by the finest talents of beatdom.

The day they met she was dressed Being & Nothingness ballerina beat. Her long blond tresses were pulled back into a bun, and there were wonderful golden bangs in front. She wore black dancer's stockings and black high-heel spikes with those stylish spear-toes. Her brown leather vest, with laces up the sides, was the rage of Bleecker Street, worn over a tight black turtleneck with no brassiere, the ultimate of boldness in 1959.

Her eyes were Nefertiti'd with great Juliette Greco streaks of kohl and lots of green eye shadow. No one would have ever, she was anxiously certain, thought *she* was a tourist from Queens. She *knew* she looked like an authentic Villager.

They sat and talked for eight hours that first mesmerizing day. They agreed to meet after school the next day. And then the next. And the next.

Well, to dress the way she did was one thing, her parents reasoned. After all, it *was* New York and not some whistle stop. But to begin to, to, to hang around with, and god knows what else with, a filthnik in Greenwich Village, well that was unacceptable to parents, grandparents, uncles, aunts, and cousins in the sprawl-lands of Flushing, New York. They banded together, the family, to ban the nascent love. She was seventeen and her eighteenth birthday was only two months away so they had to move fast.

They wrote, they phoned, they sent telegrams to the beatnik, to his parents, to the school. They hired investigators. But all threats passed right through the young lovers' consciousness into the tunnel of chaos. The parents tried to in-

16

sist that she transfer to an out-of-town school, a classic technique of parents who dislike the loves of their son or daughter. Fuck you, she countered, I'll just not go to school.

They ran away the Christmas vacation of '59. They tried to check in to the all-male derelict hotel on Bleecker Street and were laughed out of the lobby. They stayed up all night in a Times Square movie house watching *The Blob* and *I Married a Man From Outer Space,* over and over. The parents called the police on New Year's Eve with a missing-person report but the officer asked them, "How old is she?"—followed by "Does your daughter have a boyfriend?" Since she had just turned eighteen, there was nothing to be done.

They prowled the "beat scene"—frankly starve-eyed, looking for a rational salvation. They wandered the streets, caressing each other in the open day, living that famous final line from Auden's *September 1, 1939* with every lust-spackled muscle. There was no poetry reading, no art show, no film, no ritual of abandoned filth, no concert in an obscure loft, no lecture, no event of sufficiently rebellious nature, that they ever missed.

And the Fourth Avenue bookstores! How many hundreds of afternoons they spent in the twenty or so dusty stores with the worn wood floors; noses whiffing that excellent store-air, a mixture of dust and floating minutiae of antique leather bindings and frayed linen. What a heaven of data, to stand on a rickety ladder at the top of a fourteen-foot wall of out-of-print verse!

Their main problem was no place to plank. His landlord at the 11th Street rooming house would not allow guests of any gender up to his pitiful closet, and he could scarcely afford the rent plus deposit plus deposit for lights, to get his own pad. The parks of New York were their boudoir. They planked in them all. They were the only ones who had ever

17

made love under the streetlight in the midpoint of the arching stone bridge near the Central Park Zoo, according to the policeman who broke up their coupling at a most urgent mutual moment of just-before-groinflash oblivion; ears aware of the approaching footsteps of Eros, but not of gumshoe.

They tried it, lying up against the little jungle-gym park in Washington Square after the park was closed. They planked on the cinder riding track near 72nd Street on the west side of Central Park and were interrupted by police horses—again at a critical moment. They planked sports-car-style on a bench at 72nd on the *east* side of the park (the same night as the cinder track interruption).

They loved to make it in Inwood Park. One New Year's Eve they climbed high in the rocks above the Columbia University boat basin at the north edge of Inwood, and were lean/lying on a steep icy incline between huge boulders—when, right in the middle, they began to slide, were unable to break it, but still kept fucking, and her buttocks were treated to fifteen feet of thrillies down the twiggy glaciation.

That incident was absolutely the last straw. They sold everything they could lay their hands on, and hocked and borrowed, and with the loot rented a small pad on East 3rd Street and Avenue B, which caused a further useless shrill shriek from the parents.

When he dared to drop out of school for a semester, the hatred of her family nearly got him in trouble with the Feds. The father learned of the drop-out and wrote a letter to the FBI sternly complaining that a scurrilous draft-dodging beatnik, who had missed a charge of statutory rape by a mere two months, should be flouting the law by not attending college while still enjoying an exemption from the draft. Why did the FBI hesitate for even one minute—the father raged—to arrest this communist beatnik churl? Or why was he not forced immediately to join the army?

The letter did stir some attention directed against the beatnik on the part of the FBI. They visited the Lower East Side pad of the young lovers who luckily were not home.

The procedure of the FBI in those days was standard when they found the person not at home. They slid a three-by-five index card under the door, bearing the following thrill-producing message. They wrote at the top the full legal name of the "subject" with whom they deigned to babble; under which they wrote, "please contact Special Agent Edward Barnes, Federal Bureau of Investigation." Under that was the FBI phone number and the agent's extension.

The poet, of course, had not known that the father had sent in the letter. Eerie Police State fears crowded his mind. The pot in the pad was flushed immediately. Was it some sort of crackdown on beat poets? Absurd. He had signed a petition urging clemency for Caryl Chessman—maybe that was the reason for the visit. Whatever the reason, he was haunted by the phantom sound of handcuffs and the sound track of the FBI radio show.

He telephoned the agency and they asked him to bop up to the FBI office on East 67th on a little matter regarding his draft status. Uh-oh. Uh-oh and terror.

He was interviewed in a cavernous room full of desks and agents. They informed him they were not out to "get" him or anything but that, once requested from the chain of command above, the agents were required to file a report. He assured them that he was going to be back in class the very next semester, carefully attempting to paint a picture of his future father-in-law as a trembly-fingered nut.

Because of her father's letter to the Feds, the couple felt

19

it reasonable to assume that the father had written to the New York police also, perhaps a letter about drugs. For the next several years they hid their grass in carefully prepared stashes. They used, for instance, the hang-the-bag-of-pot-out-the-window-on-a-string stash with a razor blade nearby. Another stash was the pot-on-string-hanging-above-the-toilet stash. It was boring to have to take such precautions, but it was very common at that time. The couple knew one fellow who had a dog trained as a living stash-of-grass-gobbler, should the fuzz raid. In fact, during the beat era, one of the considerations when deciding whether or not to take an apartment, was the presence of built-in stashes such as crevices, shaftways, etc.; or how long the door would hold up in a dope raid.

The next crisis occurred when they got married, at which time the family considered putting her, or him, or both, into a nuthatch. An uncle in the family was a doctor. There was a lot of phone pressure on the uncle to look into committing the beatnik, "to save Marie" the mother cried, tears dripping on the receiver. In response to this the beatnik sent the message, You'll never take us alive, into the family tree and things grew quieter.

Children eased the hatred. For his part, the poet wrote and was silent. Faced with a total cut-off in seeing their grandchildren, the parents began to soften up. They could all walk down vomit alley was the poet's attitude after the years of warfare. If they got on his back, he decided that he would snarl or glower and say nothing whatsoever. A sneering, glowering beatnik dressed in weird rags was a match for many a middle-class mom visiting the slums for a peep at a grandchild.

So the years of poverty roamed past, roach-ridden, garbage-strewn, happy with rodents. Sometimes they were re-

20

duced to using T-shirts for diapers, unable to afford the disposables. Once they seized the T-shirt of a visiting National Book Award poet, right off his back, just days after he received the award, to use as a diaper.

On occasion they gathered their first editions of poetry and novels and sold them to the rare-book dealers. They were always getting writers to sign their books. At poetry readings at the 92nd Street Y, they usually managed to hang out backstage grabbing the 'graphs, man. A *signed* first edition, ahhh that was a pleasure.

In rare desperation, he joined the line of humans at the Third Avenue Blood Bank to get his arm sucked for the ten-dollar pint. Ten dollars: $1.98 for Chux disposables, four packages of spaghetti 70¢, one box spinach egg noodles 35¢, one pound ricotta cheese 69¢, sugar, potatoes, gallon milk, eggs, three marshmallow cookies at Gem Spa, two cans beer, one cola—and they had a bare three dollars remaining. That meant tomorrow was another partial day of schemes—but schemes interspersed with hours of mimeographed treason, learned chit-chat in Tompkins Square Park, four distinct hallucinations, numerous strolls in the direction of the Fourth Avenue bookstores, and f r e e d o m.

As the years went by there began to occur the phenomenon of the shopping bag. That is, when the mother-in-law made her occasional quick Saturday or Sunday afternoon visits to the squalid, enemy pad, she bore shopping bags of largess. Often she would pick stuff from her own pantry, wild "Bohemian" substances like ungobbled tins of palm hearts, Streit's brand chocolate-covered matzohs, pickled watermelon rinds, or partial boxes of kasha. But the shopping bags also contained staples such as diapers and milk and sugar. The mother-in-law apparently never threw

21

anything away. One of her thrills was to present to the grandchildren baby clothes that the mother, her daughter, had worn at the same age. Ditto for toys and dolls that had belonged to the mother twenty years previous.

Occasionally the mother-in-law would show up in the middle of a political meeting, say for the planning of a demonstration, and some of America's most notorious radicals, men and women on whom the government spent millions bugging, harassing, auditing, and burglarizing, all would shift apart in silence as the mother-in-law walked through with the bundles of choff. The father-in-law was the last to soften and remained rather intransigent in his hatred of the "beatnik punk with no excuses." Once he even injected green vegetable dye into an unopened gallon of milk brought to the hovel on a shopping-bag Sunday. They opened the milk later. There is nothing quite like pouring a glass of fresh milk and viewing green fungus juice from Mars coming out of the spout. But gradually even the father began to calm down and to tolerate the marriage.

There was no hovel, no geodesic summer dome in the woods within driving range, no junkie-ridden tenement so foreboding as to prevent the m-i-l, carrying thirty-five pounds of raw produce, clothes, notebook paper, vitamins, magazines, in two or three Care Packages as the couple called them, from climbing up however many flights of steps it took.

In the summer of 1964, the couple and children spent several months in the woods off a logging trail in the Catskill hills near Phoenicia, New York. They were living in an old striped party tent from somebody's Long Island estate, above which were second-story sleeping quarters in a clear plastic-roofed tree house. They lived in fond desolation for several weeks until one Sunday afternoon they heard

22

skwonch! skwonch! skwonch!—approaching footsteps in the twigs and dry growth, as toward the tent, laden with protein and cheer, walked the mother-in-law.

As the years passed, they were not surprised to learn that the phenomenon of the mother-in-law as the Demeter of Bohemia, was widespread. Wherever writers and artists banded together to struggle, they were present. All hail the mother-in-law.

Total Assault Cantina

I AM WRITING this from the valley of shrieks and the alleys of despair. The cellar in which I live is damp—brown roaches shine on the wall posts in the candle glare. I am sleeping on a bunch of rags bundled up in buttoned despicable shirts like rag torsos, eight of them, my bed. The food which I consume is garbage. Occasionally I go to the breadline. As I write I look about me and see nothing to which to look for specks of hope. Only filth, only mobsters hiding out in orbiting algae farms, only chop-snuff. I hook the newspapers, wet with slime and yellowed with egg, from the garbage cans and when they are dry I lie down on my floor to read them. And I am disgusted. And there is nothingness. No rungs in the ladder of whiteness; for no longer is there any ladder—but only two poles remain, the rungs are shattered—and the poles are used upon the shoulders of mourners to carry the dangling bodies of defeat home to squalor.

My landlord is a verminous crook. He raises the rent on my cellar without mercy. May he die in rush-hour traffic. No,

24

may he live. I don't care. It doesn't care. The Milky Way is nothing to know. The floodlights of the concentration camp have not yet flooded through the windows of my wet cellar, and I don't care. *Grex* is the Latin word for herd. Grex hex sex specks flecks.

I have thought about crawling about or crumbling supine, maybe strapping roller skates to my forearms and shins and scuttling thus, beating the pavement with small boards. But they would put me away. They might. And I remember well what Judith Malina told me so many years ago: Never do it alone, always conspire.

I want to describe for you my cellar. For I have memorized it and the Xerox-like replica of it in my mind is just enough removed from reality that I can bounce fondness-beams upon the page in contemplation of its image. It is dirty, wet, shiny with roaches; the two windows are narrow, located at the top of the front wall; they look like small New York curbside sewer grates. I can hear the feet stomping my metal doors and if I stand on my chair I can watch the legs walk by. To garner warmth I merely open the furnace-room door and a humming breeze lightly cuts the chill. There is nothing to report about the floor other than when the concrete was poured no one bothered to scrape it to a level condition. It is blobby, wavy, stinky with fifty years of coal dust and blotched with the garbage of my forays.

I was once a rising author. The reviewers used to look forward to reading my "next novel." My creations are on my cellar shelves; I had not much to say other than to urge the rebels to stand up in the slice-lines, take it, struggle. And now rotting springbinders hold the cobweb-streaked pages of my youth. What was it? It was a bitter mingling, brothers and sisters. And time is not the guide. Quiet despair. Quiet desperation. Quiet! I screamed till they knelt down to look

25

through the slits into the cellar. Then I lay still. Maybe I shall walk to the New York Public Library to continue my all-important ten-year research into narco-hypno-robo-wash. It doesn't matter. For I am sorting through my files. And as soon as I have them thoroughly ordered, I shall find a university to accept them and maybe then I shall eat grass and live upon the roadsides of America, a plastic container with a moldy spoon of potato salad here, a plastic container with a leftover onion ring, a small untouched ketchup pouch, there. This is what I tell myself. Then we shall roll, brothers and sisters, then we shall hear the trumpeteers and saxophones again.

There is a purple grape shining between the thumb and forefinger of Dionysus. There is an olive in the fist of Demeter. But in the fist of the monster on the front page is the sigil of robot war. I am grunged upon by that monster and sorely affrighted.

There is an ancient bale of hay down here in my cellar, black and greasy with grime. But the baling wire still holds it together. This hay has been here for twelve years, ever since 1961. I laugh whenever I sit upon it to read. For it reminds me of the Total Assault Cantina and of the time twelve years ago we threw a bunch of rifles into the East River that had been smuggled into the U.S. by a gang of right-wing creeps. Ha ha ha. Now that was a caper.

You see, the cantina was located on the floor right above the cellar where I now dwell; that is to say, on Avenue A at 11th Street. Don't bother to look for the remains of Total Assault Cantina now, for the building has been burnt out for years. After the cantina folded the Mafia used the place for years to store jukeboxes. Then they set fire to the place in an insurance scam.

We were crazed with the strange release granted to us by

the civilization. LSD was years away for us but already we were driven specks of foment. We were walking ergot. But no one was so driven with urgency in those days as the proprietors of Total Assault Cantina. They felt the need. They burned to struggle for the socialist revolution. They beat their fists into their palms considering ways to further the nonviolent struggle. Both were in their early twenties at the time; both had grown up in New York City. John McBride was thin, nervous, with a thick red mustache and short red brown hair. Paul Stillman was more relaxed, meditative, with his hair drawn back and knotted behind him.

Together John and Paul operated the Total Assault, a nonprofit establishment intensely dedicated toward yanking the corpses of J. P. Morgan's neoconfederates through the amphetamine piranha tank. It was just that way—their agitation kept them walking acrobatic along that perilous thin path of roachclips—one side of which lay Gandhian ahimsa, the other side bitter street battles and the violent insurgency of a potential New York Commune. The personalities of the two operators of Total Assault whirled in intellectual combat on the question of tactics. Both wanted to crash that TV tower off the top of the Empire State—but their approaches were somewhat different. It was sort of anarcho-Mao v. anarcho-Tao. The budda-budda-budda of machine gun fire for John became Buddha Buddha pacing rebels for Paul. Both were convinced for the time being, however, that nonviolent direct street action was the correct Way to proceed.

The first café they had operated was a tiny place on 9th Street between B and C. They had called it Cantina de las Revoluciones. They managed to float for about a year before poverty and debt forced it to close. Then they located a much larger space on Avenue A and 11th Street, comprising a whole ground floor with a courtyard. The rent: $100 a month. It was eternity.

It wasn't long before the license inspectors came around, and that meant instant trouble, because John and Paul did not cooperate with the concept of licensing. "Gonna close you down," the inspectors told them. "Can't sell food without a license."

"We are revolutionaries. Taxes don't exist. The Department of Licenses doesn't exist. Why don't you sit down and help us with the twelve-cent soup?" But the licenseers gave them a summons and would not help with the circle of friends peeling vegetables for the Gandhian ambrosia.

Soon they were forced to trek down to the Dept. of Licenses to fill out the forms. They wanted to call the restaurant Café Hashish, a proposal that was immediately banned by the red-tapers. "We're going to the Civil Liberties Union to see about this, you fucking fascists," Paul snorted after a long argument with the officials of the department. But there was nothing to be done.

A few days later they tried again. They were ushered into the office of Mr. William Karkenschul, deputy director of licenses, Liberal Party appointee, a human who was at that time trying to close down coffee houses which offered poetry readings. Mr. Karkenschul read from the notarized business form: "Hmmm, let's see"—mumble mumble, "John Z. McBride and Paul A. Stillman d/b/a Vomit, a Restaurant." Karkenschul stared at the two. "You mean you want to start a restaurant called Vomit!?"—a slight curl of revulsion lifting his lip. "First you come in here last week trying to name your dive with an illegal name, now it's Vomit. Is this some sort of game?"

"Look here, Karko, we *want* to call it Vomit. Now what about it?"

"It cannot be allowed," he replied. "The public won't stand for it."

"How about The Karkenschul House of Puke?"—Paul sneered. That suggestion got them thrown out of the office. "You, Mr. Liberal Party poetry-banner! You show us the regulation that says we can't call our restaurant Café Hashish *or* Vomit, or anything we want!!"

A few days later they were back at the Dept. of Licenses with a name that sailed through the bureaucratic ocean: Total Assault Cantina. The License Dept. blitzed them repeatedly. They seemed to inspect them once a week. I had a friend that brought the cantina a stationwagonful of hot cigarettes from South Carolina once a month. They were almost caught by the license creeps who certainly would have snitched John and Paul out to the Feds. We carried the taxstampless cigs down into the cellar in the nick of time. As it was, the licensoids required John and Paul to obtain what was called a "License to Act as Retail Dealer in Cigarettes in the City of New York."

When they began to hold poetry readings, Karkenschul picked up the announcements of the readings from the *Village Voice* and sent raiders out to issue summonses, informing the two that they'd have to cringe and beg for a cabaret license if they wanted to continue poetry. There was, and probably still is, a law in New York that allowed entertainment in a restaurant by no more than three stringed instruments and a piano: allowing *no* poetry and *no* singing. Otherwise, a cabaret license was necessary, a bureaucratic nightmare involving bribing building inspectors, and requiring employees to register with the fuzz and to carry cabaret identity cards, and so forth.

Another thing that pissed off the authorities was that Total Assault was unable to resist allowing people to sleep on the floor although it drove the landlord nuts. The police would shine flashlights through the front window in the middle of the night and the floor looked like a packed meadow of sleeping bags. Crashers could only cop about six hours sleep however, because John and Paul had to wake everybody up by 10 A.M. in order to sweep and to get the breads in the ovens in time to open for the noon-hour soup rush.

Total Assault was more of a community center than a mere café. A bu-gaze across the room revealed a kitchen containing a quaking Salvation Army icebox, a huge oven, storage cabinets made of packing crates, and a long varnished-pine serving counter. There was a whole wall devoted to collages and bulletins, leaflets and the like, and in the back near the courtyard was a printing-press area marked off by beautiful black Chinese screens, the origin of which Ptah only knows. There was another wall crammed with bookshelves. The Peoples' Library, as John called it, out of which the people steadily drained the books ne'er to return. There were numerous found-in-street divans placed around a large central table for those who liked to dine reclining. The walls were spotted with can-lids nailed over rat holes. The more serious breaches were sealed off with a mixture of Brillo pads and plaster. Near the front window was an old upright piano, stacked atop which was a neat pyramid of sleeping bags for the nighttime mattress meadow.

With regard to the wall devoted to leaflets and collages, by the end of a year there were maybe a thousand leaflets, new overdubbed upon old, from floor to ceiling. In my cellar I have a box containing all the posters and stuff from that wall. Come and get me, New York Graphic Society.

Meetings meetings meetings, they must have held a hundred meetings a month at Total Assault. They held a *New York Times* Sneer-in every night at 7 P.M. where everybody took turns singing and declaiming articles from that day's edition, accompanied by great jeers, chortles, and spits of anger. The ten top stock advances of the day were soundly jeered. And when the market went down a few points, there was a tumult of applause. Sometimes when the market really went bad, Paul would put a sign in the window announcing the good news.

I used to love the Town Meetings on Tuesday nights. They were wonderful shouting matches and many a grandiose scheme was hatched in the air. A free medical and dental clinic was born out of these meetings and still thrives, but much of it was kiosks of ego-babble, though I got to practice my yodeling a lot when the debates grew laborious.

In spite of the good Dharma-commie karma, the cantina was a fiscal disaster. There was a prophetic sign above the cash register reading: THERE WILL BE NO PROFIT! The biggest money drain was the food-scroungers. There was a porcelain bathtub in the window in which John and Paul created a huge, daily vegetable salad. Next to it was a crock of free tea and another crock of soup. People seemed to drift in the door with glazed eyes like food robots and would serve themselves from the salad tub and soup crock, then there would rise the quick slurps of filling stomachs, after which they vanished without paying. There were so many hungry. But there were a lot of people with plenty of cash lining up for free food also. I must confess that I too, shekels clanking in my pockets, also ripped free hunks of rye and bowls of soup from Total Assault Cantina. At first they tried to hand customers chits but these were left damp upon the tables or used to wipe up spills. Each day John and Paul cooked fresh bread. Humans began to steal whole loaves. They would saunter in, order coffee, and whistle out the door with a loaf, and on the way home from work at that.

31

The cantina was written up in one of the Sunday magazine supplements as being a "groovy place to get delicious free food." That nearly caused a riot. People were driving in from New Jersey to score free beatnik chow. There were hundreds lining the sidewalk and packed inside. That's where John and Paul should have cleaned up, maybe giving a little free soup and charging for everything else. As it was, people were spilling into the printing area where I was working and it pissed me off because we were trying to print some draft cards and fake I.D. for draft resisters at the time. So, to put an ebb to the weekender spew, we printed up a disgusto menu featuring things like eyeballs au gratin and frog-ani skewered on toothpicks and we taped ten or fifteen copies on the cantina windows facing out. Then we filled the salad bathtub with a concoction of Martian cookie-toss that was genuinely disgusting. We cut the heads off a few dozen realistic rubber snakes and plopped them in the gruel, adding doll heads, weeds from the park, a couple of rats, with a sign taped to the tub: FREE.

I ran the print shop, where we specialized in protest posters, poetry mags, draft cards, I.D., & leaflets. I worked hard and they would come in from the streets to babble in my ears for hours as I zombi-stood at the press. Strange people with involved tales. There were those who insisted that immediately I drop everything and print a book of their verse, or a resumé, or six years of diaries depicting their experiments in Zen-Sufi trance-dance in Arabia Petra. I was even supposed to pay for the paper. Then I got into trouble with one of the local street gangs—I forget their name, maybe the Face-Axers, something like that. They really got angry; I wouldn't let them use the printshop tool kit to work on their zip guns. That night the front window was caved in.

There was no money to fix it and certainly no insurance

so it was a find boards in the streets scene. About this time there was some sort of drug panic and the junkies stooped so low as to rob Total Assault. They stole fifteen "tuned" gongs belonging to The Celestial Freakbeam Orchestra. They stole the electric soup-heater from the front window. They stole my electric typewriter, but left the offset; probably it was too heavy for them. When they raided, late at night, they were surprised encountering the zzz-ing mattress meadow so they tied and gagged eleven people and left them zipped up in their sleeping bags. In a further dour overdub, the phone was stomped after a so-called friend made a four-hour call to London and didn't tell anyone about it. Poverty was imminent; John and Paul tallied their main debts:

gas/electric	60
paper bill	80
lumber	160
2 months rent	200
food	200

"Now, how are we going to make seven hundred bucks?"

"I hope it's not going to be a Times Square ankle-grab scene"—Sam joked.

They held an emergency hookahside scheme session. First they contemplated the traditional Brentano's art book rip-off scam. But who could carry seven hundred dollars worth of Skira and New York Graphic Society publications? Next they seriously considered a nonviolent bank robbery. They spent considerable time trying to compose a note to be handed to the teller which a) would reassure the teller, b) would in fact cause the teller to fork over the money, c) would *not* result in their immediate arrest. But there was just no way nonviolently to rob a bank.

One thing they did do right away was to hold a benefit poetry reading, one of those 8 P.M. till 4 A.M. versethons where thirty-seven poets sat nervously waiting to read. That raised a punkly seventy-five dollars, although it was a great thronging social success. Someone left a flute packed to the mouthpiece with amphetamine under a table which they quickly sold and the night's take was upped to a hundred and ten bucks. They thought of selling the printing equipment but why have a revolutionary cantina if you can't print?

The next afternoon John called his aunt in the Bronx. The family had a produce business at the Hunts Point Market where Total Assault had managed to run up a sizable bill. John wanted to hustle a few more weeks of foodstuff from his aunt and in the course of the conversation she told him, "Larry's in from Hong Kong. He's been trying to get in touch with you. He wants to talk to you about something."

Larry's in from Hong Kong meant there was dope around, for cousin Larry regularly brought in lots of hash and grass when his ship returned to New York. Aunt Mildred gave him the number and a balking approval for vegetable credit. John called Larry right away, "Got any hamburger?"

"You bet I have," Larry replied. "Listen, I been trying to get in touch with you for three days. I'm in a desperate situation. Can we meet?"

Larry grabbed a subway to the Lower East Side and conferred at Total Assault, offering a deal that would save it. If John and Paul would store ten hundred-pound bags of compressed grass for one week, Larry and his confederates would pay them a thousand dollars.

34

"Whoopee!" Paul shouted. "Ra is hip to us!!"

"There was a foul-up," Larry told them, "down in Memphis, and they can't pick it up till next week. I have some other, uh, deliveries, to make and I just can't wait around in New York. Where am I gonna put it, in dad's potato bins at the market?"

The deal was simple. All John and Paul had to do was to hold the dope safe and dry until a certain individual would drive up in a red van and announce himself with the code phrase, "Agnus Dei." With an ahem, Paul asked for a small advance against the thousand dollars and cousin Larry forked over two hundred dollars!!

Late that night, trembling with paranoia, they unloaded the heavy bags down into the cellar beneath the cantina. A few hours later, Paul began to swear that he could smell pot-fumes oozing up through the rather open floorboards. Maybe it was paranoia, but John and Paul both soon thought the pot smell was overpowering. Early the next day they borrowed a truck and drove out to New Jersey where they bought a few bales of hay which they placed in the cantina as "sofas"—hoping the hay fumes would cover for the grass. For double protection they picked up some hundred-pound sacks of flour, pinto beans, and peanuts which they lugged down to the cellar to cover the sacks of dope.

Exactly a week later a man appeared and said, "Hi, I'm Agnus Dei." It was broad daylight.

Paul threw up his hands and said, "You mean we have to load up the hamburger in daylight, in front of a streetful of people!?"

"No"—laughed Agnus Dei, "I'll be back at one A.M."

And so by dark of night they loaded the half ton of grass into the red panel truck. Talk about fear. They scanned the streets again and again. Each passing auto was the Feds.

35

Footsteps were copsteps. They frenzy-finished the job in about two minutes flat.

The man handed them their eight hundred dollars. "See that box?"—the man winked. They looked into the van and saw a packing crate behind a partition. MADE IN HONG KONG was stenciled on the side.

"Yeah, what is it?"

"There are fifty automatic rifles in there for the Operation Thunder people." Operation Thunder was a racist right-wing paramilitary outfit in the Midwest that operated in the early sixties, later branching out into political assassinations.

"They're paying us a hundred bucks apiece."

John and Paul looked at each other. Paul asked, "How are you going to get the weapons to them?"

"I don't know nuttin. All I know is that I'm supposed to park this van at Twenty-third and Seventh Avenue and leave it overnight. The Thunderbolts, or whatever they call themselves, they'll take care of the rest."

"Let's steal the guns"—Paul whispered as soon as the van had split.

"Yeah, let's dump them in the river."

"But, how will we carry them? We can't load fifty machine guns into a cab."

Then they remembered the ancient pushcart outfitted with bicycle wheels that had been in the cellar when they first rented the place. They raised the iron cellar doors and grubbled in the boards and debris in the back of the passageway till they found it. Forthwith, they trotted with the pushcart up to 23rd Street and Seventh where they found the van parked on the west side of the avenue. It was empty, except for the Hong Kong packing case. John smashed the back window and opened the door.

"See if there's a tool kit in the front."

36

"Yeah, here's one."

"Give me a pry."

They crow-barred the crate-top open enough to see that there were in fact rifles inside, but the box was so heavy they couldn't even move it an inch. John stood on guard duty keeping an eye out for right-wing creeps. Paul removed the lid and started hooking out the greasy weapons. "What'll we do with them?"

John spotted a manhole cover right behind the panel truck. He pried away the cover and said, "Here, in here, we'll dump some in here and cart the rest, whatever we can carry, down to the river."

Paul handed out armloads of the weapons to John who slid them down into the hole. "Make sure they're barrel down. We don't want the workmen to think that any might go off in their faces."

When they had thrown enough away so that they could budge the case, they oof'd it out and onto the cart. They nailed the lid back on and then it was a paranoid sprint to the East Side. They raced to 23rd and Avenue C, then down C to 14th, then to 10th, hanging a left on 10th and they hit Avenue D in a full panic'd gallop. Uh-oh: straight ahead was the East Side Highway. Zzzzzt zzzzt! the drunken midnighters whipped past. They grabbed the gun box and hernia'd the rifles across the lanes in a sweat-bath scene. They dropped the box on the far side and raced back to the cart, carried it across and heaped the box back on it, frantically looking for an entrance to the park which lay between the highway and the river. They sped south and finally found a path, oops, it dead-ended in a handball court. "We should have brought a flashlight"—Paul groaned, trying to stop the cart before it crashed into the wall.

They spotted a murky opening that seemed to lead

37

through a ballfield with the river just a couple of hundred feet away. Huffily they pushed the cart through center field on the way to second, to home, to the dugout and aha! to a gate at the water's edge. Armload by armload they hurled the rifles into the sewery East River. This done, they collapsed on the ballfield. It was an hour before they could move.

Far, far into the night they celebrated, heaping hookahs of praise upon their lungs, triumphant over the puny smugglers of The Order of Thunder.

It was another year before Total Assault Cantina went bye-bye with the waning desires of the proprietors to face the hassles. Paul left the city and now lives down in Arroyo Aeternitas, New Mexico, whence he has sent back word that he expects to be reincarnated into a pine tree.

John is still +6, but he is caught in the knowledge that they send poets to insane asylums in Russia. "I know I won't be able to live in my own revolution," he wrote me just the other day.

Myself, I began to live in the cellar several years after the Mafia insurance fire. You might say I stumbled upon it. You see, I was working as a part-time research reporter—a stringer they call it—for an uptown newsmag. I was getting a hundred bucks for every report I filed, which was more than adequate at that time, to provide me the leisure to finish that "follow-up novel" that the critics had assured me in their reviews they were eager to encounter. Anyway, one night I was out researching the post-hippie disaster area of the Lower East Side—you know, for one of those Where Have All The Flowers Gone articles. I was tottery drunk from investigations in Pee Wee's Bar, and I staggered down Avenue A at 2 A.M. past the old Total Assault Cantina. John had told me that some of the hay from the grass-caper was still lying in the cellar, so I lifted the metal flaps, lit a match and stumbled down the steps. Then I passed out. And so it was. I loved the friendly cellar, once I had defeated the rats and water bugs. I approached the landlord who thought I was crazy but gave it up for forty-five a month.

And I am still living here probably even as you gaze. I am typing this account with my typewriter atop the hay bale from the past. But it is now my dinner time. And I am going to push up the metal flaps and emerge upon the street. Then it's off to the pizzeria on St. Marks Place and a grovel at the source of sources: the white round-topped metal wastebin with the shiny aluminum flap that says PUSH. The wastebin is always crammed with yummy eighths of pizza hunks smushed into those squares of greasy wax paper; not to mention an occasional tablespoon of grape drink hovering in a crushed cup.

In fact, I'm usually dining from the pizza trashbin every evening about six o'clock, if any of you who used to hang out at Total Assault should care to drop by and nibble on the past.

Chessman

HE SWITCHED ON the radio. Oops, it was news. It was hard to dial what he wanted, namely some jazz and some horns, in the guts of his smashed sidewalk radio residing in a shoebox.

Caryl Chessman, convicted on May 22, 1948 on seventeen out of eighteen counts of kidnapping with bodily harm, robbery, sex abuse of two women, and auto theft, will die at ten A.M. on Monday in the gas chamber at San Quentin prison in San Rafael, California, a few miles north of San Francisco.

Chessman was known as the Red-Light Bandit, prowling lovers lanes in Los Angeles County using a red spotlight to capture his victims who thought he was a policeman. He has steadfastly maintained his innocence in the twelve years he has lived on San Quentin's death row where he wrote his best-selling book. Governor Brown had granted a sixty-day reprieve to give the California State Legislature a chance to enact laws against capital punishment, but the reprieve is fast running out and the legislature has failed to act.

40

*The odds are very great that Monday, Chessman will get a
lungful of the peach-blossom fumes of potassium cyanide . . .*

He switched it off, a shuddering fantasy of death-gas rising. "Poor Chessman"—he muttered, still slightly zonked
from a late night mesc drop and a morning of fitful energy
spent memorizing the opening verses of *Out of the Cradle
Endlessly Rocking.*
He decided to get some air, so he hit 4th Street for a
stroll to Tompkins Square Park. He spotted his friend Scoobie and Scoobie talked him into walking over to the West
Side, Sheridan Square, to cop some gage at J.A.'s—a popular
scrounge-lounge of the era located where the Prudential
Savings Bank is now. They walked together in the loping
high-speed hipster manner of the time, almost a run, across
the tundra which separated the East Side from the West.
As they passed the Sheridan Square Bookstore, someone
handed Sam a leaflet announcing a protest march the next
day against Chessman's execution—the march to proceed
from Columbus Circle down to Washington Square to be
followed by a rally at the Judson Memorial Church.
Sam stopped to read the leaflet; Scoobie stood nearby
blowing a complex solo through a tight funnel of rolled
newspaper. "Y'know, Scoob—I think we're going to have to
march for Chessman"—depositing the leaflet in his jacket.
For years Sam had read about the Chessman case. Even
after tens of articles and broadcasts, it was hard to understand just what Chessman had done to require him to have
to take that final toke. It was like in the fifties trying to find
out, by reading *The Arizona Republic,* just what it was exactly that J. Robert Oppenheimer had done to lose his security clearance.
In Chessman's case, the newspapers were filled with

41

veiled contra naturam babble—of "unnatural acts" the Red-Light Bandit had forced upon his victims. Much was made of one woman who later was sent to an institution, supposedly wrecked in mental health by Chessman's depredations.

The law under which Chessman had been sentenced to death had been removed from the books during the twelve years he had spent on the row, so Sam figured Chessman was being gassed in the name of an hallucination. The state of California was spending hundreds of thousands of dollars to enforce a death because of a forcible act of oral intercourse?

There was a world-wide rise of anger about the impending execution. The Pope was upset. The foreign press railed against it. There were thousands of letters and petitions flooding into the state of California protesting its little metal octagonal death-cone. Sam's brother-in-law was typical of the attitude of most New York demi-liberals. "Oh, of course capital punishment should be abolished. Certainly it should. However, it should be abundantly clear that Chessman should not be the test case for abolition. He is an atheist. He is a sex fiend."

Hope springs eternal. As a matter of fact, the very afternoon that Sam and Scoobie were walking from the Lower East Side to Sheridan Square to cop, out on the West Coast Stuart L. Daniels, editor-in-chief of Prentice-Hall, the publisher of Chessman's successful books, was having a conference on death row with the author. After the conference, the editor was asked what the meeting was about. And Mr. Daniels replied, "Believe it or not, he wanted to discuss his writing plans for the future."

Nineteen sixty was an election year, and, as such, certainly not a time of visible pity for any supposed Red-Light

Bandit. For instance, in early April 1960, the Union of American Hebrew Congregations sent telegrams to the seven men mentioned prominently as possible candidates for the presidency. Richard Nixon replied that he dug capital punishment for kidnappers: "While we naturally must be concerned about the lives of the criminals that we take, we have a greater concern for the lives of innocent people that might otherwise be taken by criminals if they did not fear this deterrent."

Sam bricked himself out of bed in time to subway up to Columbus Circle for the Chessman march. Sam had never before considered that he would *ever* have taken part in a protest march. As a first experience, it filled Sam with an unutterable urge to march again, to sing again, to protest again. Here was an opportunity to confront the pieces of shit that had ruined it all. The signs were as neat and clear as any Sam would ever encounter, ABOLISH CAPITAL PUNISHMENT, SAVE CHESSMAN, and LEGAL MURDER IS ALSO MURDER. There was a truck bearing a cardboard representation of a death-row cell that went along with the hundred angry and remorseful humans marching at 2 P.M. along 59th Street past the ritzy hotels, waving at the banqueteers at The Plaza tabbing their lips with napkins and gazing down upon the walk. "Come join us!" they yelled. "Join us!"

The march grabbed a right at Fifth Avenue and then it was a slow three-hour trudge down the avenue fifty-one blocks to Washington Square where Norman Thomas and Elaine de Kooning addressed a rally at the Judson Memorial Church. It was young Sammy's first flash of solidarity. His first coordinated anger-flash lined up at the barricades. Little could he guess the thrills the sixties had in store for him, in the matter of sneering and tumbling at the gray barriers.

For Sam, the rest of Saturday was a profligacy of hash, bistros, and yakkety-yak through filters of filth. Sunday, May 1, 1960, was a dry day of listening to the radio. And the Chessman media watch, peppering the airways with snuff bulletins. It wouldn't go away. Sam was nervous, feeling his first twinge of social-protest frustration. He felt like the whole continent was going to the chamber.

Out in California, Chessman gave a press conference and said it was fifty-fifty. If all should fail, Chessman announced, "I intend to walk in and sit down and die."

Also on Sunday, A.C.L.U. lawyer A. L. Wirin visited California's Governor Brown to ask for an additional stay of execution pending a new justice for the California State Supreme Court who would be installed on June 1—maybe the new justice would change the four-three vote on the court that had three times snuffed Chessman's various appeals. Episcopal Bishop James A. Pike also asked Governor Brown for mercy but Brown told them to go jump in the lake.

Steve Allen, Marlon Brando, Shirley MacLaine, Eugene Burdick, and Richard Drinnon, all went up to Sacramento to ask Brown to continue the stay until the people could vote in November on the question of capital punishment. Brown said that such a stay would abuse his power and violate his conscience. After the Brown refusal, the lawyers for Chessman had a quick dinner and airmailed a last-minute appeal Sunday night to Washington, D.C. for the U.S. Supreme Court.

One hundred college students walked twenty miles from San Francisco to San Rafael Sunday night in order to vigil for Chessman throughout the night.

At 5 P.M. Caryl Chessman was taken from his sixth-floor death-row cell to the elevator in handcuffs clipped to a leather belt. He was taken down to the first-floor "holding cell" to spend his last seventeen hours of oxygen. "I'll see you in the morning"—he told his buddies on the row as he left—a traditional adios given by the condemned as they go down for the final seventeen.

There were two holding cells a few feet away from the eight-sided gas chamber. Chessman was given a new pair of blue trousers, a blue shirt, and cloth slippers. Walking to the holding cell, he was unable to see the gas chamber (so merciful was the architect) located down a small hallway to the right.

Throughout the night, throughout the morn, Caryl Chessman worked on legal papers and wrote his final letters. When they came for him in the morning, he merely put down his pen and prepared to die.

The state supreme court met to consider a petition uttered Saturday morning for a writ of habeas corpus but again voted four-three against it, at 9:10 A.M. of the morn of death.

At 9:25 A.M. an attorney asked the court for a stay to appeal the decision to the U.S. Supreme Court. Again the motion was denied, four-three.

At 9:55 attorneys Gordon T. Davis and Rosalie Asher in the chambers of Federal District Judge Louis Goodwin, requested a brief stay of gas. At the same time, Justice William O. Douglas, having received the airmailed papers in D.C., sent word of denial of stay of execution.

However, Judge Goodwin sent two clerks to tell his secretary to put a phone call through the warden at San Quentin to effect a stay. It was approximately 10:03 A.M. The phone number was sent along orally and was misdialed by the secretary. Frantically the number was correctly ascertained and the call made again but the assistant warden at Q told her that the cyanide pellets had just been dropped.

At San Quentin, the place was jammed with spectators. There were sixty witnesses in the witness room, two-thirds of which were radio, TV, and newspaper reporters. Half of the execution capsule jutted into the witness room. There were oblong windows through which to peer into the capsule. There was a sign: POSITIVELY NO SMOKING INSIDE, which was positioned by the entrance door to the green witness room. A handrail was on the outside of the exposed half of the gas chamber, with the sign: KEEP OUTSIDE RAILING AT ALL TIMES.

They all got snuff-pay. The warden as chief lord executioner received one hundred and twenty-five dollars according to the exact ritual. The lieutenant in charge received fifty dollars. The guards, responsible for seeing that the victim proceed orderly without freak-out into his seat, seventy-five each. The chaplain fifty.

On the morning of the gassing they unlocked the front door to the gas chamber. The door was oval shaped, as if the prisoner were stepping aboard a demon airline. The guards checked the chamber for airtightness, for verily not they nor the warden wanted to get wasted by cyanide seepage. Inside the chamber were *two* metal chairs, adorned with fabric shackles, so that two by two the state could, in event of mass executions, perform more serviceably.

The "cyanide eggs" were carefully counted and wrapped in cheesecloth. An officer with rubber gloves hung the cyanide death-balls on mechanical arms beneath the chair above the acid buckets. They measured the acid and poured it into the receptacles that channeled it later into the buckets, so that when the eggs were dropped the prussiate of potash would spew up the peachy fumes. They checked the phone line to the death chamber to see if it worked properly for any possible last-minute reprieve.

Precisely at 9:50 A.M. the warden of San Quentin and the chief medical officer came to Chessman's holding cell. The warden read Chessman's full legal name, and announced the gas hour. The warden shook Chessman's hand and left with the doctor. Chessman's last words to the warden were to deny that he was the Red-Light Bandit.

Prisoners used to be allowed a couple of shots of whiskey in the old days prior to their execution; now they are offered downers and an all-American cigarette and coffee. The guards made one last check of the door to the gas chamber—opening and closing it—to be sure and sure again of a perfect seal. The death-watch guards took a green carpet from the cell adjoining Chessman's and rolled it into place along the ten-foot passageway between his cell and the oval door.

Then it was time to change clothes. The guards walked to the victim's cell to supervise it. The doctor joined them. The victim stripped. The heartbeat was located. A beat-detector was strapped upon Chessman's chest. He then put on a white shirt with the black rubber tube of the detector dangling out. He donned fresh blue denim trousers. No underwear because of shit fit. No shoes, but he was allowed stockings.

There was hope all the way. After all, Dostoevsky was given a reprieve even as they lined him up in front of a firing squad. Chessman said goodbye to the prison chaplain, then walked out of his cell, with four guards accompanying him. He turned right and walked along the green carpet to the chamber, stepped up over the lip of the entrance and walked to the right chair and sat down.

The fabric straps were tightened, one across chest, one over his legs, one over forearms. The detecto-tube was hooked to another tube which led into the wall and connect-

47

ed to a stethoscope in the room where the doctor would monitor the beats. They finished the strapping. One guard touched the victim's shoulders and said "Good luck." The legend is carried that a guard usually says, "Take a deep breath as soon as you smell the gas—it will make it easier for you."

The door of steel was closed and screwed tight. The doctor stood poised with his stethoscope headset and clipboard and split-second timer clock. Chessman looked to his right and saw two reporters through the viewing windows and mouthed a final message: "Tell Rosalie I said goodbye. It's all right."

The victim faced the doctor and the prison warden who were stationed in the so-called "Preparation Room." Eye-to-deatheye contact and the spectacle of a coughing, drooling, vomiting victim, could be avoided by lowering venetian blinds placed on the windows of the Preparation Room looking into the death-cone.

At 10:03:15 A.M. the warden nodded to the sergeant who pulled the lever dropping the cyanide pellets into the acid—plop plop. The victim heard the plop and the plop. About ten seconds later Chessman took a breath and slumped into unconsciousness, head nodding, the heartbeat in the headset wild and erratic. At 10:12 he was pronounced dead. The doctor noted the time on the clipboard and took off his headset. The witnesses signed the register and filed outside.

In New York City, Sam was sitting in the library by Washington Square Park, checking out some books, when suddenly he glanced up at the clock. It was 12:59. He gritted his teeth and filled out the library slips. A minute later he began to fantasize about the execution which was occurring right at the moment out in San Rafael. He began to mutter and to curse. The librarian was staring at him.

"Do you know what they're doing *right now*! They're gassing Chessman! Those goddamn killers." The librarian said nothing but turned and saw the light on the book-elevator and trotted over to pull out some tomes.

The Cube of Potato
Soaring Through Vastness

I

THE STEAM CABINET bore the oleaginous outer form similar to an old Kenmore washing machine, the gritty quakes of its shakings slightly disturbing the shiny parquet floor-sections beneath it. His secretary was reading Keats to him as he sat in the pure heat: images of dark castle halls and silken bedrooms from *The Eve of St. Agnes* bounced billiardlike within his steam-heated noggin. Emil Cione, the author of the slightly arrogantly titled Pulitzer Prize book of verse, *Am I Goethe or Am I Schiller?*[1], was working on his biology, "my body-tones," preparing for the symposium. His body-tones were of a great concern to him, for certain female graduate students had taken to gazing barfishly at his flaccid ectomorphic body pouched with asthenic bar blubber.

---

[1] Or *Am I Nothing?* as the tome was known in the basement poetry section of the Eighth Street Bookshop.

"How much did they say they were paying?" he asked, interrupting the poem just before the lovers 'scaped the castle.

"Two hundred dollars."

II

"How do I look?" asked an anxious voice in another part of the city.

"Like Copernicus, Cheevy, like Einstein," replied a soothing word-stream which once again pointed out his whispered likeness to the great men of science. "Like pale glaciers on bearded mountains . . ." But the word-stream was unable to continue after that particular image, and swirled against the dam.

"How do I sound?" Cheevy asked several minutes later, interrupting the bardic wail he assumed for such occasions, practicing from his triple-spaced all-in-caps opening statement for the Symposium on the Death of the Beat Generation. He was sure he needn't have asked—for not in vain had he slaved those many hours droning into the tape recorder, mutating his public speaking voice, deepening and thickening it. And now, on whim, he could attach a groovy Russian Orthodox choir bass line to his normal voice—a voice which usually veered dangerously close to rhinowhine. Voice reworked however, he declaimed with the sort of deep throat-drone for which, in later decades, NBC would pay a bundle to narrate documentaries on the wild world of jackals. At the same time, Cheevy's detractors viewed these attempts to sing along with Mel Torme as mere ludicrous jiveass wheat-stalk-in-mouth Shakespeak.

He severed his Torme torrent on a sudden. "Actually, I'm quite glad these bastards are dead—these fried-shoes boys—

51

these little sniffers after Rimbaud—A figurative death, of course," he continued, looking up with chin agrin at his wife's somewhat worried face, to reassure her.

III

Throughout the day of the symposium, editor of fiction Doris L. Malek was busy in her small cubicle at *Cuff & Collar, The Magazine for Men* reading through the 275 short stories, and more than elated at not having to spew an eye on the crinkly, fluffy seven-and-a-half-inch-high pile of poems and cover letters, that had piled up during the week.

Every now and then she uttered a shudder and a tsk tsk and a sneer sneer. There wasn't, she weened, a decent act of amatory culmination in the entire collection of veiled erotic desperation—goddamn fakers!

IV

The rest of the panelists were mulling the muffins of eternity.

Warner Cleftine went to a party at the Living Theater in the late afternoon, but couldn't get close enough to Judith Malina to try to impress her either with his brilliance, or more preferably with a mix of lust/brilliance/admiration/importance.

John Farraday couldn't find Sy Krim at the San Remo bar, so scrounged for an hour and a half at the Figaro reading the French newspapers on the long poles.

V

Now nodding, now shaking their heads, they read the offset announcement, fresh from the morning mail, describing the agenda for the symposium. At the bottom of the flier was a hasty note inviting them to a presymposium cocktail party at the faculty club.

Others would have felt proud to be among the security-cleared few beckoned to the party, but not Al and Ron. Both waxed facially baleful and sore of thought. Jaws of angst pressed molar tooth-roots down into the pained canals.

"They're not serious," one whispered.

"They are," the other replied.

"Stupid fucking punks! They sure are eager to kill it off. The most significant literary event since Pound hitch-hiked into Venice, and they couldn't wait to pull the bell for it!"

His friend was torrid with agreement. "I am certain," he began with a slow, almost chanting voice, "that it is appropriate forthwith to enact a feasibility study relative to Operation Potato Salad." Both broke at once into Hunchback of Notre Dame belfry cackles.

Shortly thereafter, Al and Ron paused at the glass counter in the front of Smiler's Deli on Sheridan Square, bent upon indecision. The dilemma was whether to buy two pounds of oily German potato salad or the other variety creamy with mayonnaise.

They chose the whitish mush-gush for its photogenic qualities, for its great skushiness, and the certainty that it would adhere with smeariness to the skin. Al caressed the white cardboard container with the wire handle, lost in trance-thought. Ron bought the paper plates.

A few minutes later they were practicing hurling plates of salad at the bust of Homer in Ron's apartment.

VI

It was a cold and bitter night. The wind was nearly as exhilarating as the amyl nitrite they were popping in the taxi.

53

VII

In the lobby of Furie Hall, the Crabhorne Bookstore had set up a small but rather interesting beat generation book booth. There was a painted-over Ace Books metal rack packed with publications like *The Beat Scene, Casebook on the Beats, Howl,* various City Lights Pocket Poets, *Beatitude, Semina, Black Mountain Review,* numerous Jargon Press publications, *Kulchur, Yūgen, The Shriek of Revolution, Marx-Ra, Gone Muh-Fuh Gone,* and other booklets and mimeographics of the day.

Leaning nearly perpendicularly upon an easel was an elegant velvet-covered gold-handled board 'pon which were pinned a history-will-absolve-me collection of twelve letters from publishers stating thanks-no-thanks to the manuscript of *On The Road*—a bit irritating and a bit overpriced at 350 dollars.

Almost like a carnival stall, there was a "manuscripts published in heaven" section—complete with its own little marquee, where one, under close surveillance, could view the original manuscripts of Edward Dahlberg's *Garment of Ra,* Ginsberg's *Sunflower Sutra,* Corso's *Vestal Lady,* the beautiful Reed College calligraphy of some early Phil Whalen, and the rather out-of-place editors' correspondence and annotations regarding publication of the book, *The Beat Generation and the Angry Young Men.*

The owner of the store was kept adance here and there tidying book piles, flashing his eyeballs back and forth in a closed-circuit-TV goniff-sweep—ever attentive to potential bibliokleptoi, i.e., tome-grabs. A sampler woven of Alka-Seltzer wrappers was sewn upon his soul. For the Crabhorne's rule was this: the very same poet who sells you a signed otherwise unopened *A Lume Spento* may very well lift your mint-condition *Pomes Pennyeach* on the way out.

Business was brisk. Oddly enough, the symposium was held, as if belying its funerary theme, at the beginning of the era of that mysterious rise of library beat-buy. Suddenly there was oozing oodles of mon in the budgets for the college libraries to buy beat relics and manuscripts. Even on the night of the Symposium on the Death of the beat Generation, a full run of the magazine *Beatitude* was sold to a representative of the Ohio State University Library for $25.00. The curator of the Harris Collection of the Brown University Library—wince, Howard Hunt, wince—spent a small fortune that night on early Ginsberg letters. An inscribed first-edition *On The Road* (to Martin Buber) with mint dust jacket brought $17.50. Throughout it all, vectors of Parnassus abounded as several poets stopped by the booth to autograph the piles of their books.

VIII

Emil Cione arrived with an obedient but otherwise cynical bevy of graduate students.

IX

The symposium was sponsored by *Foment Magazine,* which for thirty-seven years had lead all periodicals in its promotion of excellent literature and liberal, almost demi-socialist thought. *Foment* was so nearly radical, in fact, that the CIA-Literary-Complex passed it by in offers of grants and crypto-stipends. There was one period of years after the war during which few would have cared to enter the Café Figaro without the latest *Foment* tucked 'neath the axillae of their jackets, protruding enough for the cover to gain cognizance.

It was impossible for pulse-grabbers at the throat of culture to deny the beats. The information in the minds of the editorial board of *Foment Magazine*, however, was bedded in the enormous spew of mass attention paid to *Howl* and to *On The Road* and to the congeries of poets who had converged in the midfifties in San Francisco. The living thrill of it, the spirit of it, the birth and sweaty foment of it, had escaped the ken of the *Foment*ers. And there was a real hesitance—one might even call it embarrassment—even among the genuinely sympathetic—to bestow garlands of respect upon a coterie of "neo-Buddhist roamers who suffer visions." Beatificism therefore was criticized with a sort of golden worldliness and quote-clogged mockery—but a wary mockery with plenty of exit signs, for a critic would want neither to appear a square, nor would want to be adjudged in later history to have been a sea-tide of whale dooky, as were the brusque critics of Keats.

That is, one had to continue to cull the attention of the querulous young, didn't one? And, if one didn't want to lose the young's respect, one couldn't very well be in the position of hurling garbage and leaflets down upon the stage in the middle of a Tristan Tzara poetry reading, could one? For everyone was aware of the frequent fate of literary garbage-hurlers: that later years, even later centuries, find plenty of case-files opened on the garbagers, and plenty of pens poised ready to garbage the garbagers. All considered, the editorial board of the magazine deemed it suitable to hold a gentle wake, as it were, in honor of their recently deceased b. g. comrades.

The format of the Symposium on the Death of the Beat Generation was as follows: The first half was devoted to the origins and social etiology of the generation. The panelists were to have delivered hopefully short opening statements followed by a round robin of comments by the panelists in response to each others' remarks. Then there would be a twenty-minute intermission, certainly the high point of any such event, with opportunities to gossip, relive the past, climb climb climb, and to stare with abandon, face upon face.

After this, there was the second half, devoted with loving tenderness to the roots of demise, that is, to the alleged dissipation and dissolution of the b. g. Then the panelists would receive questions.

It was felt there might occur considerable acrimony from the floor, so within the program for the symposium deposited on the Furie Hall seats was a blank sheet for questions. Just before the event began, editorial scheiss-slaves wandered down the aisles collecting the sheets.

The thick pile lay shortly later upon the moderator's central position, as if it were the thickery of the *Foment* morning mail. He glanced at a few, and winced.

"Is there a sense of God still to be portrayed in modern fictional analysis?" the first sheet asked.

"Will the sky-brain survive the supernova?"

"Did the atomic explosion at Hiroshima destroy any human souls?"

"Why was Norman Podhoretz not invited to be on this panel?" And on the same sheet: "Why did Mr. Cione, when he was employed as manuscript reader in 1954, refuse to urge Random House to print the great American novel, *Spine of Ferrous Willow?*"

"Good God," the moderator spake curtly, "it really *is* going to be one of those nights."

We cannot here depict this Intellectual Beatnik Wake in

full—for we want, in this tale, for you to have time to attend the party after the symposium. You can however, obtain the microfilmed transcription for about $2.50 from the Library of Congress, where the CIA Poetry Operations Division, after analysis and inspection, has deposited it.

First of all, it is necessary to know a few details about the panelists and of course about the partisans of Operation Potato Salad. And you must not think it rude of us if we point out certain spastic mis-chips in the facets of their diamond souls.

Panelist A: Doris L. Malek. So-called "acid wit."— scriptwriter, editor, novelist, alky. An atheist by ascience. She is always careful to be publicly bored, because "it's all been done before." Chosen for the panel, and willing to attend, because of vague memories on the part of the choosers of her flaming youth among the poets and radicals of the early twenties. Museum basements were amply supplied with oils of Doris Malek in the Rebel Girl mode from the Greenwich Village Cafeterias.

Her secret, alas to report, is that she is a compulsive snitch; has written maybe five hundred letters, particularly to J. Edgar Flabflab, snitching out various "crimes" of her acquaintances. With the growth of drug use, she has enjoyed glorious snitch-years.

Panelist B: Emil Cione. The prizewinning author of books of verse every three years. He has had one successful novel, *The Mountain of Reason,* which missed the prizes, because the central characterization lead to litigation, based as it was on the private life of a leading literary critic who had dared to dribble spittle on Cione's first book of verse, in the *New York Herald Tribune.* But that is a story for another occasion. Cione is a real-estate dealer on the side, an interest picked up in his youth when he had taken a graduate

58

course on the pre-Socratic philosophers, and had learned of the famous olive scam of Thales the Milesian.

For a jive snickerer had approached the eminent mathematician and astronomer, and had regaled him: "How come, if you are so smart, you are poor and hutbound?" Thales thereupon scanned the winter sky and determined that there was going to be a heavy olive crop. He paid deposits on all the olive presses in Miletos and Chios, and when the crop indeed was superabundant, he rented out the presses at rip-off rates and made the mon. Cione was ready to tattoo this vignette on his forehead.

"My olive presses are all the buildings of upper Broadway. I'll own them all!" Cione told a horrified friend. Some of the finest verses ever to grace a CIA-sponsored magazine were written by Cione standing in county assayers' offices reading old maps of property lines, trying to locate the so-called "litigious few"—i.e., a few feet of borderline controversy o'er which to go to law.

Cione took too much amphetamine to have time to become an alcoholic—that would come later, when he kicked A in terror after his toenails dropped off. His politics, so he bragged, were similar to Pindar's and Simonides'—he was a cold war poet among c-w poets. His feet were swathed in the russophobic ice. But perhaps we are being unfair, for he did have softness of heart for every one of his students, and cried over the comrades of his youth.

He loathed dirt. He shuddered with disgust at the concept of the "sweaty moil," of brutes mating on mattresses to the pierces of insectual saxophones. Dirtiness was his fear. The dirtiness he *knew* suffused the backroom communist cell meetings; the dirtiness of North Beach fingernails; and above all the dirtiness of the Dirt Road—as the bulgarian aperture was known on Times Square. The thought of a

59

membrum entering an anus—an act sometimes lauded in Beatific verse—such a thought, through its repetitious occurrence in full-color dreams, nearly sent him into a nuthatch. In fact, the CIA psychiatric profile on Cione indicated existence of a recurrent dream wherein a stubble-faced beatnik, breathing on Cione's neck with Chianti vomo-fumes, forcibly buggers him while forcing Cione at the same time to hold in his own hands and to read aloud Podhoretz' article, "The Know-Nothing Bohemians," from *Partisan Review*.

Panelist C: Corgere "Cheevy" Samuelson. Alky. Fifteen hundred empty pocket-sized Seagram's 7 bottles are filed in the unused basement furnace hidden from wife. Cheevy was America's great expert, when it cared about such things, on the proletarian novel. His career had begun in such radical splendor that New York Red Squad agents, disguised as poets, followed him from cafeteria to cafeteria in the Greenwich Village nights of the Great Depression. By the era of the symposium, Cheevy had changed. Fear of being found the color pink caused him to shit in terror. After all, where could he store his twenty-seven thousand books if he had to go on the lam?

He maintains a secret admiration for Stalin and the Chinese Revolution, but has sublimated his sensitivities so that he no longer writes poems about hobo camps in the Midwest while sitting in the Yale University library. In later years, while waiting patiently for a magenta astral projection above the White House, he has grown rich from a family-operated chain of bookstores in college towns.

We must feel kindly toward Mr. Samuelson, for he nearly cried that night in desperate inner unhappiness because Viking Press had just that day rejected his book of essays—and the snickering word of exultation had not even snickered yet to those on the panel.

Panelist D: Warner Cleftine, the editor-in-chief of *Foment Magazine*, and moderator of the symposium. His whitened hair arose in a beautiful Conway Twitty-like puff above his smooth bulging forehead. Compulsively serious. He was fired up with hatred for injustice, and a few years later no one was more effective in arranging the financing of the moratoria against the war. He was adept at getting his friends out of the draft by phone calls to his friends and former college mates at the Agency, till 'Nam soured friend against friend.

Warner could set up for certain writers 730 straight days of financial security and social grace by mystic and unknown means of which they received that great one-two of a Guggenheim Fellowship one year, followed the next by a Rockefeller Fellowship. Ahhh followed by Ahhh.

He was a specialist in invitations to government-sponsored conferences. A packed suitcase lay 'neath his bed at all times.

Panelist E: John Farraday—the nearest thing to a beat that could be cajoled upon the panel. Farraday was more of a hipster tough guy than a beat. He attached himself eagerly to the energy of the movement, but was not a believer—sort of like those humans who waited until 1970 to struggle against the Vietnam War.

Farraday felt, for instance, guilt at not being able to write spontaneously. Each paragraph took days; it was not the creative agony of Joseph Conrad, but rather it was "why? why? why?" muttered over and over, head leaning on the Olivetti.

It was strange that Farraday had agreed to appear on the panel. Some ascribed it to the pressures of his literary agent. Others that he had been asked while drunk, forgot, and was horrifyingly reminded by a thank-you letter from *Foment.*

61

He did have a self-defeating urge to insult, which may have supplied the reason—as spice for a possibly tepid evening.

His secret: He is a twenty-sixth-degree member of a sect of Kali worshipers. Will his real mother, to whom he is intensely attached, find out about the Big Mother? Alky.

The two provocateurs of Operation Potato Salad were not from heaven. Al was a notorious rakehell and trouble lover. "When in doubt, riot"—this was his principle apothegm. Above his writing desk, inflaming his mind, was Degas' *Absinthe Drinkers*, a lifestyle he ever strove to emulate. At the time of the symposium he had a secret wife hidden in ratcage poverty in the Bronx with four kids. His salvation, he felt, was in the following: Even if I'm a punk, a poor father, a profligate, and a piss ant, if my *Verse* is there, then history will not empty out its offality upon my impish ways. Do you dig how they couldn't destroy Poe, man?

Ron, the second provocateur, was an outstanding translator of Persian verse, and an excellent poet in his own versestream. One thing might have hindered his meteoric career in translation and poesy: his fetish requiring the devoration of cockroaches. O, come now! Do not avert your head in disgust! It's not as bad as that. After all, does not Emil Cione lick the cold cream off used broom handles?—which is equally as questionable an act.

The trouble began with traumatic experiences suffered on Wilderness Survival Training for the U.S. Airforce, where, after his secret supply of Milky Ways had run out, and futile searching for small beasties at streams, he ate in the moist crackly cafeterias beneath rocks. And in the wonderful words of William Burroughs, "Wouldn't you?" Any hardshelled bugs will do: preferably the protein-rich June bug. In New York, however, the song is "Cucaracha."

Time and time he is almost caught, by his wife, by his

boss. Clandestinity always won, for he knew all too well if fashionable literary circles should hear the merest hint of poet as roach-eater, he would be finished. The Apollinairean Poet as Prophet was at last acceptable, but not *un poête insectiphage*. (The reader will take comfort to know that the urge was yelled out of him in an Esalen encounter session in 1967.)

x

By crowd-noise standards, it was a low roar. The panelists were in place. Water was poured in the glasses. The notepads were placed in front of each chair. The microphones were checked by a number-mumbling attendant. All was of the stone steps leading up the ziggurat of truth. And Warner Cleftine, editor-in-chief of *Foment Magazine*, whizzed a "humph" into the microphone, followed by the tinkle-tankle of his watchband against the water pitcher, and the low din subsided and nine hundred babbling faces pivoted toward the stage and the table and the poised minds there behind it.

Cleftine began. "We are gathered here to discuss and to analyze and hopefully to come away with better understanding of a recent kind of literature strongly mirrored in the magazines and newspapers and faintly mirrored in our cultural soul." He'd advanced just that distance into his statement when John Farraday rose from the table and began to pace in an oblong ellipse on the stage behind the panel. The muttered curses were not picked up by the microphones. Farraday probably had intended to leave the stage getting the hell out of there; yet he was somehow held in orbit—unable to break away. Throughout the symposium he either paced, or sat near the wings, swigging

63

a tequila flask with the curtainman whom union rules demanded to be at hand.

"Balzac Balzac Balzac!" Farraday muttered from the pacing. Sprinkled in the audience were ten or fifteen young professional novelists—professional in the sense that they were not poets who as the times grew rough dialed their minds into prose instead, for bread, in dread: brain dead. These properly cool rising novelists, hungry for the blackedged best-seller box in *The New York Times* Sunday literary section—all smirking, look at that pitiful Farraday up there! Look! I am not there. I! I! I! I!

There was an embarrassed group in the audience of Farraday's publishers and editors, the Maxwell Perkinses of his career, who thought he just might be a tube of one-shot lighter fluid. They refused to print his manuscripts in the order of composition. The era of Dickens is over, young man. Instead they urged him to write a quick book on the private lives of the creative poor. "Your experiences, young man, write them up, but with logic, syntax, normal punctuation, and believable characters. Then you'll be rich, son; you can learn to die in every climate in the world, following the sun . . ."

After Warner Cleftine's opening remarks, the evening sputtered forward. The learned comments of the panel were noticeably intertwined and the staff upon which they were twined was this: that the cortege bearing the body of a literary movement—whe'er Futurism, Vorticism, Imagism, or beatery—is a sadly beauteous sight. The audience therefore heard the beats praised as a "bellwether" against "cultural polio" and against "creeping paralysis and tepid conformity."

Cheevy Samuelson had an interesting analysis of the b.g., comparing it to the era of the Dadaists in Zurich and Paris 1916–26. As Mr. Samuelson began to speak, one could view in the front row the famous magazine reporter writing in his legal-sized yellow his sneering notation of Cheevy's "Cuban beard, so fashionable these days among those who admire Dr. Castro."

"Like the Dadaists," Cheevy slowly spoke, "the beats wrote a few interesting books—influenced a few others—inspired a dozen good articles, created scandals and gossip, and had a good ole time. They insulted the public, and perhaps our complacent *res publica* needed it. But they did nothing more. The b. g. diverged from Dada on the metaphysical plane however. . . ." A smile appeared on two panelists' faces at the word *metaphysical*—ole Cheevy and his mysticism, you know. "For it had no known tradition behind it, broken away with finality as it was from the Judeo-Christian tradition. It was visionary, it was a promise of a new American Contemplatio! So Now, so new, that it hardly existed. Yet, on the literary plane the beat generation can aptly be interpreted as a deliberately effected cultural maneuver on the part of its adherents, to leap into that Art-clogged river of the Cubists, Futurists, Vorticists, Imagists, Expressionists, Constructivists, Dadaists, Surrealists, and Action Painters, and to claim thereby direct descendency! The beats sought to claim such an adornment. O, would that it were so!"

In spite of his energetic presentation, Cheevy sat down to applause as puny as fingersnaps at a coffee-house reading.

Miss Malek announced, to great laughter, that human beings had been jumping off the Bel Air Hotel "waving genitals and manuscripts" for over thirty-five years and she didn't see what all the fuss was about. "I mean," said she, "it's all been done! These people have—rather, had, nothing to give us, nothing." She confessed without a blink to being unable to read for pleasure but rather, or so she implied, for possible borrowing of ideas, techniques, plots, and characterizations. "I read in a businesslike way and believe me, there's nothing to (lift from) these books, not even Kerouac's!"

An interesting man arose at this point, his long broomy white hair twined Hasidically into tangled dangles in all directions, and waved aloft the current issue of *Trans-Quake Quarterly*, and announced that, if any should desire, he would repair to the lobby at intermission where issues could be bought, for they contained his recently completed trilogy of novellas, the title of which was lost to us, for an insecurity spasm, or something, caused him almost to whisper the title.

And he continued: "I should like to address Miss Malek with a question. It is this, in two parts: Don't you think that extreme narcissism helps the growth of the spirit and psyche within the hostile iron clouds of the robot interlude? And, secondly, have you had a chance to read those short stories I sent you?"

The gavel pounded immediately. "We shall have to reserve questions,"—Cleftine leaning a little too close to the windscreenless mike—"until the second half of the program, after the intermission. Thank you."

It is fitting to note that the panel, down to a member, agreed that "injustice is unjust." "I *do* hate injustice," Miss Malek said in closing, "and I love life." Several short derision-hoots, even sneers, issued forth from the audience before the applause drowned out the heckling.

One would think there would never be a fistfight at such a sadness scene, yet hostility bounced from the chandeliers when Emil Cione began to talk. To improve his babble-flux, Cione had lowered his head to his lap and quickly had slipped two Benzedrine tablets into his craw. To wash them down, a trusted student had brought him his glass of vodka

66

disguised as water. All this was going down as he was being announced, and he had become confused. He half-arose from his chair as if to walk to a podium, then jerkily checked himself, realizing it was a sit-down scene—nodding at the introductory applause.

Cione had a prepared statement, a rule he never broke— for you could never tell when you might be too drunk or too A'd, and one certainly did not want to appear to rave from the sibylline tripod. His intention was not to be hostile, nor to rave. But something caused him to snap.

Only a small segment of the audience seemed to react to Cione's shrillness, as if he were a gospelist. This portion was crackling with shouted yesses! and short clacks of applause. It was like watching blue-haired snuff buffs—those senior citizens who hang out at murder trials—shift and twitch in excitement as a jury files in to announce a yes-vote for a death penalty.

"The civilization in its mercy, in its democracy of the moment, gave them their say, gave them God-knows-how-many headlines and articles, but the beats mumbled and stuttered and slipped aside.

"I have tried to read these so-called books, but I can't finish them!" Cione barked. "None of these people have anything interesting to say. Type type type, locked in their grimy hobo towers, but what is it? Typata-typata-typata! It was an entire ersatz Byronic nightmare!: bad sex, bad logic, bad breath, bad linguistics! For these little 'personal madmen poets'—to quote Jack Kerouac, who could have been a good writer, if he had only written . . ." Chuckles arose from Cione's faction on the floor.

"But the fact remains that these deadbeat beats are beaten upon their beat feet with the bastinado of indiscipline!"—pausing, though not a throat of laughter was heard

67

to utter, to let the line slide home. *"And"*—beret of inglorious berets—"they are st*u*pid!"pronouncing the *u* at great length as if it were a line of molossic dimeter.

"Booo!" boo'd a large half of the audience, for there were many students of the Big Beat suffering spasms of nausea—kicking themselves first of all for paying two bucks to partake of this jive-o-rama.

"One does *not* admire their chaos!" Cione cooked onward. "But, it *is* a cunning chaos, is't not so?"—voice shrill for a flash, on the *so*. "For if they could get us all into their pads and lairs—that is, break down the structure, then they could overpower us and force our awe!"

"Bullshit!" someone shouted. "Hallucinations!" another. "Bravo!" a third.

"I will never, for the life of me, understand why publishers, and we do not here mean to cast aspersions on the essential worth of publishers—but I cannot understand why, just to fill their annual publishing lists, they should stoop to print such unblinkingly stupid yahoo grime."

He embarked upon a litany of b. g. transgressions, including "their free-associations in poorly remembered languages, their pleonastic verse which seeks to follow the berserk fingers of hop-head jazzmen . . ."

Meanwhile, Al and Ron had edged to the front during the past few sentences. Cione—eyes out of focus near the chandeliers of the ceiling, railed onward about the many indignities suffered because of "these howling Zen freaks" and "these vermin in the cellar of the communist storefront" (which caused Cheevy Samuelson a certain uneasiness).

Cione next uttered a long sentence which, except for its ending: "next to the offal mattresses the candles drip down upon their demijohns of bad Chianti," was impossible to

68

hear, because it was at that point that Al and John enacted Operation Potato Salad.

"One, two, three," Ron counted off; then in tight harmony they sang, "Am I Goethe"—followed by a barber shop quartet "hummmmmm." Then, raising the harmony, "Or Am I Schiller, hummmmmm." Then, a Beach Boys soprano sang, "Or Am I Nothing?"—and Ron threw a high arching shot at Cione, the plate following behind the main glob of potato salad beatifically—the glob spreading into a face-covering ovalness.

A precise cube of potato broke away somehow from the main salad glop, and was traveling about six inches in the avant-garde; the cube of potato looking like a mayo-smeared marble sugar cube by Marcel Duchamp.

Cione was unaware. "Livid with shrieks but . . ." The glop still on target. "but lurid in license . . ." Glop still zero'd in on bard-nose. "and lost in laziness . . ."

Someone watching this on slow-motion film would have noticed that the soft edge of the potato cube actually entered Cione's left nostril whereas the rest of the cube broke away and traveled up his cheek, bounced against the upper eye socket and arc'd up o'er the table.

It was a situation with the validity of a microsecond however, as the bulk of the salad was hard behind the sentry cube, and, by an act of Ptah, the plop-smush hit Cione's face almost one-on-one, followed by the crimp-edged plate itself and the bard was fair covered by the oniony wetness.

Yarr. Har. Har. went the audience, forgetting its high purpose for just a moment. Even his grad students, dutifully jotting notes, wiggled and giggled. For verily their mentor, eyes besmirched, could not view their levity.

Immediately the moderator whacked the gavel and announced the intermission.

XI

After the toss Al ran away from the stage. At the wings he slipped on a scattered gob and fell back cracking his noggin. Supine, he spotted Cione's billfold fallen upon the stage beneath the table. He lunged for it and ran to the back of the room, checking the contents as he ran. The thirty-five dollars he added to his own five. After finding a love note to Cione, apparently from one of his students, Al sprinted into the bathroom to read it. It was a long note, speaking in rhymed iambics of trees and leaf-drift and arcane hints at trysts "in the tower"—i.e., the Holiday Inn on Route 22. Al strode to the Crabhorne Bookstore booth where, to his discredit, he attempted to sell it.

Doing so, a smirching olive-quarter fell from Al's sleeve upon the *Garment of Ra* manuscript, perhaps diminishing its value by twenty-five dollars. "Well, we're really not interested," Mr. Crabhorne replied, "but you may leave it here. We'll hold it for him."

XII

Cione sputtered, potato chunks spewing from his lips. "Call the police! Guard! Guard!" He threw a handful of mush back, missed; hit one of his pupils bent down taking notes. "Fool!" he shouted. "Why are you sitting there? Do something!"

Then Cione spotted Ron walking up the aisle getting slapped on the back by chortling friends. Cione leaped off the stage and tackled the young roach-eating translator of Persian poesy. Cione opened an extremely tiny pearl-handled penknife and grabbed Ron's wrist and yanked it down to a rest on Emil's knee, and proceeded to inflict a series of barely skin-piercing stabs into the hand, while leaning down close to Ron's ear whispering, "Death your verse, death your verse, death your verse . . ."

XIII

The intermission was wonderful. Samuel Beckett could have written a sixty-five-page sentence describing the movement of eyes from face to face in the intensity. Eyeball set EE_1 looked at eyeball set EE_2 who was looking at EE_3. EE_3 glanced at EE_1 who panned slowly across the field of EE_2-EE_3-EE_4-EE_5 . . . . EE_n, and EE_6 looked wantonly at EE_5 (Emil Cione) while EE_8 etc. . . .

XIV

She was carrying about fifteen books, including all five editions to date of Cione's *The Mountain of Reason*. She paused longingly by the faintly oil-stained jacket of the bard. She clicked her ballpoint into position. Cione waved it away. "I never sign with ballpoints"—as he hooked out his thick Montblanc with a flourish of wrist-flick. He paused to close his lil' pearl knife with the slightly rubicund blade, and wrote his name and the time of the occasion in each of his many books.

XV

The couple was standing at the book booth. The man said, "I don't care what you say. Everybody's entitled to their opinions. Those boys were *not* respectful!"

She was not paying any attention to him. Suddenly she found it: "Aha, I knew it, I knew there was something about throwing potato salad in here!" She was holding a mint-condition inscribed first edition of *Howl & Other Poems*. "Shall I read the section?" she asked.

"Sure go ahead."

Who threw potato salad at CCNY lecturers on Dadaism and subsequently presented themselves on the granite steps of the madhouse with shaven heads and harlequin speech of suicide, demanding instantaneous lobotomy[1]

"Look," he responded, "I don't care if it was in *The Iliad*. Those young men were disrespectful to a great American author."

XVI

The party was held at one of those shiny-floored fifteen-room New York apartments with the rugs all rolled up for the night and jammed into the children's wing. On the walls were the twenty-five expensive paintings, all with melted-snow sections of pure canvas and pencil lines.

The salad tossers had mumbled at the man trying to find their names on the front door list, and pushed their way in. They began their *Absinthe Drinkers* impressions at once. Ron took two senior editors from *Time* and a major newspaper critic into the bathroom with some pot and locked the door, causing a major congestion of the bladderially tense outside.

---

[1] Ginsberg. *Howl & Other Poems*, p. 15, City Lights Books, San Francisco. This is an example of an image influencing an image. For Al and Ron certainly did not know that the *Howl* 'tato-toss had actually occurred, performed by Carl Solomon and several friends, who hurled upon Wallace Markfield in the course of a Markfield lecture on Mallarmé.

Al sidestepped into the bedroom and dialed his wife in the Bronx. "How come you never take me to any parties?" she wanted to know when she had pried his whereabouts out of him.

"My career, baby, it's for my career, I don't actually *like* these shindigs"—his hand casually moving from coat pocket to coat pocket in the pile on the bed.

"Well bring some milk home. Have you forgotten that Number Four is sick, Mr. Terrible Father?"

Indeed he had, as he clicked the receiver in time to grab the hostess down upon the furry pile of garb, attempting a quick act of coat-pile gropery, which failed and nearly got him thrown from the revel.

XVII

Cione's Village Hideaway was known to no one, not even his accountant. Nor did his wife ever discover that he had recovered the thrown-away sheets from the garbage for his lair of license. It was here the novel of novels would be conceived, he told himself, although there were cobwebs in the toilet bowl and curdled six-month-old milk in the refrigerator.

"Do you want some tea?" he asked her.

"Yes. Do you mean grass?"

"Uh no. I have Earl Grey and English Breakfast."

"Oh, no thanks." She stood in the doorway of the bedroom. Cione was already on the bed, his hands behind his head, his belt rakishly half-undone.

She walked into the kitchen and counted the liquor bottles crowded on a wheeled metal cart. There certainly is a lot of alcohol, she thought, gazing at the dusty bottles, many nearly empty, of

73

Smirnoff Red	Creme de Cacao	Wild Turkey
Smirnoff Blue	Kahlua	Gordon's Gin
Seagram's 7	six-pack of Bud	Old 1889
Stolichnaya	Sloe Gin	Jack Daniels
Cherry Heering	Heaven Hill	Metaxa
Creme de	Four Roses	Banana Cordial
Menthe	Three Feathers	Remy Martin

plus four dried and moldy lemons, a mummified quarter of lime, and an old Chelsea Hotel towel stiff and brown from ablutions long completed.

He interrupted her as she was insistently, even amphetaminishly, recalling those recent events of Furie Hall whose witness she was from the front row. He oozed into her word-stream at midsentence, and began to talk himself about the essay over which had had been long poised in creation—how he must hurry, for the conference was just two weeks away. The rrrrhuht of the zipper sliding open down her back, and the knuckles of his hand feeling the heat of her skin as the fingers zipped downward, triggered off at least a third of a sonnet but he did not dare reach over to the bedstand to make any notes.

Instead, he asked, "Can you type?"—reaching up to grab her; his hand nudging a breast then speeding down the arm and smoothing out over her long wan fingers, the instruments which might, he hoped, whip his rough scrawls into shape.

All at once she sat up and shook her hair loose upon her shoulder. Without a word she stood, put on her dress and walked out of the apartment.

For an hour Cione lay on his side staring at the wall. He bit the lace at the corner and at last drove a fist into the pillow. "Why won't anybody make it with me?"

Johnny The Foot

HE READ THE reports. He accepted the reports.
He internalized the reports. What reports? The reports of
the dirty beatnik. What a thrill to live in scarabaeic dingi-
ness. America was a bear skull, the poems raged. The
morons of Moloch rafted through their sewer of ad-blurbs,
censorship, commie-fear, and wreaked their beaks upon the
shiny eyes of the nearly deceased, like vultures of plunder
above the mired. And what need, pray tell, was there to
wash? To please the delicate nasality of those who only
came within sniff-range to put you down anyway?

That is, zones exist. Don't come in our zone. If you do,
please love with leg-fling frenzy, or go away. On the other
hand, our zone is the future.

And they walked past the Provincetown Playhouse looking for the ghost of John Reed, or waited for e. e. cummings
to dart across Sixth Avenue for the daily walk. They sat in
the bistros to watch the poets read shriek-songs. They yelled
for help in the putrefaction, but settled for kicks and dirt
and thrills—or ear-verse in the Jazz Gallery half-light pray-

ing for Sonny Rollins to beat away the mucous of soul mal.

Yea, Plains of Gold, Nebraska had lost its finest artist when Johnny took a suitcase full of sketches and headed for the Greyhound terminal. And what was it that Washington Square Park gained? It gained a stunned young mammal scribbling with joy, who plugged into a heaven of body-burning solipsism, sex, pot, liquor, and beatific Buddhism. Just to walk unnoticed in the harsh city for months, that alone was Total! to Johnny. "Je est un autre. Je est un autre," he whispered to himself sketching on a bench.

And then to make friends with other escapees, ahhh what fulfillment in the park. As weird as you wanted, you were still One with the parklings. And the only people who asked any questions were the police.

The energy came from a desperate search for some indication that the universe was more than a berserk sewer. Johnny scored obscure mimeo'd magazines in the Eighth Street Bookshop and began to memorize the data right on the street as he walked around. The problem was transformation: that principle of mathematics that said there had to be equations of transformation from one system to another. O how sorely Johnny yearned to be transformed, and looked for the symbols of transformation in holy verse, and in the language he heard in the streets and bistros: the words of the "Bop Kabbalah"—as one bard phrased it. And he also wanted to feel holy—and, if not holy, like, cooled out, as they said, cooled in the cosmos, at least as much as Siddhartha by the river. As if thinking that the "crowned knot of fire" that Eliot wrote about in *Little Gidding* could be ordered at a coffee house, or summoned as a wraith from a page.

In the First Christian Church of his youth he'd stood up to sing that tune about the "Beautiful words, wonderful words, wonderful words of Life," just before they passed the collection plate. To Johnny, that was bunk from a punk. But now, as he heard the Words of Life as performed by the anarcho-SkyArt dharma-commie jazz church of the New York streets and pads, he felt the purest Hieratic Vastness, felt plugged into the Ladder. Greed ceased as a possibility, and the eyeball on the pyramid's apex, back of the dollar bill, rolled out of the park, through the Holland Tunnel, all the way to Minneapolis where it made a blind person see again. That was the sort of possibility that Johnny felt. He was ready for the spaceships to land.

He abandoned soap, abandoned the seasons, lived upon the concrete tracks of lower New York as if they were the props of a stage production. Dirt captured the hill. His socks became a toeless ring of frayed rot. His T-shirt mutated through the gray palette on the way to anthracite. If there was something important to do like trying to score a blue breadline card, he would wash those things that jutted into the air, namely his face and his hands. Winter and summer he wore the same outfit: a black turtleneck sweater, black despicable engineer boots or adios'd tennis shoes, green corduroy jacket and, in a bow to the past, a postage stamp on his forehead.

And his feet. He did not wash his feet from April 4, 1959 till November 15, 1961. His feet were his masterpiece. He felt they were art. After a few months of no-wash, his feet began to mummify. They developed a dry charcoal-black surface similar to the crust in the pocket of a catcher's mitt when it is not oiled properly. Contrary to public opinion, the professionally aged and unwashed mummified foot does not give off any particularly obnoxious toke. It both looked and smelled like burnt toast, and it offered to the bold feeler a texture of great crusty complexity, like a painting.

77

He tried to enter his feet in an art show in the gallery of the Judson Church in the summer of 1960, but was politely rejected, although he offered to stand quietly in a far corner atop a milk crate where he proposed to lean an empty gilt picture frame against them for proper setting. He even promised to spray them with fixative to prevent untoward vapors of vom vom from offending the delicate gazers.

As vengeance for his rejection, Johnny sprayed his feet with gold spray paint and stood on the gallery porch all through the show with a picket sign of protest on his breast.

Denizens of Washington Square named him Johnny Filth Feet. Johnny had a case file opened on tourists. He didn't know whether to love 'em or to hate them. He settled upon a role as promulgator of revulsion. The scam worked wonderfully in the summer tourist season and netted him a continuous flow of money. The first step was to place the all-important hat by the fountain to catch the shekels. Then he'd launch into a sharp-toned drawl trying to act like a carnival barker. "Beat feet! Beat feet! Come see the despicable beat feet! Never been washed! Put your quarters in the hat! Beat feet! Beat feet!" Somehow, that created tremendous crowds, who circled him thickly, some standing on tiptoes for a better scope, like a golf crowd trying to watch a championship putt.

And it could not be believed how this foot-shill routine kept Johnny Filth Feet rolling in cappuccino and baklava at Rienzi's Coffee House. It even paid the rent. He did other things to bedazzle the tourists that crowded the Village in the beatific era. Growling and slobbering, he often fell at the feet of a passel of map-clutchers. There was one weekend in August of '60 when he fell to his knees, head tumbling forward, and began to lick a Dreamsicle stick upon the ground in its wet, crumpled Dreamsicle wrapper.

Tongue-trails wetted the perimetric tar. He groaned, he slithered, a crowd developed. He was arrested. The police dispersed the crowd. The squares put their Brownie Hawk-eyes back into their purses.

But what could the fuzz hold him for? Felonious slurping of a Dreamsicle wrapper? They held him in handcuffs in the park department building in front of Judson Church. When he was left alone for a moment, he immediately removed his shoes and socks, brackish tarsals wiggling in the air.

And then the fuzz returned to haul him off to the paddy wagon but stopped in their tracks when they spotted the slime-spackled appendages, and averted their eyes in disgust. After a monotoned conference, they unlocked the cuffs and told him to get out of the park and stay out.

There was another thing Johnny noticed. The tourists loved to get close to the beatniks—some even reached out to cop a touchy-feely. Others were bolder. Never would he forget the razor-nosed woman wearing wing-shaped glasses and her husband, a marvel in bermuda shorts and a baseball cap, who approached him one afternoon as he sat on the ledge of the statue of Alexander Holley. When they were about two feet away from him, the woman leaned forward and almost collapsed to the ground. Johnny thought she had stumbled and reached out to prevent her from crashing her face into Holley's torso. That's when he heard an unmistakable sniffing sound. Her face was only an inch and a half from his mottled jacket's axilla as she filled her questing lungs. With great and severe dignity, the woman straightened up and continued onward with her husband, undoubtedly prepared to regale the relatives at Thanksgiving dinner about the hideous beatnik armpit she nearly crashed into.

After a few feet they quickly turned and hauled out their

camera, took a fast snap, executed an about-face and marched out of the park.

Johnny Filth Feet guessed that in the golden era of 1958–61, he had his picture taken about ten thousand times in Washington Square. Countless were the vacation albums in the Midwest containing pictures of him lounging in such a position, as was his pleasure, so that Henry James' old house at the park's north side would be seen in the background.

Filth Feet's greatest moment in the park was the Folk Song Riot of April 9, 1961, an event which turned him for several years into a disciplined, leaflet-crazed rioting maniac. Up to that day, his only protest had been when he sprayed his feet gold outside the art show. April 9 was a Sunday and all that morning Johnny sat surly on the edge of the fountain suffering a brain-throb diagnosed by his friends as a hashover. Added to that was the horrifying rejection of his body the night before relative to the underwear question.

It used to disturb women that he wore no underwear. The time, of course, was 1961. It was all very well that his 3rd Street apartment, a quarter-hour trudge from Washington Square Park, probably set for all time the outer parameters of gunge. One bedroom was known as the "garbage room" and during the course of a year had grown stuffed from floor to ceiling with brown bags of bye-bye. Rats used to commit suicide trying to jump into the garbage room from the ledge of an adjoining building. And it was fine that his beret was glazed with sky grit, that his jeans had obviously been worn for months, that his tennis shoes were a patchwork of tape and wrapped with clothesline cord. When, however, down derry down dropped the jeans and there was no underwear, they were shocked. Added to that, there were other matters, that is, certain genitalic tattoos which quoted Verlaine, the description of which we shall pass over in silence. Let it be only said that when the young woman from Forest Hills the previous evening was confronted, on a sudden, in the pants-drop gloom with an erect member emblazoned in a most rubicund manner with the words, "Oh! je serai celui-là qui créera Dieu!" she fled.

The Folk Song Riot was occasioned by an arbitrary decree of the New York City parks commissioner, Newbold Morris, who had taken strong exception to what he called the "adverse conditions prevalent on Sundays because of the roving troubadours and their followers." As a result, the police banned Sunday yodeling although for seventeen years the singers had gathered each weekend in the warm breezes.

During the week prior to the riot, folksingers had applied for official permits to sing/yodel/strum, but had been refused. So the ingredients were perfect for a stomp-out. It is rare indeed for conditions to prevail where demonstrators could feel absolute righteousness while surging in blizzardly balefulness across the rough sandy concrete basin for two objectives: 1) the creation of a lawless zone of thrills, and 2) to yodel outside the law. To defy an unjust law, ahhh thou thrill of thrills!

Johnny looked around him and saw that the large circular fountain and the surrounding mall had grown packed with potential yodelers. Tense with discipline and willingness to endure pain engendered by memorized instructions in the form of secret messages of foment coded into the mass media by beatnik weirdness-cells, the crowd waited.

The reporters for the New York newspapers, and there were many present, dutifully noted the "beat" look of the yodel horde—i.e., a surfeit of sandals, long hair, beards, and

81

eyes of fornicatorial glaze—into their stenopads. *The New York Mirror*, for instance, bannered the riot on its front page: "5000 BEATNIKS RIOT IN VILLAGE." When Johnny Filth Feet saw that headline later, he nearly swooned with riot-gasm.

And then it began. Within a half-hour Johnny the Foot learned a key principal of agitation. The rule was not, as he had before felt certain, "When in doubt, riot"—but rather it was "It only takes a few." For an electric unification seemed to pass into the crowd when the trigger-pack, "a group of 50, many in beatnik clothes and beards"—as *The New York Times* haughtily reported—began to march from the southwest of the park (MacDougal and West 4th) in close-order yodel-formation toward the waiting-for-inspiration yodel mob, goaded all the while by trained left-leaning folklorists and known novelists.

The congeries of bearded banjo boys and "girls with long hair and guitars" (*The New York Times*) at the fountain, went nuts. Otherwise stable humans with patches of the Bronx Folk Singers Guild proudly sewn on their field jackets, railed with defiance. Carried by the trigger-pack were signs which carefully presented the righteousness of the riot. Among them were MUSIC TAMES THE SAVAGE BEAST, and WE WANT TO DO WHAT WE HAVE ALWAYS DONE.

Filth Feet's spirit soared! Long-suppressed abilities to hallucinate were unleashed and the visions began at once. Before his mind-screen a glassy-eyed endless plateau of beats chanting Zen koans in unison were marching, marching, devouring every barricade, stone wall and stanchion, toward its goal: a beard on every other face, a poem on every lip, money for all.

The trigger-pack reached the fountain and began to strum, yodel, pluck, hoot, and to thicken their voices with subversive Appalachian accents. A woman autoharpist with

82

insolently lengthy tresses, stood then upon a hasty platform of guitar cases and began to sing "We Shall Overcome." And that was it—the police walked forward to break up the music. She was just pushing the A-Seventh bar on her harp when whonk! they shoved her and the cases went askitter, one of them hitting Johnny in his hashover.

The woman was hauled away, her harp falling to the pavement where it gave forth an atonal confusion of reverberations. Drool began to wet Johnny's lips.

After the autoharpist was hauled away, the leadership vacuum was filled by a thin young man from the Bronx Folk Singers Guild who strode forth and began to plunk his banjo contemptuously. "Stop that banjo! Tweet!"—barked out a police captain to Sergeant Mokler of the elite folk squad. And the gendarmes charged the lone banjo. Johnny began to hallucinate with vengeance, especially since the banjo plucker was only three feet away from him and he could see the raised clubs advancing. This little scuffle resulted in the ultimate prize of the Folk Song Riot, the capture of a billy club. The club was raised aloft to whack, and the banjoist was quick enough to duck, not missing even a beat of "Down By The Riverside" it will be noted, whereupon the billy club crashed into the fountain buttress instead, causing a painful punishment of vibrations upon the officer's hand. The club bounced loose across the fount basin and the Bronx Folk Singers Guildperson popped the booty into his banjo case and ran away tinkling.

When this occurred, Johnny's mind went temporarily bye-bye. Flash: Halloween '55. State police cars arrive at the tense farm community to restore order. Flashing lights on car tops punctuate an intersection. The fires in the looted country store glare. Two tall metal windmill towers are circled by a tight ring of stolen outhouses. Above the

83

towers is lashed the bicycle rack from the elementary school. Six overturned Buicks and Oldsmobiles stand in a perfect set of three-car parallel lines on each side of the outhouse/windmill construction in front of Gomell's Feed Store and the Farmers State Bank. It was the purest form of environmental art, Johnny told himself as he stood upon the roof of a nearby lumberyard, panting for breath, gazing with love at his masterpiece, which had taken him and his friends six hours to complete.

Unable to resist pissing off the state police, he jumped from the lumberyard roof and sprinted toward the railroad tracks. "There he is!" the coppers shouted. Then two sharp barks. They shot at me! He ran a quarter-mile up the dark railings, and hid in Samson's orchard, gleeful happy muttering, while far below in the valley the policemen cleared away the towers and the privy-henge, using the moon-shaped ventilators as hand-holds to lift them upon the hay wagon on the way to the town dump.

Johnny's happy fantasy was interrupted abruptly by the harsh reality of Washington Square when several of New York's Finest grabbed him and attempted to treat him like a sponge mop. They dragged him along by the feet so that his face was on the concrete brooming the Popsicle wrappers. "Hey! Ouch! I'm leaving! I'm leaving!" he yelled up. They let him go and he scrambled to his feet. He spotted the tourists staring in a thick baffled silent ring like mushrooms.

"Good. Get them!" one of them yelled. "Hurt the beatniks" another chub-chub from the outlands slowly drawled, giving his sentence a robotic hollowness. Johnny was finally angry.

And he quickly learned another principle of rioting. That is, in a riot one can find oneself in the so-called leadership cadre, propelled there as if entranced.

Johnny Filth Feet found himself jostling forward to address the throng. He tipped over a metal wastebasket to stand upon. "We have the right!"—he screamed, "the need, and the duty! to yodel!!" And then he let loose from all his lungs and throat, a drastic tarzanic high-low yodel/warble. About halfway through the prolonged yodel, someone set fire to the rubbish in the basket and the flames began to rise up, pain-tongues curling upon his feet. His mummified condition probably prevented him from suffering intense pain, for, as if nothing were trying to char-broil his extremities, Johnny yodeled onward. The sight of his feet enveloped in flames as he orated to the thronging pissoff, created genuine mania in the crowd.

Nothing in the ensuing years would ever match it. Lunch-counter sit-ins in southern bus depots, voter-registration drives in Mississippi, peace walks, running war-research computers with maple syrup—nothing would be so intensely sparging of insight-thrills for Johnny Filth Feet as the Folk Song Riot of '61.

Finally Johnny was carried from his perch into a police van. "Police Brutality!" people began to scream, a phrase Johnny had never heard. "Fascists!" others yelled. The beat-mob surrounded the van and started rocking it back and forth. It almost went over, poised in that either/or moment of car tilt when you have to jump out of the way as it comes crashing back or you can surge in jubilance as it tilts over. The van crashed back down and Johnny face-punched his way out the back and the screaming crowd demanded him again atop the charred metal. The police dragged him back into the van but for two hours the people surrounded it and kept it from leaving the park. And what was Johnny charged with later in night court? Making a speech without a permit.

85

And out of the thousands only ten people were arrested! Another ace principle learned: You can riot and everyone can escape! Johnny laughed in a convulsion of inner peace all the way to the Tombs. By midnight a total stranger had bailed Johnny out and he and the stranger were soon drinking orzatas at the Café Figaro.

It wasn't for another fifteen years that the arrest in the park would cause certain problems relative to Johnny's post-beat career. This was solved by pulling some political strings and having the records of the arrest forever sealed. For "everything oozes"—as Sam Beckett so dutifully annotated; and it was no less so for the happy roaming beatniks of yore. Within a year of his arrest in Washington Square, Johnny Filth Feet fled the set without a whisper.

What happened to Mr. Dirt Foot? Did he rise to lead the ten thousands in marches of anger? Well, he did travel south on some voter-registration drives. Did he then go back to run for the Nebraska State Assembly? Did he take over a New York publishing company? Did he fade guzzling cheapo down among the Bowery replicas? Well, I did locate him several years ago and I must say that it was startling to note how remarkably he had altered the channel of his life. He showed me his feet after I had taunted him a bit during our dinner. They were as white and polished as Carrara marble.

But I do not want to anger him by revealing his name, for he is a prime source of money for many of my projects. For instance, he supplied the money for the LSD in the Chicago water supply. So you will understand when I say that we do not want his name floating around police intelligence files. But I can say that he is currently a vice-president in the trust department of a prominent New York bank, and is moving up.

Mindscape Gallery

HER NAME WAS Louise Adams. She was twenty-two years old, a student at Cooper Union where she specialized in wood sculpture. She also worked in hand-painted pottery. More than anything, she was a painter of canvas, and a good one. Her greatest difficulty had been her parents who dearly wanted her to marry Murray of the real-estate empire. To drop some asterisks around this desire, they threw away some of her paintings. "You have broken our heart. After all we've done." Get married was the message. "You can never handle it alone. It's a man's world"—her mother told her. "Get what you can."

They were wrong and their nastiness in tossing away the paintings cost them her presence out there in Patchogue. She threw her possessions out by the trashcans except for a bed, record player, books, and art supplies and moved to the Lower East Side to paint. She told them to leave her alone. She refused to communicate with them and refused all offers of financial assistance. She obtained an unlisted telephone number and ripped the listing label off the dial.

87

They tried to come to the apartment only once. When they announced themselves at the door, she just took off her clothes and opened up, "Hi dad, hi mom, come on in. I want you to meet my friend Big Brown. He'll be over in a few minutes. You'll love him." Her mother's only reply was a shudder. She took a chance that they wouldn't have her arrested and immediately rolled a joint, which she lit with an enormous suction of smoke and held it in her lungs. "Would you like some?"—pot-puffs escaping her mouth with each word as she offered the j to her father, leaning across so that her bare breasts slid down the front of her mother's overcoat which remained on throughout the short visit.

Louise Adams soon had to give up Cooper Union. But that was fine with her—tired of being a schoolgirl and unable adequately to worship the pitiful abilities of her instructors when she knew she was a better artist than any of them.

She was tall, about six-foot-one, and rather slender. Skinny with energy. And as soon as she spewed in from Patchogue, she was an immediately sought-after, almost worshiped, friend on the East Side art scene. She just loooooved to explore the pleasures of the body, and loved to hang out at Stanley's Bar at 12th and B almost as much. She never had any trouble with any of her new friends becoming possessive or jealous because she constantly and pointedly scoffed, scowled, jeered, at the possibility. Furthermore she quickly established a complex of rules regarding her friends so that there was a great privacy and at the same time a great diversity.

She *believed* in the East Side. In the frenzy of her rebellion she would not have considered for even a minute being humiliated by a man with whom she had grown infatuated. Nor by a brother artist operating at the very same barricades as she.

Louise had lived on the East Side for less than a year when she met Barton Macintyre, a painter also, who was soon professing his fiery love for her, joining a rather substantial list of humans so professing.

At first she was attracted by his energy and his apparent dedication. Barton Macintyre worked at making it ten or eleven hours a day—churning out the paintings. Jesus, he hungered for success. Macintyre was twenty-six at the time, tall and hairy. He was maybe six-foot-two and chub-chubbed upon the scales at about 225. As for hair, his chest and arms looked like an exploded eyelash factory. His face skin was almost flour-white and possessed a wide full-nostriled nose plus a long but carefully attended beard. His mane, however, was beginning to go bye-bye.

Barton's daily garb consisted of baggy brown Sweet-Orr corduroy trousers and a sports jacket. He always carried a tie with him in the jacket pocket. You could never tell when you were going to be called uptown for a meeting regarding a sale or a show, man.

He was very careful about his attire. He had a closet full of seventeen blue workshirts, five or six jackets in grays and tans—all in denim/corduroy, and a floor full of various types of shoes and moccasins from Abercrombie & Fitch and the Bean catalogue. He was loath to stray from the current artist fashions.

Louise liked to wear long-sleeved blouses with drawstrings at the sleeves and at the neck. Discovering Ukrainian clothing, as made by craftspeople of the Lower East Side, was a joy. She must have ordered ten of these blouses, many of them sewn with flowered patterns, from Madame Braznick, a manufacturer of dancing boots and Ukrainian attire on East 7th Street.

At Christmas, the first year they knew one another, she

ordered for Barton from Madame Braznick a long black Cossack coat with cloth bullet-holders designed into each side of the upper chest. The bullet-pouches were stuffed with hand-sewn flower patterned cylinders. Barton flatly refused to wear the coat. He did carry it with him, in the gift box, down to Stanley's that night where he showed it, guffawing and snorting, to all his friends.

Barton was addicted to art openings. He made sure he was on the mailing lists of virtually all uptown galleries and museums. In the early sixties he would dash from gallery to gallery in order to attend four or five openings the same night. It was inspirational. He needed it. The out-of-sight lofts with broken windows, the half-finished art on the walls, the irrational rages, this he could endure if the leprechaun in the paint-stained beret at the end of the rainbow would only hand him a fist of MONEY!!

Whatever his secret concern for lucre was, Barton was ever concerned to project an image of controlled wildness—exposing just the "correct" amount of nuttiness, drug-abuse, alcoholism, and feigned flip-out. And his ego surged. That was what Louise Adams could identify with.

Barton viewed everything he created as something major. He labored according to The Theory of The Frame. Anything created was enshrined in a frame. If he wanted to make a sketch of something, first he made a sketch of various ideas for the sketch. The sketch of the sketch was framed, signed, dated, as was the sketch itself. Doodles, telephone lists, everything, framed. He soon had his mother's apartment in Riverdale filled up storing his frames.

There was one series of works he did throw away—i.e., his notes perfecting his signature. His first problem was his secret belief that no one whose name was Macintyre could really make it big on the New York art scene. He had long

90

considered changing his name to another, say more successful type of name; he hungered for one whose last syllable
was a vowel. But he finally decided not to change his name
for the following reason: Hell, I'm on the verge of making it
anyway. I'm just about the most well-known painter on the
set already, why not therefore just ride it all the way with
Macintyre?

So, for about a year he worked on his signature. He
wanted it to look as cool and individual as Picasso, Braque,
Dali, Miró. Barton Macintyre II was the signature he had
used since high school. He hated the way it looked, having
stayed static since his junior year. First he dropped the II.
No good. Next the Barton. If only he could make the word
Macintyre itself a work of art he would be happy. To this
end he scrawled and painted his last name at least fifty
times a day for weeks. He consulted popular books dealing
with handwriting analysis and personality. He was horrified
reading the personality traits revealed by his then-current
method of signature. So he changed it drastically. Finally
he settled on a swooping flourishing signature which he
could repeat blindfolded. "More stylish than Braque, more
substantial than Picasso"—he told himself.

He rented what he considered a dream pad, a four-room
so-called "box" apartment where the rooms opened off in
several directions from the entranceway. This was in dis-
tinction to the railroad flats which offered much less privacy
since one traipsed through all rooms in order to get to the
farthest one. He was happy. The apartment was his when
the previous tenant, a senior citizen from Latvia, was
hauled away by his relatives to Beautiful South Shore Lei-
sure-Retirement Colony.

Barton decided that it would be "out there" to leave the
apartment just as it was. The man had been a tile-freak. The

91

entire bathroom, floor and walls and ceiling, was covered with two-inch pastel ceramics. Not only that, but the entire living room and bedroom were also covered ceiling and floor. Barton left the old man's furniture just as it was although he did clear out the room overlooking Tompkins Square Park. Many a painting of Barton's was inspired by gazing down into the park fantasizing drooling brontosaurs mating in the mist.

Barton considered his Tompkins Square pad just a temporary hassle to endure on the way to the aforementioned leprechaun with the paint-smeared beret and the slight scratching-sounds of bankers writing checks and cocaine honked through ivory straws on yachts. A house in P-town, a house in East Hampton, a house outside Paris. "Houses"- he cried, stumbling drunk down Avenue C, "Houses."

When Barton Macintyre felt he was in love with the painter Louise Adams, his first move was to zap his rivals. He crowded in on Louise. He answered the phone a lot when he was at her apartment and did his best to discourage incoming male calls. He used up as much of her time as he could get away with. He spread the word among the denizens of Stanley's Bar and local cafés. To her own surprise she found herself tolerating this sweating brute who was driving away all her lovers. She believed his love and was even tentatively beginning to become dependent on it, and gave him in turn her tenderness and plans and cares.

Poverty was Louise's main problem at the time. She had her potter's wheel set up in her apartment and was able to use the kiln at Cooper Union. Her vases, jugs, and pots were placed on consignment at several West Village stores and they sold pretty well. They were very skillfully painted with ornate forest scenes and elf-satires bearing the faces of renowned artists of the day.

92

An opportunity arose for her to rent a storefront on East 9th Street between First and A, for fifty-five dollars a month. Her plan was to live in the back and sell her work in the front. According to law, she had to make use of the storefront as an actual store. She built a high loftbed in the back near the ceiling. She cleaned the paint off the brick walls and polished them. She installed with her own sweat a Sears & Roebuck shower stall. She built racks of shelves to hold the pottery and a partition to separate store from living quarters. In the back was her castle of happiness: at last she had enough room for her painting, her woodworking and her claywork.

She had no idea how good her painted ceramics were, just the word of her friends, so she undervalued them, selling for five or ten dollars vases and jars she'd spent weeks painting. They were soon gone and she was not about to glop out more in a spew of crudity. She needed money badly however, so she reluctantly placed some of her paintings on view in the store section, again at modest prices. She sold two paintings within the first week and was overjoyed. She bought rounds for her friends at Stanley's. She bought an armload of canvas and extra supplies and a pair of red dancing boots from Madame Braznick.

For his part, Barton Macintyre was slightly upset at all this. He was all for the pottery bit, the groovy storefront, but her sale of paintings, well, that was unfair. He therefore encouraged the pottery. He would pick up a pot and announce, "Say, this looks really good, almost beautiful"—while his eyes passed over in silence the rows of her new paintings.

There was a half-flight of black metal steps leading down to the store entrance. He carried the complimented pot to the front window; "Why don't you hang this on thongs in the window?" he asked as she was attaching a circle of sandpaper on the floorsander.

"Damn you! This is going to be a gallery of paintings! Paintings! not a ceramics studio!" Then she dropped the sander, and snatched her pot from his hands.

On another occasion he was holding one of her wood-carved panels, part of a series of long walnut planks intricately worked in human figures and slum scenery. "You ought to go practical with this stuff," he advised, holding it horizontally in front of her face. "This would be ideal material for a rich man's rare-bookshelves." For this, after she had seized it away from him, she shoved him out the door and banished him up the steps.

Her small successes inspired her to undertake a series of paintings she called Mindscapes. The series was numbered chronologically and when she was finished she had completed ten Mindscapes.

Her method was this. She banned her friends from visiting. She got plenty of sleep and made sure she had no hangover, methplummet, or distress. She placed the phone in the closet with cushions on top of it. Then, in a frenzy she described what was happening in her brain, as she viewed her mind-screen. Faces, images from the past, quotes, hallucinations, desires, with usually one single image dominating the pictures. Feverishly she took notes, made sketches, modeled shapes in clay, literally exhausting herself after several hours roughly blocking out the painting on a five-by-seven canvas. Afterward she spent several days finishing the painting. She began a new Mindscape each day so that at the end of ten days she was working on completing ten Mindscapes at once, moving from canvas to canvas. The Mindscapes astounded her friends. Many of them were so impressed that they brought their friends around to see the

94

works. About that time, Louise decided to call her store The Mindscape Gallery and furthermore to hold a formal exhibition and party celebrating the Mindscapes. She gave herself a month to get it ready.

For the outside of the gallery she carved a wood frame inside which she inserted small canvases in a row, each canvas a painting of a letter of the words, Mindscape Gallery. For the next month it was all work.

There were pressures unforetold. The rabbit at the lab kakked, so she had to endure a nightmare of buses and fear traveling down to get an abortion from a human known on the East Side as The Butcher of 86th Street. Barton, of course, was strapped for moolah at the time and could not share the expense. As a result she waxed behind in the store rent. She could always like sell the place for maybe three hundred dollars because she had done so much work fixing it up. But she hated to sell Mindscape even before it really got rolling. She could have gotten some assistance from her parents, and they offered to help, but she turned them down, although her heart had softened a bit and she had invited them to the exhibition.

There were so many things to do. There was a misprint on the invitations. The printer dared to want an additional partial payment to do a corrected version. She blew up at this, and decided to silkscreen her own, a project which took her days to finish.

There were further matters of repainting the gallery, aligning the lighting, purchasing wine and food for the party, and dealing with Barton.

Macintyre was eager, on the other hand, for her to accompany him on the usual rounds of dinners, strolls, hourslong grope sessions, bars, parties, galleries, and cafés. One of their favorite places was a café called The House of

Nothingness, located on 10th Street near the Tompkins Square public library. Nothingness had a garden section for the warm months which contained a really outstanding miniature Zen rock garden of raked white sand around which patrons could sit and meditate.

They were sitting by the rock garden when he asked her if she would prepare a dinner party for him, his cousin (a salesman for a book company due in New York for a market conference), and for a banker he'd just met at the Cedar Bar. And, of course, she could sit in herself at the proposed feast. She was surprised at his request since she had just been telling him of her frantic preparations for the gallery opening. "When is the dinner to be?"—she asked.

"Next Tuesday."—he replied. The opening was Wednesday.

"You must be joking. You know I have to work on the show."

"Yes, I understand. It's just that you're such a good cook. And I wanted to get the fellow from the bank interested in purchasing some pieces."

The day of the opening of the Mindscapes exhibition arrived after an allnight spurt of work. The gallery was at last prepared for the jostling, excessively cigarette-hungry, shrill party of the art-flock. The Mindscapes were hanging beneath skillfully placed lights—they were beautiful to behold. Louise was happy. The phone was ringing about every five minutes with inquiries about time, how to get to the gallery, and so forth. To shield the paintings until the party should begin, she had draped a large sheet of cloth across the entire front of the gallery.

It was 3 P.M. Louise had gone down to Houston Street to get a couple of cases of wine and some ice-blocks to chip down for the shower-stall coolery. Barton Macintyre had agreed to remain at the gallery to answer the phone or to receive any deliveries while Louise was away.

A human tapped at the front door. "Hello, My name is Victor Richardson. I am with the Creever Gallery. Is Miss Adams here?"

Barton was dumbfounded. Victor Richardson of dollarland!? Victor Richardson the millionaire?! "She's not here. She went somewhere hours ago." Barton did not take the collector behind the sheets but talked with him in the foyer where the paintings were out of view.

"This is Louise's first exhibition—of paintings, that is. You ought to see her earthenware pots! Boy, is she a skilled pottress, if you know what I mean"—smiling at the collector.

"The show has been late in getting on the walls. She may not have it quite ready by the time listed on the invitation." Barton was still smiling. "Say"—looking at his watch, "it's going to be three or four hours before she can get things ready; why don't you come over to Stanley's? We'll have a beer and then why don't you stop by my place? As long as you've come all the way over here. I've been working for months on a series myself. I'd like you to look at them, to get your opinion. I'm exhausted from the project—but elated. You'll see what I mean. If I could only. . ."

Barton could hear the phone ringing as he locked the front door of the gallery. The two men walked down the street toward the beer and maybe—Please, God, please! prayed Barton Macintyre—a sale.

Vulture Egg Matzoh Brei

I

SHORTLY AFTER DAWN they collected all the Popsicle sticks they could find from the wire mesh baskets on the periphery of the fountain plaza. They made a sticky, sooty pile of several hundred, then lined them in a neat straight row, whereupon Avram Maniac, as he was affectionately known, uncapped a giant tube of library paste and squished a dot of white on the end of each, dancing oddly foot to foot, and hooting imitation trumpet riffs through the side of his pressed lips. Maniac was a genius at the lip-horn, but a few hours of it was unnerving to the listener, especially in a hot summer tenement with nothing to eat for four days but buckwheat pancakes, calf eyes stolen from the butcher, and ripped pigeon crumbs. But they were out of the pad now, and it was a beautiful morn and no one yet felt compelled to yell at Maniac. Stomp your lips, Maniac baby!

They fashioned a tall rectangular central stick-tower rising in the grapejuice-stained dawn upon a foundation utilizing the inside top step of the circular stone fountain/wading pool in the center of Washington Square Park. It was a work of major importance, they assured themselves. The date: July 1, 1959.

There were three of them working on the stick-work: John Barrett, Avram Maniac, and Newt. Maniac, it must be noted, expected to hear the sirens at any moment, for only a few hours ago he'd oozed away from the I Am Jesus ward at Bellevue Hospital. In fact, he was wearing hospital attire stenciled "Property of Bellevue Hospital" on the back. But that was like money in the bank. Weekend beatniks from Queens would pay a pretty penny for genuine flip-out garb.

The night before, Avram had traded his maroon Bellevue bathrobe to Mary Meth for twenty-seven little white methedrine tabs, so dawn found him twitchy-jittery and wide awake, all the better he thought, for it made his pajamas appropriately soiled and sweaty with insanity, as he smeared himself with glue and shriekily hooted making the sculpture of sticks. He figured that there was someone out there right at that very moment strapping on their sandals, who would soon get on a subway headed for the Village little aware that he or she would get the honor of paying ten bucks for Maniac's nuthouse finery. The glue was also flying into Avram's hair which was normally curly and matted and strangely bebumped as if numerous small cocoons were waiting there for some future spring. But now it was like a flattened opossum on a highway—a pitiful squashed elevation of hairy-boned grime.

The boy named Newt was a twenty-year-old dancer two years out of the Bronx High School of Science. This tense specimen of indecision could never enter a conversation for more than two minutes before blurting out that he had been scientifically measured a genius. He was short, not over five-foot-four, and extremely skinny—his rib cage could have been used as a rhythm instrument in a jug band. In fact it was, many years later, when he was sacrificed by a Kali-worshiping rock band in San Francisco.

"I am a sunflower surrounded by gleaming careers!" he shouted again and again as he leaped voraciously from fad to fad—first sketcher, then poet, composer, weaver, singer, woodworker, and finally his true avocation of the year, as dancer. And Newt danced around the clock, specializing in wild tourist-attracting herpitudinous shudders on his "stage" —i.e., the plaza near the Washington Square fountain.

Sometimes Newt would strap a roller skate to the top of his head and perform a headstand under Washington Arch, twirling and flailing his arms to draw attention. The crowds of tourists couldn't take enough pictures as Newt somehow caused the skate to move toward the fountain and the head-standing young dancer would yogambulate in a large circle around the spurting waters. Newt's disciples, and there were many, devoured that data as if it were a theophany.

Newt was ambitious; he considered himself only a year or two away from the big league of Beauty-Motion, meaning his own recitals, large halls, tours, quarter-page ads in the *Village Voice*, airplane tickets. "Newt has found the node, man, Newt has found the node!" he shouted from his roller-skate headstand, his arms gyrating like someone shaking sparklers.

John Barrett was twenty-one at the time and attempted to subsume himself beneath a supernal frenzy. He was a poet who pronounced his vocation with gritted teeth and his every waking moment was spent patrolling "the set," which in the parlance of the park was anywhere in the slums of the Lower East Side or the orderly well-preserved

Bohemia of the West Village, as long as you stayed below 14th Street. John Barrett was a bit overdressed for the weather, but felt more ready for Blake-flash when attired in a turtleneck and his year-around jacket. Beneath an exterior of scheme-filled awkwardness, Barrett thought he was at *least* as talented as Keats. Especially Keats, for somewhere he'd read about the hateful garbage the critics had dumped upon poor Keats after the publication of *Endymion.*

"Critics will never get away with that shit with me!"—Barrett muttered, smashing a fist into a palm. Barrett was the type who listened intently with reddened eyes spewing tears through a Beethoven concerto and then rasped hoarsely, "I can do it! I can do it! I *can.*" By this meaning the composition of perhaps another *Iliad,* or at least an immortal sequence of tough lyrics of slumopathic lust. Or something.

"God, I'm a good poet!"—was his permanent judgment of himself as he scribbled his eyeball-data into his notebooks, smoothing and polishing the ripped images, everything holy, everything notable. "Shriek! Shriek!"—oh how he loved that word *Shriek,* "Shriek, I'm up to number forty-seven!" This meant the series of notebooks begun on 6-15-1957 and running relentlessly till that beauteous morn in the summer of '59. The sequence did not exhaust itself until 1963 with number 128. The entire exquisite irruption being subsequently purchased by the Harris Collection at the Brown University Library where it may be inspected to the heart's content.

Oh and ahhh how he felt the Muses—particularly Erato, Terpsichore, and eu-yodeling Melpomene—all properly attired in black leather skirts and Allan Block sandals laced knee high; and all yelling Fire! Fire! Keats-shriek! Blake-flesh! Moans of Byron! in the fierce egoist lightning of his

101

soul. "Keep working arrogant Self"—he commanded. "My notes are mere prolegomenon scrawls, man, for the FINAL POEM. I am on fire to birth the last American poem! I am Pindar!"

To this end, he became an anecdote-junkie, constantly urging his friends to hyperextend themselves, to leap freaky into arcane weirdness. It couldn't be weird enough. So he stirred up people like Newt and Avram Maniac to dance before his eyeballs, his notebook filling up with verse froth.

Meanwhile, the stick-tower kept falling over in the breeze so they glued a perpendicular bracing at the top and leaned the whole apparatus against one of the thick concrete buttress posts which stood every few feet around the fount's edge. Newt produced some Tarot cards from his musette bag, a strange sight in those prepsychedelic days, which they glued to the outside of the Popsicle ziggurat. "I wish we had a camera," Newt complained, bending back to observe the art, shrugging his shoulders in abstract patterns to Maniac's squeaking lips.

By the time it was finished it was 6:30 A.M., and the parks-department sweepers were pushing their wheeled garbage carts and brooms toward the fountain to clean up the papery gunge from the night.

"You want this?" one of the sweepers asked, pointing to the tower.

"Nah, take it. It's all yours." Whereupon the sweeper picked it up and a card fell away, delivering a prophecy upon Barrett's foot. Barrett stared at the card.

"Hey, Barrett" Avram laughed, "according to that card you're in trouble man. You're gonna be talkin' to the worms, baby. That's death there on your toe. Ha ha ha."

Barrett reached down and picked up the card, still wet with glue, and jammed it back on the stick-tower. The

102

sweeper stuffed the whole thing with crunches and stick-snaps into the garbage can.

II

Sun-Ra poured its shafts of grooviness down upon the set and the park began to fill up. A dozen ears perked up when a high-pitched gargling sound was heard from the direction of Fifth Avenue, more like a Persian warble, which signaled the arrival of a human being known as Uncle Thrills, who was appropriately attired in gray bibbed Alpine shorts, a wide-brimmed straw hat, and a perfectly square black beard which collapsed on the inside into total white.

"Here I am from the God-tower!" Uncle Thrills shouted, "Thrill Freak ex Machina! ImGrat! ImGrat!" ImGrat, acronym for Immediate Gratification. "Rapple dapple dally doh!" he continued. "Glupple Globble Gloffle Gluffle! Gloppe Glope har har! Har!"

Barrett was scrawling as rapidly as his poor fingers could flail, trying to copy every syllable. He really wished Uncle Thrills would slow down, because his notes were so awfully chicken-scratchy. And what university library would ever want to purchase such an unruly notebook?

"Hey Thrills, baby," Avram yelled, "Tune us in to the Thrill Flow, man!"

Uncle Thrills obeyed at once, sprinting upon his babble trail, and young John Barrett, Avram Maniac, Newt, and all the others listened with all-suck. For Uncle Thrills was important—he had stuff printed in *Partisan Review*, in *Beatitude*, and if you knew where to look, you could find him in *On The Road*.

Barrett had Uncle Thrills' speech patterns down like someone who'd memorized phrasing off an early Jonathan

Winters tape. But he couldn't very well duplicate Thrills right on Thrills' own turf, so he restrained his imitations until he was in calculus class or among his friends down at the *Catholic Worker* for a little Theos vs. Thrills theology battle.

How poetically Uncle Thrills' face muscles twitched on the steps of the fountain, Barrett thought! "What else is there in this universe if it ain't kicks, baby?" Thrills demanded to know. "You got to feel good so the Gods can dig it. This set is zero!"—pointing to the haze above the park. His disciples dutifully followed his hand to the top of Washington Arch. "What holds this, this mush..."—his face twisting awry in disgust at the word, "together unless it's kicks, some fierce sky-punk's kicks, man? Kicks!"—shuddering with some unknown urging; perhaps it was self-approval. "Those old trees over there, see them?"—pointing to the tall oaks to the west. "They grew up on corpse sweat, yeah! You know what's under this fountain? Poor dead shreds of pissed-on motherfuckers of a hundred years ago, that's what. This was Potter's Field, baby, and a public hanging ground. There used to be mandrake roots growing all over the park."

"I ain't gonna be no chump! I want thrills. Not yesterday, you dig, not tomorrow, you dig ... but now! ImGrat! ImGrat!" He began to stamp his foot. "That's what I want, Lord. Thrills Now! Thrills Now! Thrills Now!" He began to chant it, and a circle of his friends joined him. The din of thrill shouts aroused the police from their post on MacDougal and they came running over to quell the spew.

Suddenly Uncle Thrills broke away from the chanters and trotted toward some early-morning tourists. "Say man, you got a cigarette?" he asked, making puffing sounds with his lips, holding two fingers up to his mouth. "Lay a cig on Uncle Thrills, huh, muh fuh?"

104

With an ashen face of near heart attack the tourist forked over a Pall Mall to The Thrills, who walked away toward the pissoir, already having unzipped his Alpine shorts, violating various exposure laws, singing, to the tune of "I Love the Lord Jesus," "I lick the Lord Jesus upon his bland bod. . . ."

He had a way of forcing the place alive, and the fountaineers were cackling with laughter as Unc' Thrills walked away. Barrett looked at his fingernails, and took a painful nip of one. Several hurt badly from peeled and infected strips of edging. He consoled himself by counting the fingers *not* chomped, sort of a negative confession, and noticed today that fully six of ten were pure and chewless.

Thrills began his shouted lecture even as he returned from the john to the circle. "The Superior SQUISH! plugs into your every movement! You had *better* know it! Let them have their thrillies, the Gods. Aiee! the Gods definitely go nuts on your body, young lady!"—flashing a quick grab in the direction of the buttock of a stroller. "You *can* lick and chew the silver threads from Sky to Earth! Wow!"

That was Uncle Thrills when he was happy. More often he'd moan like a dog pack. His favorite shriek was a line from *Waiting For Godot*:

> *I've puked my puke of a life away here,*
> *I tell you . . .*

Quoting that drove Thrills into a foaming frenzy. "*Waiting For Godot!*" he shouted so hysterically that his voice went up about half an octave. "God the Idiot! God-ot! Bah! Oh how I've peeeeeuked my peeeeeuuuuuke of a life AWAY!!!"

Disciples of Unc' Thrills used to practice that line to

105

catch those great sneering inflections. Barrett remembered his high-school classmates doing the same thing, swaggering out of *The Wild One* to practice sneering like a Brando biker in the bathroom mirror.

Uncle Thrills loved the attention. His scheme of life involved the careful construction of a legend of himself as a genius. To this end he had contrived three careers: as novelist, as inventor, and as artist.

For eight years he had been working on a long multilanguage novel, bragged to be over ten thousand pages in length, entitled *Cryptozoic Aeon,* the epic story of the genealogy of a human genius (Uncle Thrills) which began in the warm germic algae soup of the cryptozoic aeon and passed through some 14,023 sequential life forms until somehow arriving in his current life form, U.S. Genius 1959. Now that was egotism. It must be said, however, that all anyone had ever seen of this monumental endeavor was a musty springbinder of untyped pagination.

As an inventor Uncle T. held several patents. One was for the so-called battery-powered Thrill Beeper®—which was really more of a tiny cattle prod and was supposedly able to activate wonderful pleasure nodes within the brain when applied to certain areas of the scalp. (A scalp-map depicting proper zap spots was supplied to the purchaser.) Uncle Thrills loved to chase young beatlings around the fountain waving the Thrill Beeper.

Another invention involved a bathtub meditation system. This grew out of Thrill's habit of submerging himself in a hot tub every morning for spiritual communications with Poseidon. He stayed beneath the water for over a half-hour, breathing through a copper tube which extended up and over the porcelain lip of the tub. To facilitate his visions, he sewed a black wool canopy which fit tightly over the top of the bathtub. He also created quite exquisite stained-glass tub-covers enabling the meditator to look up during submersion for vision-inducing Gothic colors.

As for his painting, one is afraid that, without Uncle Thrill's complex mythological explanations, which he gladly supplied to each purchaser, the works sagged sadly in merit. His long interpretations of his paintings seemed to fool many collectors, who would buy a canvas titled, say, *Chaos Charted on a Hesiodic Map*, or, *The Angry Spirit of Protein Spits Verbs at Deus*, when the paintings in question were constructed of platefuls of spaghetti thrown on the cloth and sprayed with fixative, the spaghetti blobs encircled by ink-sketched coronels of organic molecules.

Which brings us to the checks. Man, could he grab the checks. In a dazzling blitz of hype, Thrills would learn of the address or phone number of a collector or rich patron, perferably patroness, of Art, and within a day would gobble a check, sometimes even a blank check, out of them.

You scoff? It was strange, especially since it would not seem to be so easy to acquire an instant check, but those who wouldn't normally think they would *ever* fork over money to some mumbling nut waving a manuscript, would, as if in a trance, find themselves scratching away at an elegant French writing desk. "You just write Uncle Thrills a check—I'll cash it over at the Eighth Street Bookshop—I'll be finishing my translations from Ibsen soon. This will make it possible."

Thrills liked to use the innocent-faced John Barrett in some of the check capers—which meant that Barrett might find himself guarding the door of a bedroom at a party— Thrills inside droning hypnotically at a trapped countess, shoulder straps sliding helplessly down a spa-smoothed

107

back, "write a check, O beauteous Imperatrice, write a check, write a check . . ."

Thrills would do anything—his favorite gimmick was a peyote-methedrine mickey in the champagne, followed by a seance wherein the spirit of Walt Whitman would urge all to write, write, write! out that generous check to this great man of our times.

Accordingly, it was with regard to copping a check that Uncle Thrills began to huddle with Newt and Avram Maniac by the fountain. "You see," he said, "I know some European royalty, married to American money. She just *adores* novelists, can not resist that urge to help. And I just happened to have brought my manuscript—bloof!"—as he blew dust off the springbinder, "with me. She lives up at the Dakota Apartments. Let's go."

He waved over at Barrett. "Hey Barrett, you coming with us? We'll cut you in." Barrett demurred and off strode the trio in quest of the Holy Check.

III

Barrett watched his friends depart—and soon his mood sank down into that negative trough, to face his three-headed enemy: boredom, confusion, fear. Hi!, Barrett greeted the hallucination. He filled the holes with filled holes, so to speak, for a while by doodling on his hands and arms with fountain pen. "RA is Hip to It All" he mock-tat-tooed 'pon his forearm—then rolled up his sleeve, so all could see, and stood up and strolled around the park. This is a thrill-stroll; this-is a thrill stroll; this is-a thrill stroll, he told himself. Maybe someone will be blowing some gage; nothing like a fear puff to tighten up the day, he thought.

It must be remembered that Washington Square Park was

108

steeped in the Eisenhower era—i.e., squaresville, baby. The beats, the derelicts, the surrounding campus of New York University, the parents of young children, all vied for the use of the turf. No music was allowed (except Sundays), nor poetry readings, nor drummers. Only recently, known beatnik rioters had acted to close the park to dangerous auto traffic that once swarmed through the park's center. But the rules for the park's use remained strict and robotic. The police were always instant breaking up a crowd listening to a poet, or bumping lovers from the grass. And speaking of grass, which was what Barrett was keeping an eye out for; smoking a reefer in Washington Square in those '59 days was an exercise in total fear that was forever burned in the memory. With sneers of derision spittling upon the concept of the taxation of hemp, the dharma-commies lingered upon a remote bench sucking the pale clouds upon the alveoli of the lungs, while the senses were on Anslinger Alert: eyes left, fear-scan, eyes right, fear-scan, eyes even scanning the sky—and ears: ears attuned to the farthest footstep, mouths ever ready to swallow the smoldering kernels of aphrodisia, should fuzz pounce.

But there was not a puff of pot in the entire park, which was just as well, for he heard the gong inside him, a gong that sounded the poesy hour, the high point of his day. He found a bench beneath N.Y.U.'s main building, opened his knapsack, removed a small stack of books, and spread them side by side upon the slats. "Ah holy books," he whispered, stroking them like those secret painting-patters whose greatest thrill is to jack the leg of *Oedipus and The Sphinx* at the Metropolitan Museum.

There were *The Cantos* of Ezra Pound, *Howl & Other Poems*, Allen Ginsberg, the *Collected Poems* of Dylan Thomas, *Wasteland & Other Poems*, Eliot, *Echo's Bones*,

109

Sam Beckett, *Buddhist Texts Through the Ages*, the new issue of Roi Jones' *Yūgen* (with Ginsberg's *Kaddish* IV & V), plus *Beatitude*, issue #2.

He read with a tension that made him breathe heavily. He became so excited he had to pace back and forth in front of the bench, pausing to lean down now and then to pick up a fresh book. He read them aloud, alternating stanzas from different books. At first it was Pound's *Canto 45*, with its beautiful litany 'gainst Usura, which began to make the young man tremble; and then a few lines, right after the *Canto*, from Ginsberg's *Kaddish*, Part V—the Caw Caw crows shriek in the white sun over gravestones in Long Island section—followed right away by the first sixteen lines of *Wasteland*, cut back to *Kaddish*, Part IV (oh Mother what have I left out, O Mother what have I forgotten), and Barrett by that time was literally jumping up and down.

Finally, risking the reproach of cops and park attendants, he vaulted the bench and ran into the forbidden grass, threw himself down and began to reap the slender golden-headed wheat flash into his notebooks, his fingernails jammed with wax from candled poverty.

He could *see* the Verse Flood! a river of lines from various bards—O it thrilled him to see his own lines mixed in his mind with the verse flash flotsam of his heroes. It was as if he were unconscious, as he wrote. An hour, posing as a minute, passed. Now, these *are* the thrills, he thought, as the pure jolts poured back and forth, pen to brain, brain to pen. "Melpomene! Baby!" he shouted with glee. Μελπομένη—that is, God-dance.

IV

If Melpomene in fact was watching Barrett's scriptive convulsion, she saw how pitiably attired he was in a coat caked with candle wax from his hovel of no electricity, with buckwheat noodles crusting his lapel like melted Secret Service pins. Every day he seemed to knock a candle over, bespewing himself with the tallow. How like a seized bard, he thought. And the coat, which had suffered duty as his winter coat also, had acquired by its ceaseless service, an olfactorial hint of zebra anus, offending nearly everyone it came near.

That morning he had lost the heel of one of his shoes and the exposed nails were slowly drilling into his foot. The New York spring rains had rendered the shoe leather swollen and brittle. Both shoelaces had broken a long time ago and the halves had been realigned as laces, ends slowly frazzling. The halves themselves snapped next and with only a quarter of each remaining, he could barely tie two holes together per shoe. On wet days he wrapped tinfoil around his socks to keep the seeping moisture from sourly souping the griseous inner foot-soot.

It's time to go to the *Catholic Worker*, he thought. I'll visit the breadline and maybe I can con some clothes. He packed his books and walked over to the Bowery, and on east to Chrystie Street, to shed his sark. He still felt a nag of guilt that said, "Barrett, thou dost not deserve a new coat"— his preferences for socialism, or rather anarcho-peoplesrepublicanism not being sufficiently developed for years to come. He also knew he'd have to bullshit with the woman who staffed the second-floor clothing cage for maybe hours before he could summon nerve to ask for a coat, and maybe some shoes, if he had enough energy left.

He raved a bit with the *Catholic Worker* staff, muttering nolo credere at the possibility of the Christ Lamb. He aped Uncle Thrills right down to ImGrat! ImGrat! Where Barrett had been born, atheism was the coolest stance, in that you

111

could cause, say, a locker room of football players after practice to become a frothing mob of potential killers by insisting on discussing the virtues of atheism. Even as he softly whispered "ImGrat, ImGrat, ImGrat," the lady who ran the clothes box coaxed him into a prayer circle, and Barrett found himself reading aloud from the Bible when his turn came up. He forced back what he kept telling himself was a mote-caused tear. He reproached himself severely for the lachrymosity later. "Toughen up, Barrett, toughen up!"

Nor could he allow himself to deny the free *Catholic Worker* lunch, which he gobbled aplenty. He conned a few extra slices of that good C.W. whole wheat home-baked, for his pocket; later he'd buy a can of sardines, some halvah, and suffer an evening banquet by the healing waters of Washington fountain. He was the healthiest human in the room full of the sanguine hispid-faced hungry men and women trembling with age and alcohol. "Yum yum!" he blurted out, trying to catch a thirds on the pea soup by flirting with the ladler. Not that he ever later on gave a penny to the *Catholic Worker* when he was out there on the poetry circuit pulling in fifty a year.

After lunch, Barrett waded into the clothes cage which was overstuffed with groovy winter attire. He found a wonderful brown riding jacket, sewn on which was a great draping rust-hued cape, with copious pockets suitable for pounds of notebooks and the apparatus of scrounge.

For his feet he found a pair of rubbished bowling shoes, each of a slightly differing size. They must have been discarded rentals from an alley—since the left shoe, red and green in color, was painted with a 9 on the heel back, whereas the other, plain brown in hue, bore the number 14. They were extremely comfortable, free of rot scent, and worthy of the stroll of Apollinaire past the riverine book booths. Donning his new attire, Barrett felt a spew of raw genius.

V

He was full, he was happy—the angst of an empty stomach emptied away—for e'en a nascent Keats is de-ego'd and deprived of depravity by the talons of the Food Hawk. He was in the mood for a stare scene at Rienzi's Coffee House where his antlered eyes might be assuaged by eyeball data, pulchritudinous and groovy, sandals on taut tanned calf muscles, muscles under flamboyant attire waving and bulging, existential stares from the window as he passed the San Remo Bar. He dazzled the Bowery, he was sure, as he oozed along in his new bowling shoes and apollonian/apollinaire jacket, to Bleecker, up Bleecker to MacDougal, right on MacD, to Rienzi's.

He chose a white marble table with inlaid chessboard at the front window. For what good was a long sit in Rienzi's without a full view of the MacDougal Street parade? During Barrett's years in the Village, he developed methods of gazing that would have been useful fifteen years later had he decided to have formed a psychedelic cult of eye-trained followers, instead of becoming an English professor/bard.

He lit up a little Henri Winterman Café Crême and sat, just sat, drinking espresso tinted with lemon rind, followed by a cappuccino, then another strong espresso, raising his energy to the level of, say, a Wash Park pot puff fear-scan, as he impaled the passing grooviness, haughtiness overdubbed above unselfconfidence, pausing to jot down in notebook the fleeting flashes.

He would not have called it boredom, but after a few

minutes the window-stare caused an inner confusion or mild desperation like that of a cultist trying not to fall asleep in front of his guru during a meditation session. Therefore, he was happy to switch his attention to the observations of face muscles, for he found a sad lack in English verse of the description of the activities of the human face during moments of love, tragedy, and heavy action. For instance, what were the face muscles doing during the seduction scene in Keats' *The Eve of St. Agnes*? And was not Ezra Pound in book after book telling everybody to "Make It NEW"?

To Barrett, such concerns provided possibilities to enter literary history with a bang, as opposed to that other odious possibility of entrance, e.g., whimpersville. So he turned from face to face in the coffee shop, jotting down face-muscle data. He paused at a boy and girl sitting at the table next to his, and decided to time-track, so to speak, their activities in his notebook, perhaps as a vignette for a short story—for he certainly did not want to get lost in a career as a poet without having acquired the ability to spin up a story for a magazine in a time of poverty.

He could not pick up a copy of the *New Directions Annual* in the Eighth Street Bookshop without feeling sore remorse that a story of his was not contained within. A story, not a poem, for he felt his lyrics much too completely unpublishably ununderstandably totally garbageably brilliant to risk printing, yet—again possessed with a stubborn belief that critics were going to vampire his career.

The girl was attired in a tightly fitting blue suit with a white lace blouse beneath the vestlike suit top. Barrett's notebooks are unclear as to the color of her hair, but it was cut just above the shoulders, was parted in the center, and there were bangs upon her brows. Beneath the bangs were wide brown suffering but sensual eyes sadly encircled with the apple bruises of tiredness—or maybe the languor of summer-school final exams. With her was Levine, a poet whom Barrett had met at a Ginsberg-O'Hara reading at the Living Theater.

The girl reached into her briefcase and drew forth with hand atremble a clutch of typed verse, maybe fifteen pages in all—and handed it to Levine who read them most attentively for at least ten minutes, his jaw muscles munching a phantom cud of Old Mule chewing tobacco. Levine turned back to several poems for a reread, nodding and humming through his nose in apparent approval. Then it was chopsville.

Slowly Levine unscrewed the fountain-pen cap, his head bent down, his eyes staring slightly upward in a baleful Ivan the Terrible glance into her returning stare. Barrett watched this unaware. The girl certainly did not ask the guy to edit or to emend her work.

"I hope you don't mind," was all Levine said as, in a quick slashing of 's, rubouts of phrases and sentences, and even, horror of verse horrors, rewrites of entire lines, he chaos'd her poems.

She watched this quiet and white-faced. "You see this line?" he asked, twisting the page so she could view. " 'I have learned nothing,' " he read. "Well, instead of nothing, I usually write 'naught' or 'aught'—you dig? Because 'nothing' is so, uh, unnoticeable, but 'naught' is, sounds more, like, what a poet would say."

She was not so sure. Her lower lip jutted and trembled. And you could tell watching Levine hold her poems crunchingly, he did not consider her a poet. " 'I have learned naught' " he read, then he scribbled the change.

At the same instant as Levine read that sentence, a hu-

115

man in a frayed purple top hat just beyond them leaned down toward his companion's face, holding a lightbulb up next to her nose, and shouted, "You prove this lightbulb exists! Prove it!"

Barrett was overjoyed, heading for his notebook to jot those twain of pearls.

> I have learned naught.
> you prove this light
> bulb exists.   Rienzis 7–1–59

You can check it out at the Manuscript Collection, Brown University Library.

It was after his second espresso and second hour at Rienzi's that John Barrett headed toward the restroom. There was a thick post located near the stairs down to the john, with a table on the other side obscured from sight. As he started down the steps, he noticed a spade cat at the table, in a beret, sun glasses, and smoking a cigarillo in an ivory holder. Barrett nodded hello.

The man gave a quick look to his side, like a basketball player before a back-pass, then, in the manner of dope dealers of the time, blurted a mumbling rapid sentence softly, "Would mumble mumble buy mumble grass, man?"

At first Barrett wasn't sure what the man said. Then it clicked. "Maybe a nickel bag," he replied, and walked down the steps. It was really stupid to buy pot on MacDougal Street. Barrett knew it. But somehow he felt he had to go along with the offer, like someone who can't leave a bookstore without a purchase to please the cashier.

First of all there was the problem of quality, because notorious burner-hustlers worked the Village coffee houses, and it was sure injurious to the beat image as tourist pot-seekers from Indiana University were sold a pitiful mixture of catnip, oregano, a faint dusting of real cannabis, and maybe a sprinkle of de-doped canary seeds.

"May I see it?" Barrett asked. There was a flash of disgust on the guy's face as he slid a hand into his pocket and palmed a thin foil of crinkly substance into Barrett's fingers, all the while fear-scanning over the shoulder and up the steps for the narks.

"Hurry up man," he said. "There's fuzz everywhere." It was in the Rienzi's urine parlor that the first beatnik narkos flourished—becostumed in berets, beards, sandals, black turtles, and shoulder holsters. It was supposed to be humor-out to watch a beatnik policeman head for the john every five minutes to try for a collar.

Barrett unfolded a corner, peeked at the green, and sniffed. The grass was mysteriously almost as verdant as a pool table and it smelled like the spice shaker over at the pizzeria.

Barrett loved any real opportunity to get righteously indignant. And now was the time. He only had twelve dollars as his entire worldly hoard. If he spent five for the bu, that left him on the poverty line with seven to last through a week's spaghetti, day-old bread, and whatever he could grab off free and pungent in the sun at the Fulton Fish Market. It also meant he couldn't pick up the book he'd ordered at the far-famed Orientalia Book Store on the techniques of Japanese Nōh Drama—another area of scholarship the wily writing of Ezra Pound had inspired him to consider.

Therefore, Barrett was relieved and the Nōh book was as good as bought when the odor of the grass indicated it was a Zippo-lighter scene. "Why're you trying to sell me spice, man!" Barrett demanded in a loud whisper. "Fuck, I can go across the street and shake this shit free out of the pizza

117

shaker." And He left the bu upon the washstand, walked up righteous to his table, paid the chit for the overpriced beatsville coffee, and headed out into the glare of MacDougal, such a narrow and overarched street that it was almost like walking room to room.

Barrett headed up MacDougal for the park. Suddenly the burner passed him, nudging him with a shoulder. The burner turned back upon him, adjusting his beret to the back of his head. His words were a hiss. "I don't want you telling anybody you *think* I tried to burn you, or you and me are going to go through some changes."

"Leave me alone, burner," Barrett almost moaned in reply. The burner vanished left at West 3rd Street toward Sixth Avenue, dancing at the heels of a pack of tourists, then was swallowed into their midst.

VI

"Man, you shouldn't *ever* buy grass in Rienzi's!" They laughed. "Hey, Barrett just got burned in Rienzi's! Ha Ha Ha!" A circle of loungers at Alex Holley's statue as Barrett took a slurp from a Thunderbird bottle someone passed him.

"Check that motherfucker!" one of them exclaimed.

"Yayah! Here comes J.S.D.!"

The sucking circle of T-birders at the statue's ledge were excited. You were always excited whenever a friend would stroll, saunter, cringe, or crawl, into the park. Barrett looked up and there he was, loping into the plaza, stilt-legged J.S.D. J.S.D. was maybe twenty, and extremely tall—the type coaches start taking out to dinner by the time they're thirteen. J.S.D. was wearing a pair of tan Levi's about six inches too short, and a fishnet T-shirt which was very popular at the time. J.S.D. had a habit of pointing his finger and shak-

118

ing it while tilting his head to the side—according to Barrett's notebooks—before he began to speak. The barman at the Jazz Gallery gave him his name from the first letters of jazz/sex/dope, which triad comprised the substance of J.S.D.'s worldly interests. He was a Wurlitzer of saxophone solos—all you had to do was give him the name of the record, and the instrument you wanted, and he was ready to give you an oral recital. Obscure alto recorder parts, for instance, that you could barely hear on early records, J.S.D. knew them all. He was the Mozart of the Jazz Gallery. If Sonny Rollins came out of retirement to play the Gallery, J.S.D. would sit all night, head in hands, at one of those one-dollar side booths at the club, and memorize the entire gig. The next day he was at the park ready to perform it all. As for the other initials in his name; id est: sex and dope, those occurred hourly daily nightly.

"What's happening, J.S.D. baby!" Barrett exclaimed, holding a palm out for five. J.S.D. whacked palms, sat down next to John Barrett on the shady side of Holley, drained the Thunderbird, cadged a cigarette, and asked the immortal question, "Anybody got any pills?"

Twenty minutes died in the mirth. Barrett looked over at J.S.D. whose head was tilted aside, attracting Barrett's attention, and his finger was pointing wildly. One would have thought J.S.D.'s eyes were going to liquefy, he was so torridly impaling the advent of a girl known when she was not around as Racy Tracy—portions of her body in various orbits of wiggly jiggly—all of which drove J.S.D. into a brickbat down-scope with respect to his middle initial.

Tracy looked just like the red-haired woman staring out from Édouard Manet's *Le Déjeuner sur l'Herbe*. And that was her scene, the picnic of the senses. There was one slight difference, she was not yet quite as chubby as the picnicker

119

sur l'Herbe, but the face was one-on-one. Barrett tried to bring this fact up, but Tracy was already aware. She said that she was mad at Édouard M. for not having at least *one* of the guys nude also at that famous creekside foursome.

Tracy was a watercolorist, specializing in portraits of the denizens of W. Sq.—particularly the spade cats. She was good at it—she worked hard—although her name has never appeared in subsequent years in *ARTNews* or The *Voice*, or on SoHo posters, so it is difficult to know if she kept it up. Each early morning she grabbed the D Train from the Bronx, with a pad of paper and her case of colors, and headed for the park. There was, of course, the sensual side of it too, she being addictively an adept, in the votive sense, of the "onyx lollipops"—as she spoke of it, as of FLASH! Man, was she popular.

J.S.D.'s favorite summer pastime was tar-beach sex, and the arrival of Tracy triggered off such a possibility of paradise that he brought it up immediately. " 'Ey Trac'! What's happening. Let's go over to East 9th and roof it! My friend's got a sun tent set up over there, and we can use the shower in his pad." Tracy and J.S.D. were famous on the set for the number of roofs they had made it on. They even once broke the lock on the door, and went up the spiral staircase to the roof of Wash. Sq. Arch where they celebrated the birth of Himeros, God of loin lunge, out of Chaos.

J.S.D. and the others did not pay much attention to her paintings and that pissed her off. They were always trying to set up house with her—having in mind more of a wash-the-dishes scene than her being a painter. Barrett was somewhat upset that whenever Tracy was around she seemed to look through him as if he were gauze. He didn't exist. "Look at me," he spoke breath-level, "please."

Tracy laughed, and showed J.S.D. her latest portrait, but

120

sensed at once that his mind was dialed into a mono-chan-nel. "Not today, J.S.D. Maybe tomorrow. I'll be down here about noon. Okay?"

"Okay, baby, see you then." J.S.D. turned to Barrett, "Hey, let's go over to Dom's and cop some stuff."

VII

Dom's pad was above an outdoor fruit market on First Avenue and the arising air always had that scent of potato buds and acrid cantaloupe. When they arrived Dom was standing at the stove cooking a pan bread of beat-up matzoh crackers mixed with corn meal in a large iron skillet. He was sweating and his oleaginous muscles were bulging as he shook the skillet, his laced sandals occasionally slapping the linoleum. Dom's voice was almost a caricature of a Deep South accent—mayan for man, squayah for square, Zin for Zen.

Dom lived with June, a nurse at Bellevue Hospital until very recently when a ward nurse had found her grabbing fingers in the hospital dope cooler. June wore her yellow hair in a near crewcut; she was thin, with hips elegantly sliding perpendicularly from her thin stomach for about an inch before angling downward. She was a bit of an A-head and was a familiar figure at the fountain in her uniform after work. She liked her white nurse's stockings and wore them that day beneath a Mexican wedding dress embroidered with briar roses across the bosom. J.S.D.'s head tilted to the side and his finger began to point, and Barrett copped at once the real purpose of the visit, watching the pants-down stare passing back and forth between June and J.S.D. out of Dom's sight in the living room.

In the kitchen Barrett belched with nervousness looking

121

through the cupboard doors upon an Old Mother Hubbard barrenness. The only things to eat in the pad were a box of matzoh meal, a box of matzoh farfel, a box of corn meal, and a pint of cooking oil and that would all be gone soon as Dom heaved the pan bread out of the skillet onto the plate, a gray curl of corn-oil smoke arising from the hot iron.

He and June were totally broke in a New York summer—hardly a time to be down and out in the beat apple, although wintertime on the Bowery by the burning barrels had to be infinitely worse. Besides, Dom had his dope business to keep him going. He was rumored to be able to supply virtually every substance mentioned in Robert S. De Ropp's book *Drugs And The Mind,* and his living room attested to that claim with many shelves stacked with pharmacist's jars of semilegal substances such as *Lophophora williamsii,* wild lettuce from Mexico, belladonna, yohenbine bark, Indian tobacco, ginseng root, and even some sort of dried worm from Sumatra that purportedly placed the user into the Land of the Warm Fog. Illegal drugs such as coke, meth, bennies, pot, skag, yellowjackets, goofballs, mescaline, and opium were kept ingeniously stashed in the ceiling light fixture of his neighbor on the floor below. Dom had drilled a hand-sized hole in his floor just above the fixture. Dom said that you had to be very careful in retrieving pharmaceuticals from the bowl-shaped light because it was easy for the arm to miss the fixture and find itself waving in empty air. The residents in the apartment were very religious and Dom was afraid that if they ever looked up and saw a hand descending from the ceiling they might consider it some sort of epiphany and start screaming.

Dom had just flown back from Tangier where someone had dropped a total burn on him in a hash deal. He tried to make the story humorous but his words were crispéd and sere. "There I was, man, pushing a cart out of this market-place; my eyes were seeing dollar bills and the lease on that summer place in Vermont. When I loaded the stuff into my trunk it turned out to be, I guess, a bunch of camel dung bricks mixed up with pieces of clove. I lost everything but my plane ticket. All I got out of the whole trip was a sack of vul . . . ." He paused, suddenly snapped his fingers, turned and walked through the curtain of beads into the living room.

Dom came back holding a lumpy bundle tied up in a bandanna. He undid the kerchief and placed six brown-speckled oval objects on the table. He lifted one of them up to his ear and shook it.

He explained that he had bought them last week in Morocco and he'd been solemnly assured by the purveyor that they were fresh vulture eggs from nests in high mountain crags. He had meant to give them out as gifts but now, with the Food Hawk screaming 'gainst his eyes, began to meditate aloud on the possibility of frying up a bit of ome-letic vulture. "Lordy, I hope they're fresh enough to eat," he said.

He closed his eyes and broke one into the sizzling skillet, wrinkling his nose at the same time as if expecting a miasma of rotting buzzard to issue upward. But the egg looked great. He broke the other eggs and mushed them up with a fork, sprinkling matzoh farfel into them and a splash of oil. Right away the orange-yellow plexus began to spew forth soft odors of yumminess so that all four of them crowded around the skillet, freshets of salivation forcing them to swallow.

"Man, I don't know, they look fertilized," Barrett cautioned.

"Fuck it, man," Dom growled in reply. "We need protein.

123

They can always pump it out of us up at Bellevue if we get sick. You got a dime to call the ambulance?"

Barrett nodded.

The V.E.M.B. looked like a flat circle of yellow modeling clay upon the serving plate, but boy was it delicious—the only known instance in the beatific era of vulture egg matzoh brei. And it may have been also the only instance in the same era of vulture-egg protein stoking the fires of fornication. For June and J.S.D. began to send little ships out of each other's eyes to meet and negotiate a body brei. And the meal was barely ended when J.S.D. took June's hand and guided her to the fire escape, whence he spat a glance over at Dom as if to say, cool out your wrath South boy—and then in a slow turn of his head he focused his attention on June, smile spreading. They giggled and bent over to crawl out the window and climbed upon the metal slats.

Dom and June had a tar-beach roof cabana reachable by a ladder from the fire escape. There was a mattress out of sight behind the water tower, which was shaded by a couple of those large umbrellas borrowed from hotdog carts. June and J.S.D. went up to fuck almost every day that summer—not exactly groping in front of Dom but it was a silent rule that Dom would keep away while they were up on the tar.

Barrett thought he saw a quick bite of the lip, but Dom turned his head before John could be sure. Dom kicked the floor with his sandal, and muttered. "I don't know. I'll just never get used to them."

"What do you mean?" Barrett asked, "them making it on the roof?"

"Nah, man, I guess I mean spade cats."

Barrett wanted to change the subject. He also wanted some fresh data. "May, uh, I go up and watch?"

Dom looked startled, but said, "Suruh, go on ahead."

124

John B. reached the top of the ladder and paused, his head and most important, his eyes, just clearing the rim of the roof; he could feel a very pleasant breeze float up the back of his riding jacket. He looked down the six flights to the trashy alley. Shudder. Then he lifted his eyes unto the action.

June and J.S.D. had just about reached the mattress, their arms tight around each other's back, June's long fingers sliding under J.S.D.'s belt, under tan jeans, over the darkling buttock—a little insistence of pain perhaps, as she scritch-scratched her way.

"Ow! Watch it," J.S.D. laughed.

John Barrett himself laughed as J.S.D. slid down his Levi's, folded them carefully, then laid them across a TV aerial. June couldn't wait—she knelt down as if to worship the Afro-herm, rubbing her hands down both sides of him—and then took as much as possible into her mouth. For a few seconds, from Barrett's vantage point, her head looked like someone nodding frenetically listening to an anecdote at a party.

Then J.S.D. pushed her away and June sank slowly down to the hot, slightly dour-smelling Sealy Posturepedic, rolling her white stockings off most efficiently—it reminded Barrett of a baker rolling dough for pretzels, and he nearly fell off the metal ladder trying to put that comparison 'pon his note-pad. After that, she lay back coyly in her briefs and J.S.D. was on her and she was barely able to remove them before shyly but adeptly she glided the dark guitar-neck within her. "Come on come on come on," she said, "come on."

Barrett fought away a curling of drool from his lips—and found himself aroused against his gabardine trousers. Another long stare and then he forced himself to look away, more specifically to look fearfully downward as he attempted a thumpless silent creep back down the fire escape.

John found Dom jacking off lotus-posture on a prayer rug, looking at a wall map of East St. Louis. Is that what he really saw? It sure looked like it—although Dom quickly removed any indication of manstupration when Barrett lunged through the beaded curtain. "I've got to get out of here before things get weird," Barrett spoke deadpan, "but first can you deal me some bennies?"

They were a bit overpriced at six for one dollar, but Dom had already wrapped them up in an empty Rolaids package before he could complain. When Dom found him browsing in the other room by the dope crocks, he suggested he try a speedball, which was a "steal" at fifty cents. Barrett wasn't sure exactly what was contained in a speedball and was far too cooled-out to pull a Q & A scene to relieve his ignorance. He thought it was a mixture of cocaine and either morphine or Nembutal—like, a ride up ride down same ride. He knew he'd probably never take it, or leave it around collecting dust in the paperclip bowl, try to offer it to a shocked graduate student ten years later, so he bought it.

Barrett was pretty tired so he blew fifteen cents for the crosstown bus back to Washington Square. During the ride he noticed a mother with young child sitting on her knees. She was teaching it various words, and after running the child through the obligatory "mama" and "dada" and "gonkit" (blanket) she pointed over at Barrett and said, "See the beatnik, Tommy!"

"Come on, honey, say beatnik, beat-nik!"—breaking the

126

word in two. And the child rolled a drooling face toward Barrett, smiled, and said, "jeep jik!"

That made Barrett's day, and he spent the next hour and a half in the musty silence of his favorite bookstores, The Eighth Street and The Phoenix. He was still able, at that early point in his career, to experience mysterious bookstore flashes or energy tranferences by, say, standing very near the New Directions rack in the basement of the Eighth Street, or reading the mimeo'd *Ezra Pound Newsletter* at The Phoenix. Ahhh sweet bookstores of New York.

He finished the latest issues of *Semina* and *Kulchur* and caught the time off the wrist of a clerk, and sped back to the square to log some time working on the sequence for his first book of poetry. He sat down again by the statue of Alex Holley, but far enough away from Uncle Thrills, who was holding court at the fountain, that he could barely hear Thrills' shrill wail, and escaped into the sentences.

Siobhan McKenna
Group-Grope

THE TAN FOG of particulate dooky lay low 'tween the high clouds and the barren skyline cenotaphs of New York City. Within the closure of lower Manhattan, in tenement slums of the poor, a poetry reading was held in late September of 1961 at The House of Nothingness on Tompkins Square North. It was an open reading—one where any and all were allowed to read their works.

In warm weather the readings were held out back in the court where there was a beautiful rectangular garden of raked white sand with a triad of small boulders bunched in the sand at one end. The garden was modeled after a similar garden in a Zen temple in Kyoto.

There were seven humans—three women, four men, who were walking through the streets after the reading toward an apartment at 704 East 5th Street just off Avenue C. Each of them had read their poetry. That is, when they arrived at Nothingness, each had approached the person running the readings and had placed his/her name on the reading list.

128

There were twenty-three readers that September night, divided into three approximately one-hour sets. Readers were requested to limit themselves to ten minutes each but occasionally someone droned through a 115-quatrain translation of the Pyramid Texts of King Unas so that after, say, fifteen minutes, people began to shift impatiently at their tables. In all truth the majority of those attending had come clutching springbinders of their own verse to read and viewed time-hogs with disapproval.

Of the seven walking through the midnight East Side, three were editors of their own poetry magazines. They knew each other's work intimately and discussed it whenever they met, which was just about every day. Their life was the world of poetry and poetry publications and the recounting of the anecdotes of poet-life. They lifted a common nose of disdain upon the rest of the world, especially television and newspapers with their ceaseless spew of right-wing death.

In spite of the horror, terror and vileness of the *res publica*—the ennui, the mental spasms that sent them down plateaus of nothingness constrained to watch the blobs convulse and mull and melt—in spite of it, they met that fall after the readings to listen to poetry records, and, while lyrics softly babbled from the speaker, did lie down toward the Galaxy to pluck the vast lyre of grass-grope. For no right-wing government can prevent the sneers and derision of the people smoking pot in private.

Compared with the bunch-punches of the psychedelic years to come, it was tenderly innocent—but it was thought to comprise an historical first, the premiere instance in Western Civilization of such activities.

They specialized in Caedmon/Spoken Arts records—committing skin-clings to the best minds of three generations,

129

including Dylan Thomas, e. e. cummings, Marianne Moore, Delmore Schwartz, William Carlos Williams, Edith Sitwell, and even T. S. Eliot although it is to be admitted that Eliot reading *Murder In The Cathedral* made it somewhat difficult to keep up the stoked fires of fornication. (A complete list of poets, to whose verse were held the parties, is appended.)

It was actress Siobhan McKenna's reading of Irish poetry that the group played again and again in their fuckings. God, it turned them on. They exhausted their love-surge listening to Siobhan McKenna. They talked about writing her a letter inviting her to attend one of their midnight specials the next time she should visit New York. They were especially excited to find out that McKenna had performed as Lady Macbeth in Gaelic at a theatre in Galway.

"Let's find out if she had made a recording of the play in Gaelic!" someone exclaimed, bright-eyed with eagerness.

There was no theory behind the group-gropes—unless the theory of the heated bottom. "Who loves himself loves me who love myself"—the bard sang; and that was the gropers' theory. They didn't discuss it really—but fell down regardless into the furrows of the avoidance of coma. If anyone asked, "Why do you think we do this?"—someone carried the hookah-tip over to the person or toppled them onto the mattress with a grope-tackle.

Some were hesitant, waxing bold later. Others the reverse. It was like that Ezra Pound poem, *E. P. Ode Pour L'Élection de Son Sépulchre*, Part IV, only as applied to phonographic fornication. Ava, for instance, wrote long-line poems of religious nature and wore extremely demure attire, but once the police lock was poked into place, became a torrid participant. Brash-mouthed Bill however, who was a veritable Tourette's disease of obscene expletives, became almost unparticipatingly shy, although he was eager to hop around the mattresses with an ancient box camera. For the most part, the seven relaxed into a common soul and grew to know each others' bodies and desires and energies to a labyrinthine degree.

When the sex-hungry poets arrived at the pad: Ava, Bill, Rosebud, Nelson, Rick, Trudy, and a human named Obtak who considered himself to be the reincarnation of Shelley, they drank a round of yohenbine-bark tea that Rick had made during the day after a street-scrounge for mirrors. Right away they stacked the poetry records atop the turntable. Rick had a gentle thing about mirrors and that afternoon he'd collected as many as he could find in the Bowery area from thrown-away dressers. He hauled up five cracked, pitiful specimens which he lined around the mattresses. That was his chief thrill, to watch others reflected fucking in mirrors, at the same time listening, say, to Edith Sitwell, while Ava massaged his pornic area with a banana skin.

There was a small offset press in the back room on which Ava printed a monthly verse-paper. Ava and Obtak had to work awhile in the room fixing the inking mechanism which had become maladjusted so that only the left side of the page was being printed. When it was fixed, they fell fucking beneath the machine on a blue air mattress, unable to wait for the poesy. Someone in the bedroom put on an e. e. cummings/Luciano Berio composition. After a few minutes, Ava and Obtak came out of the press room, Ava laughing, "I guess it's time to go to bed." She leaned against the bathtub and whipped off her blue velour pullover, dropped her jeans skirt, flaming over to turn on the water. She took a bath with the assistance of Nelson, and then appeared at the mattress, dabbing at her hair-ends with a towel.

There were two mattresses side by side, one double-sized,

131

one single. Before anything they smoked a lot of grass, via the toilet roll dope blow. They took the cardboard inner cylinder and Rick punched a small hole into the top of it, inserting a thick burning bomber in the aperture. At both ends mouths were positioned. One end sucked their lungs full of dope. Then, on signal, he/she blew the lungful through the tube into the sucking mouth-lungs of the other, in a fast whoosh. Then it was off to the zone.

There were variations of this, for instance when Bill inserted his cock through the roll when there was a lit roach burning perpendicularly and several of them took a toke.

For serious bedside smoking, however, there was a five-tube hookah made out of a jug from an office watercooler. The toke-tubes were long lengths of rubber lab tubing wrapped in velvet ribbons. The carved burl was kept packed with grass and throughout the festivities anyone could lean over from the mattress and snerk.

They started with an arpeggio of e. e. cummings, Marianne Moore, Dylan Thomas, and a flash of *Howl*. Then it was the McKenna hour. Siobhan McKenna's voice, soft, full, beautiful, triggered off a cross-mattress grope spasm that turned the arms and legs of the lovers into a quick frenzy of motion like a dropped fistful of jackstraws. When she read Yeat's *The Stolen Child*, with the chorus in Gaelic, three suffered orgasm immediately. "Siobhan! Siobhan!"—Bill moaned, as he was engaged in E3- with Obtak, Ava, Rick, and Nelson. E3- was a term used by them to denote concomitant double-handed beatoff plus fellatio by Ava, with simultaneous impletion of Ava from the back.

There were numerous combinations but usually they paired and trio'd off by the end of the records. Ava and Nelson slept together. They always seemed to pair off and indeed, of them all, were the only ones to live together. Ava pushed her slight frame against him. Soon she was atop and seesaw bumping. She was able to come that way, rocking, rubbing forward, sliding into the happiness. Next to the frenzying Ava/Nelson, Rick and Rosebud lay side by side, Rick bringing her to a moaning cliff-leap by means of an extraordinary device fashioned from a furry pipe cleaner.

Obtak and Trudy, she side, he at her back, eyes shut tight, making it on the single mattress. Trudy was able to lift her leg and move it back and forth across the partner's chest during conjunction.

As for Bill, he usually fell asleep after a single act of love culminating in a long warbling scream they called the "yohenbine yodel." Bill had read a poem that night at The House of Nothingness titled *Homage to the Buttock*. Later on, Bill and Ava were seeing how hard they could whack themselves together and the pops filled the air from the pubic cymbals. Perhaps thinking of his poem, Ava whisper-urged him to climb upon, nay, to impinge himself within, her buttocks. He became confused and soon had to stop, thinking she had bidden buttockal pain upon herself because of his poem—for verily there are few who trod the paths of Mt. Bulgar.

He continued to think so except that he gradually learned that she genuinely was an adept of buttockry. Forever he remembered her lying topless upon her stomach on the sleeping bag on the air mattress in blue tights and Rick pushed his hand upon her behind and into the inward-curving, rotating the muscles circularly. "Don't stop, don't stop"—she whispered. "That arouses me more than anything all night."

Bill and Trudy loved Dylan Thomas, especially when he read *Fern Hill*. It drove them crazy. That night they played it over and over, seven times, until Bill was constrained to

133

utter his famed yohenbine yodel after which he was soon asleep.

Hours oozed. They talked. They smoked. They wrote. They ate. Some departed. Some slept. Some kissed till dawn. And the gatherings went on each Monday for ten weeks before their Galaxy spiraled into dissolution. One went one way, one another.

During the ensuing decade, the seven ran into each other occasionally—at Orly Airport, in domes of meditation Colorado mountains, and so forth. "Remember those nights of Siobhan McKenna?"

"I sure do."

And always the friendship. bloomed. to renew again. the pleasures. of former. commingling.

Recorded poets grope-list:

1. *Yeats (Siobhan McKenna reading)*
2. *e. e. cummings*
3. *Ezra Pound*
4. *T. S. Eliot*
5. *Dylan Thomas*
6. *Edith Sitwell*
7. *A. Ginsberg*
8. *Marianne Moore*
9. *W. C. Williams*
10. *Delmore Schwartz*
11. *Arthur Rimbaud (Germaine Bree reading)*
12. *E. A. Poe*
13. *Lawrence Ferlinghetti*
14. *Edna St. Vincent Millay*
15. *W. H. Auden.*

Lophophora Roller Rink

HE DECIDED TO forego the reading of any more novels after he had tallied his future reading list in the languages he was studying, in the poetry of the languages, and in certain religious studies relating to Coptic sects, Buddhism, the Vedas, and the beat poets. He did not have time for many years to read novels, he felt. *On The Road* often lured him into its lonesome pages, but he was able to resist consuming much time therein. Joyce, however, was a poet in everything and the young man felt it was okay to linger within.

His refusal to study contemporary fiction was a disaster that surfaced fifteen years later when he tried his hand at a couple of novels. Even the critics who were his best friends had to turn down assignments to review them for *The New York Times* Sunday book section.

He was living on five dollars per week consumed in spaghetti, day-old bread, chicken parts (hearts/necks/wings/ani—like, twenty-five cents a pound on Avenue A), and what could be borrowed from markets by stealth just after pre-

135

dawn outdoor deliveries. His pad on East 4th Street was a three-room citadel of verminous grime. He loved it. He had rented it furnished from a policeman, who was acting somehow as the agent for the prior occupant who had recently been placed in an asylum. The legal rent for the pad was eighteen dollars a month, though the policeman charged him forty-eight.

The method of acquiring an apartment in those days was this. The *Village Voice* was published on Wednesday, but advance copies were delivered to Sheridan Square around noon on Tuesday. One waited in role as nervous pad-junkie for the delivery truck and when it arrived, grabbed a copy and ran rudely, without even opening it, to the cigar store, where there were phone booths. Once inside the booth and the door was closed, one read the pad ads, and made immediate phone calls. Less than one minute after the *Voice* was delivered, he had made an appointment to see the famous pad on East 4th, and less than thirty minutes after the phone call, he rented it, not knowing the renter was a cop.

The prior occupant of the apartment had left numerous letters around the place signed "Nancy the Lion Heart" which were long love letters from her to "King Richard the Lion Heart." The policeman had apparently been involved in carting her away to the institution. One day a letter arrived from the rent control board, addressed to Officer Smekolsk—which the young man could not resist opening—announcing that the legal rent was being raised from sixteen to eighteen dollars per month. That meant the cop was skimming thirty illegal bucks! A quick contemplation of his dope-hoard, however, made him decide not to make any trouble for the officer.

He kept the pad furnished exactly as he had found it, and filed Nancy the Lion Heart's letters away carefully, in

136

event she should escape the asylum. It was a roach farm, and the only thing he could find time or inclination to keep clean, besides his bed and desk, was the middle drawer of the kitchen table. He threw the knives and forks from the drawer into the bathtub—an act which necessitated scooting the utensils out of the way when taking a bath. The emptied top drawer was used for the dope: pot, skag, amphetamine, papers, and needles.

His only interests were books, dope, thrills, and his friends. He had not seen a TV for three years nor had he listened to the radio except for the midnight jazz shows. Newspapers were pillows for copping z's on the subway or on a park bench. The world of *Time* mag was absent, man. For instance, the advent of the twist caught him unaware. He was stumbling home wrecked one afternoon when he encountered a group of Puerto Rican kids on the stoop doing the twist to a blaring portable radio. In his apartment he turned on the radio and tried to locate it. Finally on WMCA they played a weird record called "The Lone Twister," sung by a gravelly voiced male crooner. "I'm de lone twista"—the voice sang.

"Hey, that's what I am, man, too, the lone twister!"—his roommate Wilfred yelled from the other room as he twisted the tie on his arm before the blood clouded into the dropper and Wilf pushed the rubber bulb and the skag zombied the vein. Wilfred was working his way through De Ropp's book, *Drugs And The Mind*, the beat bible of dope gobble, trying whatever he could get his hands on.

For instance, in a few minutes they both planned to take peyote. It apparently wasn't illegal to receive *Lophophora williamsii*, the peyote cactus, from mail-order "cactus ranches" in Texas and the Southwest, so there was a flood of buttons that year for the mouths of the Lower East Side, and only yesterday Sam had trudged up to Stuyvesant Station to pick up their packet from the thrill farm.

When at last it was time to chew, Sam was alone. Wilfred had gone out somewhere stealing or scoring or scrounging and had told him to sail ahead. The poet lay upon his back, after swallowing five dark spansules packed with flakes of peyote, waiting to experience the period of nausea that was supposed sometimes to occur just after ingestion. He felt no sickness-waves, however, and within a few minutes the gods switched on the lights of peyote. He looked around the room and saw colors and gradations of colors in objects that he had never before noticed. He began to stare up at the copper-colored lining on the inside of the socket of the ceiling light fixture. The copper normally would have been a mere dim blur up there in the cracked plaster but under the grace of *Lophophora* it gleamed with new fire. Minutes he stared at the flaming copper.

He had been advised to close his eyes for peyote flash-patterns which would maybe present themselves as great whirling Ezekielian religion-wheels. This he did and waited for the colors. Instead of Ezekiel, he immediately experienced a time jump and there lit up upon his mind-screen a full-color reverie of Mr. Roddle's '49 Plymouth packed with his seventh-grade schoolmates in 1952 driving to a roller-skating party in Bluff River, Colorado. Why was he thinking about the roller rink? He didn't care—he felt like someone in some small futuristic movie house watching his own bio-tape. He even murmured, "Roll it, O Zeus, roll it!"

Mr. Roddle's blue Plymouth came with those fuzzy brown seatcovers that caused hideous spine shivers whenever one's fingernail accidentally scratched across it. Sam could see the inside of the car, the kids clutching the skates in their laps. He saw himself with his arm around his girlfriend Annie Thornton!—whom he hadn't seen for many years.

Annie's father was driving the other car of skaters. The last thing Sam wanted was to be spotted by Annie's father in the rearview mirror necking with Annie so Sam remembered having talked her into riding with Mr. Roddle. Every time he saw Annie's visionary face, his stomach felt that empty ache and it was no less so eight years later as a derelict beatnik. She was a dark blond with long delicate hair on her forearms. Even in the seventh grade she had already acquired her wanton beauty, and to see her again, as if it were real, was sad indeed. Ache, beatnik, ache.

Annie and Sam had taken piano lessons together with the same teacher for about five years. That's where he had first seen her, sitting with derrière-length tresses at age seven at the keyboard during one of those torturous recitals the students periodically had to give for their parents.

Then Sam remembered the movies he and Annie Thornton used to go to on Saturday afternoons. Her father would sit way in the back while she and he sat in the third-row front. Her white jeans, the starch of her white shirt knotted at the waist. Her hair. The popcorn. The secret cigarette smokers snerking Lucky Strikes bent low in their seats. The sweat of the palms of nervous hand-holders. What a smell-mix.

He remembered putting his arms around her, fearful of rejection. And then she leaned her head on his shoulder, purest of thrills. And her hand as it held his, what could match that? Could it have been that a beatnik trio writhing nude on mescaline upon a mattress could not duplicate in any way the thrill of a hand held in a matinee of a Durango Kid movie?

The seventh-graders had begun to hold parties for one

139

another. Some went together to dancing school: organized, sanctioned body contact—an hour and a half of fox trot, box step, the jitterbug, two Cokes, then home by 10 P.M. The parents wanted to control it, to prevent any pants-down scenes. When a "weak" parent was discovered fronting parties where there were necking games, they were immediately halted. Sam remembered one party there was a game devised on the spot called "pick-a-leg" where, divided in halves, one group would sit on a high ledge and hang their legs down. The others would "pick a leg" and then there were five minutes of rubs and smooches in the dark followed by another round, new pick-legs, and new smooches. When the snitcher snitched, these parties were banned.

The solution to this "problem" was the institution of bi-weekly skating parties. Let the little punks skate their fires away.

Clommer's Roller Rink was located right on the Kansas/Colorado state line. It was owned by Walt Clommer, a local sports hero just in the zenith of his career as a major-league catcher, preparing to spend his remaining forty years operating a roller rink, a Dairy Queen, and a used-car dealership. His daughter Sophie was Miss Colorado in 1957 or '8.

There was great excitement when Mr. Roddle pulled into the parking lot. Sam could never remember anything of the interval between arrival and putting on his skates inside. He leaped from the car and zombi-ran to the front door. The next two hours would be total fun: no politics, no hidden meanings, no parents, no visions, no hassles.

Clommer's Roller Rink was a bit run down, sorely in need of paint, and rather weatherworn. The cost: fifty cents to get in, thirty-five to rent skates, if needed. The interior was high ceiling'd and heated by a vibrating furnace in the far

140

corner. The rink itself was edged by a rickety railing of two-by-fours behind which were wooden benches skaters could rest upon. There was a side room with a sacred snack bar full of Milky Ways, popcorn, hotdogs, Cokes, and bubbly orange.

The music was provided by sempiternal records of organ music. At the far end there was a cylindrical device which indicated the type of skating to be done on the floor. This oilcloth roll had a handle which could be turned to change the notice. Occasionally the music would stop and the manager, who skated around and around the floor cooling out daredevils and keeping the flow unidirectional, would utter a tweet on the whistle he wore around his neck. Then he would skate over to the cylinder roll and turn the handle till it indicated the skating he desired, such as COUPLES, TRIOS, LADIES CHOICE, WALTZ, etc.

Sam was a punkly skater. Skrunk! Skrunk! Skrunk! he practiced, lifting his feet uncertainly rather than gliding. Curves were hard to negotiate at first and sometimes he would carom centripetally and crash into the bare wood guardrail—oof!—his torso doubling over the board in sudden pain. The skate floor was ground down by the ceaseless skrunks, so that there was always a fine dust upon it. When he fell, he begrunged himself. Humiliated he headed toward the restroom to wash, for he hated to look creepy in front of tender Annie Thornton.

Each time they went to the roller rink, he always spent time working on learning how to leap and twirl. Annie Thornton, just like she was a better pianist, was a much more skillful skater than he. With a sigh Sam saw himself skating with her, gliding, twirling together, crossing arms across each other's back, holding hands.

The really skilled teenage couples sometimes dressed

141

alike, with matching pompons on the fronts of their skates; the boy, say wearing a red and white sweater, and the girl in red and white skater's skirt. In those seventh-grade days, Sam had dreamt of the year when he and Annie would skate in matching outfits too, her arm wrapped on his shoulders, he his finger hooked into her back belt loop, his senior ring bouncing on her chest.

Toward the end of the evening, Mr. Roddle left the rink and went out to his Plymouth where he sat inside with his head on the steering wheel. Sam could not remember eight years previous going outside and seeing Mr. Roddle get into his car. It was eerie. Then he saw Mr. Roddle sobbing. He certainly didn't remember seeing that. A woman came out of the rink and walked over to the car window. "Something's got to be done!"—she yelled. She reached in and began to shake Roddle's arm. "Stop it!"—he shouted. And abruptly the peyote vision fell apart, just as the car door opened and Roddle's leg appeared.

A knock at the front door poofed the roller rink and drew him back to East 4th and 1960. He found the door. It was Wilfred his roommate with an armload of mimeographed pages. Wilfred had begun to write down his dreams in shorthand. He mimeo'd his shorthand notes and used to give them out on MacDougal Street while hitting on the tourists for change.

Wilfred walked to the kitchen table, removed his works from the silverware drawer, cooked up some skag, tied up, shot up, and then walked back to the bedroom, turned on the radio for horn-shrieks, horn-mania, horn-defiance.

Sam returned to his cot and tried to retrieve the bio-tape of the skating party but the vision was like a tenth-generation photocopy. No roller rink. No teen-skate '52. What he saw stretching before him was a checkered plateau clear

142

unto the horizon and, in the distance, saw wavy blobs rise up, coalesce, melt, then rise again. "I am a nuclear potato. I am a green bat in a purple cave." He began to laugh. "I am a handprint on a burnt wall." He rolled over on his lumpy cot to face the wall, and still the convulsing blobs kept rising and sinking.

"Hey Wilf!" he yelled, "Come here and look at the blobs!" And he roared with laughter. "Roll it! Roll it!"

Luminous Animal Theatre

THERE WERE THREE of them at once, the tripod, as she thought of them. The three, who were in love with Claudia Pred, founder of the Luminous Animal Theater: The first was a playwright, the second was a tax examiner, the third a critic. There was a possible fourth, a rich New York stockbroker and book publisher who had invested heavily in *Newsreel-'84*, the new Luminous Animal production.

There were numerous others who had fallen down in groveling obeisance, even in the past half-year, whimpering near her hemline, salivating and swallowing, nervous for reciprocity. Claudia, as a matter of moneysaving practicality, fashioned as many of these salivating lovers as would endure it into Laborers of the Abyss, that is, into production assistants, artists, scene-swabs, janitors, and ticket-takers for the always-busy Luminous Animal.

Claudia Pred,
Cantatrice and Carpenter of
Beauty-motion,

144

the headline of her first big review in *Dance Magazine* had flashed, when she was just twenty-two years old, five years before the occasions described in this tale of gloria mundi. A carpenter of beauty-motion, that's what she was indeed, and she had a tremendous impact on dance in the early 1960s.

1. She had begun her career very early. Right from high school she had enrolled in the New York School of Dance and Drama, where she studied for three years, by the end of which she was already putting on weekly performances at a loft on 22nd Street. And even at that early point in her career, the *Village Voice* was monitoring her art with semiannual reviews. Fred McDarrah, for instance, who chronicled the 1960s for the *Voice* with maybe a million peripatetic shutter-clicks, already had a file-cabinet drawer packed with glossy proofsheets of Claudia by the time she was twenty-four.

2. She loved dancing; dancing she felt the fluxions of Eternity. Her energy was legendary but her legs were weak. Try as she might, she did not seem to strengthen them. Not that her tries were very forceful, for she seemed, in such attempts, to tire quite easily. And she was not about to become an A-head in behest of "dance, devadatta, dance!" But, in front of an audience, when it counted, she was all energy, all performance, all creatrix. She was Of Beauty; let us say it, for many a night we sat in Luminous Animal staring at her ceremonials of beautyway, muscleway, danceway.

3. She had a strong and oaken physique and full cheekbones able to cast shadows from upper light down upon the face flesh. Her hair, long waves which crested every two inches or so, was combed back out of the way, or worn in braids, or woven into a cunning knot at the back. On the night of a performance, she placed a goodluck hair pin in the back

145

knot made from a brass penstalk that had once belonged to Herman Melville. Often there were pendulous hair bunches she fashioned on each side, to hang down to the middle of the eyes—another item of thrill for dance stare-freaks watching the hair grow glistening wet with perspiration in the course of a performance.

4. She was radiant. But it was not the pale lux of pity, buddy, it was the harsh light of Apollonia. Severe. Strict. Melted peanut butter sandwiches in the sun. But such strictness of bearing merely turned on the stare-freaks, that is, her followers, men and women of various reasons and wishes. And she cultivated them. She focus'd a substantial portion of her rarified artistic taste on her costumes and her personal attire. Every part of her had *THE* aspect; and she was ever a subtle contortionist, presenting the bone, the visage, the palm of the hand, the portion of the foot, to the beholder in its most moving view, offstage, onstage, and under the stage.

5. She was a magnet. She had that most necessary trait of leaders, the ability to engender intense dedication to the most miniscule of projects. Her disciples were ever eager to entangle their lives with hers, and there wasn't a drama department in any New England college which didn't have a few rebel students, especially women, who wanted to emulate Claudia Pred's life in the New York theater scene. They were astonished that she held so many projects together at the same time.

6. That is, she was resolute and domineering while appearing indecisive. It was a classic theatrical management technique, at least as old as Richard Sheridan managing the Drury Lane Theatre. Her apparent indecision was really a total resistance to compromise; and since her schemes were usually well underway at any point, she could appear as indecisive as she wanted. And, to be sure, highly literate and

articulate vagueness which at the same time evinces reassurance is of inestimable value in warding off the scent-tizzy hounds of banks and creditors.

7. And she was stoic. She rarely shrieked. And never thought herself to be in the wrong; and probably wouldn't have been able to function at all if she had felt in any way to march under any other banner than that of Truth, Justice, and Socialism. She was generous—she paid many a paper bill for various groups printing protest leaflets on her mineograph machine, or for poster boards and ink for her silkscreen equipment. She ran what she would want to have called a community—but she was always aloof from her associates. Part of it was a natural coldness that is a curse to so many creative people.

8. She was a lister. She kept one-hundred- or two-hundred-unit lists for each project, and her clipboard bulged with them. Hot projects, or projects needing repair, were placed at the top. The bottom of the clipboard bulge was reserved for those that functioned smoothly, and for projects still in the visionary or spectral stage.

9. She was a diarist. She kept it all—the march of the mosquitos of manners. And she spared nothing, no one, no memory, under her theory of TROUBLE. She LOVED TROUBLE, as long as there was no violence involved. There was something in her that rode against convention with shiny-eyed glee; without that boring periodic occurence of religious fervor that such brave individuals often endure, those who trample out the fresh surfaces of ne'er-been-done-before. In her diaries, she constructed her own language to describe her complex life and loves, which is going to be a pain in the ass for her future biographers—unless she codes her hapax legomena to the English language. And her writing resembled amphetamine calligraphy on a

napkin at 3 A.M. in the Café Figaro, a fact which prevented lovers and unlovers from sneaking by stealth into the pages for some quick thrillies.

She also encouraged filmmakers to record her productions. And she tape-recorded everything she could afford, and there were thousands of still photos of rehearsals and personnel carefully annotated and saved for the aeons. The posters for Luminous Animal productions were made by the best artists, and a full signed set of them today will bring about ten thousand dollars at auction.

10. In the matter of men and morals, she had to evince an exaggerated toughness. One may remember that it was 1961. For one thing, the males kept cringing in adoration, or if not cringing, they came on whippy tough-guy. They tried to tell her what to do—always making crummy unwanted suggestions, especially on artistic matters, like, "Say, I know exactly how to improve the plot in your current production. Here is my critique . . ." Others wanted to sow confusion, to weaken her, and to overpower her. Scorn, derision, and toughness; these were her weapons.

11. She was known to torment her lovers. Lord forbid they should fail in the bristlings of Eros. Subtle hisses and boos met that sort of failure. But she liked the nuances of reconciliation and to be forgiven her temporary cruelties. When she broke up with someone, she always felt herself to be the wronged party, but it was she who usually had to endure them tacking up a list of grievances on her doorstep.

12. On occasion she felt herself falling in love with a Sister of the Abyss, as she called her dancer friends. She loved that two-month period of total tenderness the affairs more often presented; after which, she felt herself enormously more sane, and would then leap back into the theater with pure devotion. Former lovers later would see her photo in the

148

drama section or dance section of a magazine and shake their heads like someone waking up from dream zzzzz, eyes opening, seeing the face of a radio by the bed, seeing an actual face! which slowly dissolves into the radio, knobs, dial, and speaker.

13. In spite of her archivist attitude, she had a habit, which she grew to despise, of Moving On. Burning Bridges. Leaving behind begrieved humans shaking their heads. Th' earth-blob orb'd the sun-blob not too many times before Claudia began to feel guilt for things gone awry—especially certain events in the remoteness of her early career. Such guilt allowed her to be bushwhacked at any moment, like an acid flashback. Sometimes her face filled up with tears right in the middle of a performance—but her friends chalked it up to her Art. And after a decade in Bohemia, the plexus of remorses for addled projects, sour affairs, ruined friendships, was sometimes unbearable. One man gave up poetry to become a nut, losing his toenails and teeth age thirty-one in the amphetamine death trap—she blamed herself. Another leaped—she blamed herself. Another, whom she rejected, banned herself from the theater, for which she had been a designer without compare.

14. She had a superstitious magic-believing side. She blew a horde of fear-stuffed nights inside old books by A. E. Waite and Dion Fortune. She had a glass-enclosed case of old basement-of-Weiser's-Bookshop occult tomes from which even her closest friends were banned. She felt that the United States was soon going to go up in a big "hydrogen jukebox" boom boom—and that she and the other chosen would totentanz through the city ruins, collecting the paintings and artifacts of their choice from crushed museums.

She had a vague interest also in astrology, which concerns were centered on a zodiacal analysis of her career. That is,

149

she felt the stars all lined up with this message: Claudia Pred will dance inside a whirling rainbow across a vast meadowy theater filled with a billion eye-bodies silenced in amazement.

15. She attracted a broad spectrum of critics—for her political actions, for dance, for drama, for her singing, for her costumes. The same work of art would produce great praise and great hostility, both of which she could easily endure, but not derision or mockery, which when she read it, drove her into a foaming rage. Some would rail and mewl against the political statements she chose to make in her beauty-motions—mewling that she was "politically naïve"—i.e., and apparent socialist, or, worse, in the rightist cold-war babble of the time, a com-symp, which was strictly naughty-naughty-mustn't-do in a dance-and-drama scene heavily financed by the warbucks crowd.

The *New York Post* pointed a finger at her as a sufferer of "Joan of Arc complex"—which criticism twisted her into a fury. It didn't take very long to learn a useful rule: never to read any criticism whatsoever, while remaining silent in the squinting faces of critics. Even as she did so, a small temple of belief was set up in the back of her mind emblazoned upon the portals of which was a rewrite of a certain sentence from Voltaire: "the last critic strangled with the guts of the last theatrical moneyman."

The critics she hooked to her art, however, stayed hooked. The words, such as "genius" and "protean energy" and "beauteous frenzy like no other," spewed from their typewriters.

There was one lamentable situation relative to certain critics trying to take advantage of their power. That is, they would flock to her side, listen sympathetically, try to drunk-fuck her, then totter back to the cab or the train. She had several characteristics of body which the critics loved to analyze manually; most far-famed of which were her buttocks which were as legendary as those of Claudette Colbert, and were discussed most attentively by her critical fans. Critics just couldn't stop themselves from lunging, fingers fluttering grabbingly, toward this living statue of Aphrodite Kallipygos, in the course of an interview.

Enough of this description, O Rapidograph scratching in the night, for we must moil ahead with our story, though we could easily tarry for many a chapter describing the remarkable Claudia Pred, cantatrice and carpenter of beauty-motion.

Ever since she began to produce dance dramas, Claudia had dreamt of finding a playwright/composer who would write a dance-opera-drama which used maybe a small jazz ensemble—which she could stage, and star in, at Luminous Animal Theater. She thought for quite a while she had discovered such a genius in Roy Shields of East 3rd Street. Shields was known by the nickname Dirty Roy on the Cedar Bar-White Horse-Stanley's-and-Bowery tavern circuit, for his squalid apartment, and for certain indiscretions relative to his ambi-subaxillary musk farms which evinced themselves in profusion whenever, say, he decided to try out his jitterbugging techniques at the face of a jukebox. Claudia cleared up that problem when they became intimate by banning him to the shower amidst sharp rebukes which became Pavlovian later in their affair when he automatically took a shower whenever she yelled at him.

That was okay with him, because part of Dirty Roy was all desire to become Tuxedo Roy—although he would have punched you out if you had told him that in early '61. He can come and punch us out today, but it's true that his gameplan called on him, for a few years at least, to become Scandal Roy, then Calm-down Roy, then Come-to-terms-with-life Roy, then Tuxedo Roy. As Tuxedo Roy (becoming what he once despised, a liberal dispensing a check here for a worthy cause, a check there for a worthy cause) there would be those winters in richland, summers in villaland, and falls on Shubert Alley.

But we are being unfair to Roy Shields, for at the time of this tale he was the most powerful writer on the off-Broadway stage. And he was enough of a composer to be able to write melodies and lead sheets for the jazz quintet that backed some of his plays.

Roy Shields considered himself the greatest playwright since George Bernard Shaw. (A few years later, in the acid era, he took a few trips up at Millbrook and came to believe that he *was* G. B. Shaw, but, by that time a good business-man, kept this startling reincarnational belief to himself.) In fact, he considered himself vastly superior to Shaw. Aeschy-lus, that was Shield's league. For, was it not true, he asked, that only in Aeschylus could one find the appropriate com-parable abilities in combining dance, music, beauteous verse, drama, and social foment within the same sempiternal con-cretions, that I have?

"They will tremble, or more probably, like, weep, reading my folios in 2200 A.D.," he told Claudia, "trying to figure out why the civilization treated me so shabbily; nay, why it took such an obvious delight in performing a flamenco dance on my face!"

Shields loved the danger-thrills of insurrection. For in-stance, it thrilled him immensely reading how Aeschylus in-serted secrets from the Eleusinian mysteries into some of his plays (such as *Iphigenia* and *The Archers*), for which the Athenian populace brayed for his death. To Roy, the modern equivalent of the mysteries were state secrets. Oh how he hungered that someday he would get hold of advance information about some immoral government scam, such as the CIA invasion of Cuba, and put it on right away as a stage production, exposing it to the world, before the actual invasion.

In the Shavian manner, Shields wrote extensive, and I mean extensive, introductions to his plays, the intros often being as long as the plays themselves. He published his plays under his own press, Triumph Publications. They now fetch a goodly sum from rare-book catalogues, which probably makes him regret all the boxes of them he left behind unsold at the Luminous Animal Theater. He was a poor businessman—thinking for instance that all you had to do to collect from bookstores was to send an invoice with the shipment of books.

Especially for Claudia, Roy had written a long skit-skein which he titled *Newsreel-'84*. The play was based on George Orwell's *1984*, and Franz Kafka's *The Trial*, and the extensive series of books published in the 1950s, inspired by the Korean War, which analyzed brainwashing as a political tool. The time of the play was April 4, 1984, and consisted of acted-out news stories for that day from *The New York Times*. Heavily featured in the work were political trials in the form of nightmarish dance-rituals put on in public.

Roy parted from Orwell's vision of permanent war, by positing a world-wide condition of a different form of hostility. In the civilization of *Newsreel-'84* everyone belonged to exclusive, angry sects. All obedience was pyramidically spewed to the top of each sect. Friendly communications between humans of different sects was prohibited. Through

153

an intricate set of rules, leaders alone of sects were allowed to meet, behaving and talking monotonically, like zombis. Claudia played a dancing (dancing was forbidden) neo-Zombicult nun who secretly falls in love with a six-foot-six-inch black neo-Catholic priest played by a poet known on the set as Big Brown.

The production presented numerous problems. Claudia felt that the play, with its several incidents of flag-burning and partial interracial nudity (this sent shock-waves clear into the closet of the district attorney's office in the fake-sex days o' '61) was quickly going to get her into TROUBLE. Besides that, she didn't really think very much of the play's quality, especially when measured against, say, Roy's beloved Aeschylus. Roy, on the other hand, was upset over certain adjustments he was required to make in the play which resulted in more dancing and in bringing Claudia's role more into prominence.

Claudia thought the work too suffused with, well, (*boring* was the word in her mind), heavy-hounding political analysis. She mistrusted the theatricality of a standing chorus chanting for fifteen minutes at a time, in trochees, backed by a jazz ensemble wailing in trochees, the words being a lengthy socialist analysis of social conditions in a far-off era. These danceless actionless portions of *Newsreel-'84* were what Claudia felt might produce a counterpoint of snores from beyond the footlights. But Roy had trapped her on that one. For, in agreeing to give her a bigger role, Claudia had promised in return that the choruses would remain uncut.

Nevertheless, the play had a sudden-at-every-point powerful energy into which she injected her remarkable dancing and singing. As for her singing, she had that octave of basic notes, the Broadway (and off-Broadway) eight, which

154

she could sing well in different styles, from softsad plaintiveness, to high emotion, to screeching anger, which was a rare ability in such an expert dancer. She could have signed with a folk label later on in the decade, and she'd probably be deposited right now in a stone-and-redwood mansion in the Santa Monica Mountains, strumming and fretting at injustice.

There was a long ketchup-soaked sequence featuring a character known as the Lord High Chopper who was made up to look almost exactly like the then-current mayor of New York City. This had already been mentioned several times in the gossip columns as the show opened for previews, and the Democratic district leader was reported to be very upset over the "insult against our dedicated hardworking mayor."

This party official had prompted a blitz of fire inspectors, building inspectors, health inspectors, tax inspectors, to besiege the theater as it struggled to prepare *N-'84* for its opening just two weeks away.

There was nothing that Claudia could do short of self-censorship. Too much had been spent on the production. Too many were dependent on it for salaries. Besides, Claudia could not afford to get the reputation for stuttering or backing down from the pulings of political hacks. So, she pushed the performers very hard, held many practice sessions, and slowly mutated the vignettes so that the play grew eerily smooth.

She woke up when a warm hand slid beneath her gown. She quiver-startled at the touch, then rolled over, legs lifting apart for a more intimate tangency. She did not seem to mind, yet who can ever know? They held out their arms in a most un-Shavian pattern of Eros, for the usual morning clingings. Gowns and pajamas wound up under the covers at the foot of the bed. They fucked for a while, but both were freaky for hot shower slurps so they adjourned to the bathroom shower stall, where she blew him under the torrent, and then he knelt down in the hot wet and brought her to a semblance of bliss with a drive-crazy quicklick, from which he pulled away at least two crucial minutes too soon, but she rebuked him only in her head, how sad that such a didactic person as Roy Shields should lack such erotic information.

Therefore the vibes, as they say, or the vectors, were misdelivered somewhere other than a paradise pro tempore, so in the dance of her preparation of breakfast for two, the conversation tensed with bad art as well as the golden cage and the silken nets Blake sang love traps all soaring souls.

He thought he brought up the subject of the play in an oblique, constructive way. He mentioned the "tension" in the first trial scene in the third act, finding fault with her "outbound twirling"—i.e., her dance notations, a nomenclature which peeved her right away, which he felt should be "more centripetal, so as to give the cultic uniqueness its necessary implosive quality, don't you agree?"

That one sentence triggered off an argument that proceeded in the gibberish mode toward a schism in their affair. "Do you think anything *could* be done with that concatenation of casual behavior?" she wanted to know.

And so it went. His art, she shouted, wobbled prolixly between the poles, boring boring boring! and didactic! didactic! didactic!

At the finale of the argument, Dirty Roy was banned from

156

her pad, and his pitiful suitcase of manuscripts and peestains was hurled toward the door as a prelude to him returning to live at his East 3rd apartment.

"Boring!" she shouted from her door as he walked down the linoleum of the tenement steps.

"You are made of lignum vitae mallets!" he shouted back, crashing his fist into the mailboxes.

"My God, he's wearing a cravat," she thought. Not only that, but Mr. Twerthel, the tax examiner, had recombed his hair Julius Caesar–style to cover a bit of the baldness. And he was *not* wearing his usual muddy brown three-button suit with the linebackerlike shoulder pads; rather, he was wearing a White Horse Tavern tweed with matching charcoal trousers and, by all that is holy, a pair of Mexican sandals with car-tire soles.

Mr. Twerthel was bent over a small wire wastebasket into which, upon Twerthel's urging, Claudia had agreed to deposit all receipts, check stubs, phone bills, and the like. The basket was heaped nearly to the brim and Twerthel was retrieving the fiscal data piece by piece, and noting each down in his ledgerbook. "Would you like a cup of coffee, Al?" she asked, leaning by accident ever so slightly with a heavy breast in Ukrainian blouse against his shoulder, which act erased all tax data in his mind for a second and substituted certain sensations of seldom-felt happiness.

Mr. Twerthel had been assigned to her case some six months previous in order to facilitate collection of past-due federal employee withholding taxes and to audit her books.

Somehow, after a few visits with Claudia, the tax collector found himself working on her taxes so that, rather than

157

owing any back taxes, the government would be required to refund money to Claudia and to the theater! "I could get in a lot of trouble for this." That was a sentence he repeated many times.

His psyche, however, was locked into a pattern of obedience. He was convinced he was doing his share for the salvation of civilization while at the same time he could be near his damozel in tax distress. "I don't intend ever to pay any taxes." That was her position and it made the tax man sweat with nervousness.

Soon Twerthel had taken over the bookkeeping for the entire theater; he was forced to begin to dream up strange excuses to cover his time spent there, and he began keeping a separate wardrobe in his car, his Bronxville beat garb which he wore at Luminous Animal; stashing his tax-man suit and tie in the back seat.

Claudia saved maybe ten hours a week, not having to worry about computing taxes, keeping records, making notes of expenses. Twerthel did it all. He even took to verse, and carried his freshly typed sequence of love lyrics inside plastic sheets in a leather ledgerbook. Some day he hoped to show them to Claudia.

She had seen him around—he couldn't have been more than seventeen or eighteen. He came up to her as she was entering the theater for rehearsal. He was just her height, and what was immediately noticeable: his thick black eyebrows and beautiful face. What a face. He was carrying a basketball wedged 'gainst his body and his arm angled out and down over it, and in the same arm's hand he carried a rather frazzled hardbound edition of Nijinsky's diaries.

It began so simply. He asked her if he could watch rehearsals. She paused, almost breaking her rule of closed rehearsals before openings; then told him no, not before the opening, but to come around later, in a few days maybe. As she walked into the darkness of Luminous Animal she thought of asking him something, turned, but heard the sound of a basketball dribbling half a block away.

After rehearsal she walked down the Bowery for dinner at Ping Ching Restaurant in Chinatown, passing a small park where she spotted the boy shooting baskets. She yelled at him, and he leaped high for a rebound and globetrotted the ball over with quick intricate dribbles.

"Would you like a job?" she asked.

"Doing what?"

"We need somebody to act as usher and to help clean up after performances, sweeping and aligning the seats, and so forth. We've an opening in ten days, so there's lots to do."

She told him they could only afford twenty-five dollars a week, for six nights of work, but of course he could learn a lot, watch practices, help with the props. "Do you go to school?" she asked.

"No. No school," he replied, a bit of a fib.

"What's your name?" "Paolo." "My name is Claudia." She shook his hand. "Can you start tonight?" Yes yes—and he turned and sunk one from the top of the circle—yes yes.

Claudia decided to show a week of previews, and to becloud the desks of local media editors with press releases. She personally called up the Democratic district leader who had been so upset over the mayor's role as Lord High Chopper. And she sent a formal invitation to the mayor and the district attorney to attend the opening. The first preview of *Newsreel-'84* played to half a house, but with each succeeding evening there were more and more people. And the re-

159

sponse, standing applause at the end of the second preview, gave Roy, at least, those fabled rays of hope. But Claudia was still very skeptical about the show's chances. She saw it still too much a rough-hemp rhapsody, that is, a coarse weave. "This production is still too jerking, too abrupt; it's more like an old World War Two documentary film than . . ."

"Then it's your fault, Cl . . . [he almost said Clotho] Claudia!" Roy Shields snapped right back. "You're the three Fates wrapped up in one in this whole damned production. If you hadn't forced all those changes . . ."

"The reviews will finish us, no matter how many come to previews." And that was her final opinion, although she certainly could never babble it aloud. Never babble defeat to your cast, or Lord forbid, to the backers: that was tattooed on her soul.

At 2 A.M. after the first preview, Claudia was alone in the theater, except for Paolo who was making an occasional skwitcha sound with the broom among the seats. She was in her office listening to a tape of a work submitted for production by the Celestial Freakbeam Orchestra, a Lower East Side ensemble operating out of the Total Assault Cantina on Avenue A.

It was a tremendous piece of music, with orchestration by Joshua Gortz, and words by Sam Thomas, the editor of a poetry magazine, *The Shriek of Revolution*. The work was described as a Ghost Dance, and its personae were two dance/singers, personifications of Hiroshima and Nagasaki, who would perform on a stage which was wrapped entirely around with diaphanous gauze or angel hair forming a

160

mushroom. Claudia was so excited by the tape and text that she wanted to hear it on the larger stage-speaker system.

She glided noiseless up the steps to the stage. In the back of the theater she could see strange leaps. Paolo was lunging around in the demi-gloom, apparently using the inverted **T** of the large janitors broom to give him support for pole-vaultlike leaps, like an ice-skater sliding with a lawn chair across a frozen lake as if practicing with a partner.

She had kidded him earlier in the week about his basketball, which he brought to the theater every day. He grew quite angry, and asked her to come down to the Bowery court with him. She stalled a couple of days, but finally went with him, and watched him dunk it a few times, quite a feat for someone five-foot-nine. He could do it with a half or full spin also—that's when she noticed his legs, and his marvelous chest, which curved up abruptly from the top of muscly stomach to the nipples, then curved gradually back toward his wide thin shoulders. She learned that he had been coming to Luminous Animal for the past two years; that's why he had looked so familiar. In all her years in the theater, she never really learned who came to the performances, for she never mingled with the audience before or after a show. She had a closed passageway constructed from backstage to the rear of the ticket booth so she could monitor the money, and avoid the faces in the lobby.

Paolo, she soon learned, had a fixation, a fascination, a compulsion, for dancing. His father had studied dancing, or had been involved in a dance company in some way—and had died in Korea. Paolo was about as intense as they come—everything he gripped, he gripped so that his taut hands turned white: sitting in Washington Square reading Nijinsky, fingers gripping faded cloth.

Claudia walked to the lightboard and turned on the

161

stage. The leaps stopped. She put the Celestial Freakbeam Orchestra tape on the Wollensak and attached the Wollensak to the large stage speaker used in *Newsreel-'84*. "Paolo, would you come here please?" she asked.

"Would you like to listen to a new tape?" she asked when he had vaulted upon the stage. He sat at a judge's bench and read a few pages of the text. She watched his legs begin to move slightly with the music, and then . . . .

"Let's explore it," was all she said, then worked the rheostat so that the stage contracted into a very soft orange oval with darkness surrounding. She walked into the orange and waited for Paolo to enter. He wasn't sure what she meant. "Would you like to dance"—lifting her arms, "with," half-turn, "me?"—she asked, making it clear.

By that time he was in the orange oval. "Can you pick me up?" she asked, and put her arm around him; and with his surprising strength, he lifted her, and twisted her overhead. They whirled in the dark, then in the oval; he knew, from long stageside gazing, how she danced, and fitted himself into her Way.

Throughout she wore golden slippers—one of those things which strongly woodburned themselves into a memory. Years later, Paolo, long after he had become an editor at Random House, could close his eyes on a hash-oil weekend, and see in long leisure reverie, those convoluted swirlings of Claudia's golden slippers on the dark dust stage.

Claudia would always regret their finale when Paolo was left without a guide as Luminous Animal went on its first European tour with *Newsreel-'84*, and he dart-boarded Nijinsky's diaries and headed for the foul line and a career with the Princeton five. For a while anyway, it was all sipping joyjuice through a straw for both. They danced without a stop that first night till 4 A.M., achieving an ironic ecstasy through the tragic music called *Hiroshima and Nagasaki*.

She was amazed. He could memorize at once any routines she might suggest, and could repeat them in any order. And he accepted her leadership, and the Celestial Freakbeam Orchestra wailed onward.

The day she watched him dunk the basketball she had made her decision, and she moved fast. Three nights later, that is, the night after their primal dance, the dancing resembled an elegant touch-football game. Paolo was glistening with the sweat of contact, as if oiled up for a muscle-mag photo, resplendent in gym shorts and a St. Agnes Boys Club T-shirt which Claudia soon removed. Claudia was attired in a cutaway portion of her nun's habit costume for *Newsreel-'84*. This became hot indeed, she said, and so she removed it and was down to a purple bodystocking.

The music tonight was still the Celestial Freakbeam tape, but Claudia chose to interpret its often insistent rhythms in a more conjunctive manner. Her hands caressed his rib cage—and he locked his hands around the back of her shoulders. And they moved close together for several minutes.

"Take them off," she whispered, leaning upon his ear. He did so, and sank to his knees, half-covering his erection. She slid toward him, her bodystocking flung aside and lying half-in, half-out, of the oval of light; knees at the edges of a beauteous **V,** feet underneath herself, and right away she slid upon his knees and up his muscles of thigh, and he was inside her.

She pulled his arms under her thighs; then she locked her arms around his neck. "Stand up," she whispered.

He got to his feet, and stood rather uncertainly, in such a new position of the ballet of Eros. "Turn up the music," she whispered again, and he carried them over to the tape re-

163

corder, still inside, and she reached down to turn the volume knob.

"Dance," was her next whisper, and then they were silent for several minutes, until there was a burst in the music; and she undertook a particularly twig-ripping series of leg flailings, legs outstretched behind his back, Paolo having difficulty holding himself inside. Then his heart began really to tom-tom his rib cage, and he couldn't keep his eyes open, and he sank slowly to his knees, still inside her, she on top, into their original position.

She could sense that he was just about to come; she pulled off him, and reached down, cuddled his balls with a soothing cool palm—urging him to his feet with the other.

They then began to dance again—she paying just enough attention to his crotch to keep it erect. And the Celestial Freakbeam Orchestra played on.

Then, in what may have been a first in American Dance, she leaped up, using his shoulders as a vaulting horse, and jack-knifed her body, while at the same time spreading her legs. Paolo knew somehow he'd better brace himself quickly, and did so, stamping his foot down slightly behind himself in a couple of short back-steps. And then Claudia, in a move that revealed her extraordinary strength, somehow lowered herself down so slowly, slowly, and without any stuttering of the motion's fluidity, flattened her body against him, and the frightened cock, which expected perhaps a mash-job, was brought back into the warmth. Paolo evinced a few un-dancelike contortions, that is, he just about collapsed to the floor, rolling himself over and on top, and let loose, burying his face upon her mouth and her neck, unable to stop.

But the Celestial Freakbeam Orchestra tape was but half-completed. And just a few seconds later Claudia 'rose to dance some more. And it was all beauty. The come, or

164

aphros, or foam, dropped down from her legs, or fell in smooth beautiful gobs here and there, her legs soon aglistening with it. And she brought Paolo onward.

She lifted him, pressing him against the rear wall of the stage, out of the oval of light, into the darkness, and just for a second, licked the tip of him, springing it to hardness right away, then let him slide down the cool thrilly wall. And so it went.

During the next several nights, they tried a lot of variations on dance-sex, including pas de deux oral intercourse on roller skates, and various worshipings upon the pink altar while the subject stood in accomodatingly modified fourth position, not to mention a few engagements upon the couch of the dressing room.

When the initial several days were over, and they began to calm down, as of Eros, they started seriously to work on the Celestial Freakbeam tape. An idea began to develop inside her. She could be seen bent over her clipboard writing rapidly. Its possibilities meant she had to coax him into singing. He had rather a hoarse voice, she found, but it possessed that all-important characteristic, so rare on the stage (or on records); he could catch a note and hold it! After that determination, it was merely a matter of mutating his voice into an aurally pleasing contraction/constriction/construction of larynx.

It appeared to be love, or whatever it was, for she had long ago banned that word from intimate discourse. She found herself thinking of him all the time, kindling within her a distracting triplet of shyness, tenderness, and passion. She became distracted, and with her obvious fatigue from dancing all night every night, she eased up on the practice schedule for *Newsreel-'84*, for which the cast was grateful—and the show relaxed into a finer mode as a result.

She was worried about Paolo's intensity, which might have found an outlet in jealousy. But she could not stop thinking of a tripod. A tripod: with intense dance-genius Paolo, the anarcho-Hegelian writer Roy, and the Croesus of off-B'way, Ron Lawler, as legs—and she, Claudia, chewing the sacred bay leaves, drinking the spring Cassotis which was channeled into the Luminous Animal temple; she taking seat adangle in the center of the tripod out o'er the Delphic crevasse whence drifted the intoxicating mist of "mephitic" dope-vapors, triggering off not the voice of a seeress, but the action to which she was destined, god-dance. And it was with Paolo something told her it could be done. His force-field, the curves of his aura, fit in with hers. She could "feel" the curving aura. God-dance, god-dance.

Roy was less than enthused, because, banned to his pad, he'd not been alone with Claudia for over a week. If he was jealous, he assured himself that his concerns were strictly limited to Ars Gratia Cursus Honorum (sui), that is, getting the pole position in the chase after the white stag of fame.

One disturbing thing he noted was that her clipboard was occupied with several sheets dealing with some new production involving her and who?—he thought, noting the letter *P*. Paolo? Bah! It can't be—and the Celestial Freakbeam Orchestra, ha! A bunch of punks if ever Roy knew punks.

"I suppose," Roy snorted, after he had Q and A'd some data about the new project from Claudia, "you'll call your show,"—*show* delivered with a sneer, "Sex Dance with Cybele?" This was the morning after Roy, cool as a fool, had come to Luminous Animal, it must have been 3 A.M., beating, drunk, kicking, drunk, swearing, drunk. But Clau-

166

dia had bolted the night latch and the Celestial Freakbeam Orchestra played on.

"Don't insult *me*, Mr. Fourth-rate Brecht!"

Opening night for *Newsreel-'84* finally arrived. Roy was in emotional traction with angst. The toilet tank in his hall was filling and unfilling with neighbordisturbing frequency. Claudia had never felt such boredom on the day of a first night. She actually overslept, whereas normally on such a day she was up like a child on Christmas morn. It was a busy day: at least fifty phone calls to be made, the enduring of last-minute squalls of Genius and Art, a final practice. The lists piled up on her clipboard thick and black.

The espresso coffeemaker in the lobby broke down. The pastries didn't arrive. Paolo forgot to mop the bathrooms. Someone had stuck gum into the phone. Several of the spotlights on the outside had to be replaced. The ticket-beggers were a pain. All someone had to have done was to have attended high school with anyone faintly connected with the production, and they called up for freebies.

Claudia insisted on total cleanliness of the entire building before an opening, a position adopted for arcane reasons of preritual purification, which her mystic nature demanded. Therefore, the theater was given ablutions as if it were a ziggurat awaiting dawn.

Luminous Animal was located in a cavernous dank cinderblock former garage on the Bowery near 3rd Street, down the hill from Cooper Union. Oh what a pit of grease it had been when she had first rented it. A team of the most dedicated Laborers of the Abyss had slaved two weeks to foam away the grunge, and another two weeks to tar the roof and to paint it, blue on the outside, black inside.

Most of the available money had gone into a fine resilient stage which ran some eighty feet across the back of the garage. There were a few plywood dressing rooms, a lobby, and a large area enclosed by black burlap curtains to serve as the art department, which lay cluttered with silkscreen equipment, an old A. B. Dick mimeo, carpenters' benches, storage bins for scenes and costumes, the Luminous Animal Archives, and even a small darkroom.

For the audience there was a hodgepodge of backless funeral parlor chairs, street sofas, cushions, and lawn furniture. On the outside of the buildings, situated just above the entrance, was a ten-foot-tall reproduction of a paleolithic painting from Les Trois Frères cave in the Pyrenees, the reindeer-headed human figure which Claudia used as a symbol for Luminous Animal. Abbé Breuil, who had first published a drawing of the figure, had named it the Sorcerer, an appellation scorned by Claudia. She saw the figure as a deer-dancer, or rather, as a primal configuration of drama, that is, of god-dance.

Surrounding the Luminous Animal sign was an enormous bank of lights a friend of Claudia had borrowed from a military installation in Brooklyn.

The landlord chose this day of frenzy for gouge maneuvers. The landlord was known in the neighborhood as Louie the Criminal. (Today however, he is no longer a criminal. He is SoHo Lou, respected art dealer and speculator in Peruvian powders.) Louie got into trouble right after the lease was signed and had to disappear for a while, so Claudia dealt with Louie's brother, Tony.

At first the conversation was pleasant chitchat. "Hey," Tony said, "I see you've got big crowds at your new show."

168

"We'll know tonight," she replied. "The reviews could drive away the uptown crowd, or they might not even review us at all, which could be worse."

"I was talking it over with my wife. We both felt that if the play does real well that we, as owners of the building, should share in a small percentage of the action—in addition to the rent."

"Are you serious?" Claudia's voice dialed to shrill in the middle of the sentence.

"Well, I've read the newspaper articles. The play certainly is getting controversial; and it could get me into trouble, like bring heat on my other businesses. Do you understand what I mean?"

Claudia was angry. "Look here, Tony! You can't expect me to cooperate with robbery. We negotiated a fair lease. I put three thousand dollars into fixing up a decayed, incredibly filthy building. I just can't go along with you. I'm sorry."

"Well, let me put it to you another way, sweetheart. Louie's back in town and he wants his garage back. He wants to get into the auto-repair business again—"

"You mean vehicle-disguise business!" she interjected scornfully. "You can't threaten me."

"Yeah? Who you gonna go to, the mayor?" He laughed. "If anything happens to your Taj Mahal over there, I'm not going to be responsible. I trust you are insured."

She clicked the receiver on him, and sat there trembling. But the blesséd flow of gibberish swept her up right away, and she was called to the stage to oversee some repairs to the Lord High Chopper's throne, and she forgot all about Tony the Creep.

169

That evening Claudia strayed from her custom of always remaining at the theater the day of an opening, dining uptown with her chief financial backer, Ronald Lawler. She figured an elegant restaurant was the proper setting to pull off the delicate caper of securing a commitment to provide money for a new production before the fate of *Newsreel* could be determined.

This was difficult to accomplish, since Lawler, a stockbroker who also owned a big New York publishing company, believed in the Eleventh Commandment: Thou Shalt, O Lawler, Not Fail to Get a Return on Thine Investment, a belief unshakably maintained although he had become involved in the theater in order to come into contact with beautiful women. That is, in the mode of gangsters who used to sponsor burlesque performers and torch singers, Lawler tried to specialize in off-Broadway actresses. But he was always attentive to the shekels. He was ruthless, manipulative, lecherous (on the mental plane, since not even daily cocktails of vodka mixed with a half-cup of Vitamin E oil could aid his dongal impuissance), but, to himself, he was a positive, if not revolutionary, force in the American theater. He thought of himself as the Divine Liberal, in the nineteenth-century English tradition. He served as treasurer for several cultural foundations (thereby avoiding himself having to contribute).

Lawler's current problem was that he had fallen in love, and worse, the love had jelled into obsession. Whining obsession, the mode of adoratio which Claudia most easily could handle.

Her response could have been to proffer a cracker of derision for the puppy in a shoebox on her doorstep. But she seemed to like Ron Lawler. It wasn't just the checks—but in spite of the checks. And they'd never fucked, or even lain down on his yacht in sunny carezza. But they seemed to get along well. He was completely undemanding—and would never, she judged, do anything so frantic, in his obsession with Claudia, so as to injure his family relationships—a wife and children up in Mays Landing.

During the meal Lawler sought to shake into the air two questions: a) what are the chances on *N-84* making some mon? and b) when can we spend some time together?

It was difficult, just minutes before its opening, to speak of a theatrical production as a floparoo, especially to a nervous backer, but that's just what she did, gambling that his affection coupled with her persuasiveness, would enable him to envision glorious crowds of success flocking to a new production starring her and Paolo. "Who?" he asked. She tried to describe Paolo's extraordinary abilities. She mentioned his power of leg, and it was like mentioning the secret word in the old Groucho Marx quiz show on TV, so excited became Lawler—it was all he could do to keep his hands above the table.

"He's the finest dancer I've ever worked with," she told him at the end of a long paragraph of praise. "Have you heard," she continued, "of the Celestial Freakbeam Orchestra?" He hadn't, but tried to give a vague motion of his head to indicate, of course!—Do you think I'm stupid?

She continued, "They've written a wonderful, uh, morality drama, which they've submitted for production. They call it a Ghost Dance. It would be marvelous. The stage is wrapped in gauze, in the shape of a mushroom. The specters of Hiroshima and Nagasaki appear . . ."

Lawler shuddered, and broke in to change the subject.

171

Like the bazooka shell his ancestors, their millions made in the New England codfish-oil trade, had trained him to be, he repeatedly steered the conversation back to his two concerns, mon and time-with-Claudia.

She responded. "I think *Newsreel* may well be very successful. But it more likely may be too many years beyond its time. The critics will be too stupid to understand it. It's got a lot of boring choruses. Of course, nothing is certain here, and the previews have picked up. But if it fails . . ." She paused.

Ron gave a wince at the word *fail*. But Claudia dared not notice such things and continued to present her best babble, best stare, best angles, best smile, best nudging foot. "If it fails, I want to start immediately on a production of *Ghost Dance*. The costs will be greatly reduced, since Paolo and myself will be the only ones on stage. The biggest expense will be paying the Celestial Freakbeam Orchestra. There must be fifteen of them; and some will have to quit their outside jobs. They have performed a lot at the Total Assault Cantina, where we went for that poetry benefit, you remember?" Lawler nodded, yes yes he remembered.

"And I'm counting on you, Ron"—reaching for his hand. "Also, we may want to film it, if the money can be raised. That too might supply a return for investors."

Ron tried hard not to imply an affirmative answer but he found himself fluttering his hands and nodding his head in agreement.

He turned his attention again to question B. "You never seem to have time to do things. We could fly anywhere you want, any weekend you name. Or," he continued, "we could take out the boat. I have it down in Florida."

She wanted to see him, and he saw it in her smile, and the stockbroker was almost happy. Just as they left the restaurant she kissed him, I'll see you often, I promise. We might even be able to spend some weekends together. It depends on how long *Newsreel* runs, of course."

Waiting patiently in the lobby was Assistant District Attorney Arthur Mynah, a former classmate of John Mitchell at Fordham Law, belching nervously. Mr. Mynah's suit was tight and was the color of phlegm-tinged split-pea soup. His stomach was taxing the ability of the Arrow shirt company to cover it, a blubbery dingle-dangle brought about by daily visits to smoke-filled greasies near the Criminal Courts Building. The assistant district attorney still tried to button his suit coat, a mistake of crimping and winkles that should have sent him over to his Delancey Street tailor, but didn't, for five years had not passed, and therefore it was not yet time to obtain a new suit. Mynah's assignment: to prepare himself for possible criminal indictments growing out of *Newsreel-'84.* There was the shameful matter of ridiculing His Honor, the Mayor. There was also possible criminal interracial lascivious (*lashivus* was the way Mynah pronounced it) carriage in one torrid dance between Claudia-the-nun and the Priest, a dance which had caused flocks of A.D.A.s to visit the theater for a look-see. And finally there was the matter of the burnt flags. This arose out of a vignette where competing sects burned each other's flags in public ceremonies. The flags which were burned appeared to be the actual flags of major world powers, including England, France, the U.S.S.R., and the U.S.A. Burning a Russian flag, that was fine. But burn an American flag, and you were in trouble.

Throughout the play, A.D.A. Mynah kept a glazed stare

173

upon the proceedings. The theater was packed. Every last weird divan and packing crate was filled. The play was interrupted several times with loud applause not to mention numerous gasps of surprise as when the flags were burned or during the torrid intimacies.

As soon as the curtain closed, Ass. Dist. Att. Mynah raced backstage where, like an umpire, he removed a whisk broom from his back pocket and brushed the flag-shreds into a paper bag. "If this is a certified American flag, you are in deep trouble," he said with a smile, leaving his card with Claudia as she prepared to open the curtain for a bow.

The audience stood and applauded for four minutes and thirty-six seconds according to Roy who was monitoring his wrist. The reviewers were ecstatic. Claudia spotted Roy waiting in the wings. She ran over and hugged him, "My goodness, it's going to be a hit!"

"I told you, I told you!" Roy was hopping with joy, a spewing champagne bottle in his hand. Roy was attired in a tuxedo and a polkadot bow tie. Roy was still employed as his building super so when he had left his apartment that evening he had paused, donning his garbage-spackled work gloves, to haul the garbage cans from the cellar to the curb, then absentmindedly had stuck the gloves into the tuxedo pockets, and now, as he glub-glubbed the champagne he noticed the incongruous fingers poking from his pockets and quickly stuffed them deeper out of sight. "It's going to be the big time! the big time!" he shrieked to himself.

Claudia finally made it through the throng to her dressing room where she collapsed, but not before pulling her clipboard off the wall and moving the lists for *Newsreel-'84* to the top. "Dance, Aeschylus, Dance!" she sang. Then there was a knock.

It was the most pretigious drama critic in Western Civili-

174

zation—a notorious womanizer, drunk, coke-fiend, plagiarist, writer of pseudonymous Ace Books murder mysteries on the side, and manic-depressive. But one favorable line from him containing three powerful adjectives was worth a hundred grand.

"Miss Pred, I'm Milton Clark. I believe we met at the Stanislav opening. I can't tell you how much I enjoyed your performance in this marvelous theater. I was wondering if you could spare some time for an interview about Luminous Animal and the production. I have rather an urgent dead-line. But I've brought my typewriter with me, it's up at the Plaza. They have a private booth reserved at Bertolucci's where we could talk without interruption. So, if you could accompany me to a late supper, then I could . . ."

"Of course!" Claudia was beaming. "But I will take a shower first. And see that everything is in order."

Paolo stood near when she came out of the dressing room, amidst a crowd of friends whom she proceeded to greet. He saw her coat. "Aren't we going to dance?" he asked.

"Not tonight, honey." She hugged him. "You have the keys. Wait for me here. I'll be back in a couple of hours."

Claudia turned away abruptly and walked out the front door, the arm of the critic cuddling her shoulder. Paolo went inside and threw a gold slipper against the dressing-room door.

After everyone had left and he had swept the gritty floors, Paolo turned on the stage lights. He began to pace back and forth, in obvious anger, dribbling his basketball. With a growl, he suddenly threw it out into the sea of divans. He danced alone, jumping and twisting. He kicked off his tennis

175

shoes. Then his shirt, his jeans. He twirled. His legs were very long, very thin—except for his upper legs which were over-muscled. His black hair was falling over his face. He practiced rebounding, leaping high to grab imaginary basketballs; then rolled upon the sooty stage, gray streaks across his back and buttocks.

Later he walked to Claudia's dressing room to wait.

An Editorial Conference

HE RENTED THE two-room apartment at 521 East 11th Street in December of 1961 for fifty-six dollars a month. It was on the third floor. One room was a combined kitchen and living room. The other was supposed to be a bedroom. There were no closets, only a five-pronged clothes rack nailed to the wall in the bedroom. The rooms were tiny and both had lumpy metal ceilings stamped with leaflike patterns in six-inch squares.

The two living-room windows opened onto a fire escape which protruded rustily upon a back courtyard crisscrossed with clotheslines and wet clothes getting gritty from the anus of satan, otherwise known as the Consolidated Edison smokestacks belching a few blocks away. Some mornings he would awaken with the inside of his nose black-caked with fallout.

Spanish music floated in from the courtyard by day by night by dawn. Someone close by had a rooster and occasionally he heard a faint baaaa. On the roof of the building directly opposite his fire escape there was a five-tiered pi-

177

geon warren which was used ostensibly to supply food for a family in the building. The super, however, swore up and down that the birds were shipped downtown to a Chinese restaurant for squab gobble.

The backroom or bedroom had a single window to the outside which was sealed shut, its panes painted lightless with many coats. When he pried the window open he saw why. The vista was of a gray-streaked solid brick wall about five feet away and a sheer drop to the rubble of the alley dotted with dropped garbage bags, a common disposal method on the East Side.

Like many dinky New York apartments, there was a window between the kitchen and the so-called bedroom. This too was completely covered with years of paint, the newest being avocado green. The icebox was strictly early American and rattled as the motor struggled to propel the refrigerant. The door was almost as cold as the interior and a piece of rubber insulation hung down from the top and prevented it from closing properly. Next to the icebox was a large low sink which apparently had been originally intended also for use as a washtub. Next to the sink was the bathtub with a removable porcelain-glazed metal covering. Above the bathtub were the kitchen cabinets—whose crooked doors could never quite be shut and whose interiors were a sour-smelling barrenness of decayed oilcloths, cockroach egg cases, kernels of roach-chewed rice, coffee grounds, and greasy dust.

The watercloset was jammed into a small booth in the hallway. There was something wrong with the light fixture so he placed a candle on the ledge. Either the user left the hall door open, or lit the candle, or voided in darkness. The toilet gurgled with spilling water twenty-four hours a day. Roaches loved the watercloset. There were hundreds of

178

them. He gave up at once trying to maintain the watercloset with the result that his friends, even the funkiest among them, were loath to lower any exposed skin upon the seat.

About forty-five minutes after he had paid the rent and deposit, he moved into the apartment. His possessions were scant: consisting of a small silver waterpipe—very hip in 1961, sixteen cardboard boxes of books, a typewriter, a suitcase of clothing, a small open-drum Speed-O-Print mimeograph machine, a milk crate full of mimeo ink and art supplies plus numerous copies of issues of his poetry magazine, *The Shriek of Revolution*.

There were eight layers of linoleum on the floor. These he chopped up and carted away by the armload. The bare floor itself had never been painted or varnished. It was raw wood. He wondered if he should leave it the way it was. Enough paint splashed on it when he was working on the ceiling and walls, however, that he decided to make it black also.

He wound up painting the entire apartment, floor, ceiling, walls, door, black except for one wall which he painted white intending to cover it with murals. The living room was red orange when he rented the place. There were many buckles, cracks, and ridges in the plaster. When painting, he left the cracks and ridges red orange so that there were these groovy abstract red lines and patterns running through the black expanses, man. As for the long white wall, he spent the next few months carefully painting it with multi-colored cuneiform stanzas of Sumerian poetry which he had studied in college.

In those days the Lower East Side on Wednesday nights was a free department store. For it was then that residents would place upon the pavement old furniture, kitchen cabinets, smashed TVs, mattresses tied up with cord, etc., for the refuse department to cart away. Sometimes, as when an

179

elderly person without family would die, the sidewalk outside an apartment would be jammed with trunks full of old clothes, boxes of books, lamps, utensils, and the debris of fifty years. This produced a grab scene almost as if someone had thrown money on the ground. Citizens were thrilled to seize from an old trunk a sport shirt from Honolulu or a photo album dated 1923.

The very first Wednesday he forayed and found a large, lidded packing crate from Japan which he lugged home, painted black, and added to the pad as a table. Some things he had to purchase. One such item was a ten-foot-by-ten-foot bamboo mat edged with black cloth. This was the living room fun-rug. Floor pillows he obtained from old sofas found on the streets. He hung another smaller bamboo mat in the doorway between the two rooms. He rigged a string from the bottom up over a nail at the top of the doorjamb so that the bamboo curtain could be raised or lowered by a tug on the string.

He walked the side streets looking for a throwaway mattress. It was a poor day for freebies. Finally he spotted an old mattress tied up into the shape of a jelly roll with rope and leaning against garbage cans at 9th and Avenue C.

The first thing to ascertain, when checking out a free street mattress, was why it was that the owner had discarded it. He regarded the mattress. Even as a throwaway, it was rather a pitiful specimen. In the first place, the prior owners had not been the most continent of humans as evinced by several widespread spills, so to speak, all over the middle of it. But, when given the firmness and bounce tests, it seemed very substantial. To the nose it was not particularly offensive and he could find no indication thereon and therein of cootie, tick, crab, or roach. Therefore, all con-

180

sidered, he grabbed the mattress upon his back and staggered toward 11th Street to his apartment.

His kitchen utensils consisted of two large wooden bowls, two Chinese soup spoons, two glasses, a can opener, a knife, and several pots. Within a few days of moving in, the power company turned off the lights and gas, sending him a letter that he would be required to put up a cash deposit for the big Con Ed turn-on. He decided to tough it. He bought candles instead and was happy for a year.

For lunch the day Con Ed turned out the lights, he had boiled a pot of broccoli and had fixed a peanut butter and broccoli sandwich on a long Italian roll. The unused broccoli was stored in the quaking refrigerator where it remained decomposing for eleven months. When anyone opened by accident the refrigerator door it was curtains for the nose. No smell ever devised quite matched the wafts of Tales From The Crypt putridity corpsing forth when someone opened the door. Even the memory of it sickens the brain cells.

Since he had no working stove, he ate raw food and the cold contents of cans. From urges unknown, he started eating a strange concoction he called Yum. Yum and vitamin C, except for an occasional pirogen and sour cream feast at the nearby Odessa Restaurant, was his exclusive diet for months and months. What was Yum? Well, first he made a thick dry two-inch bed of oats in the wooden bowl. On this he spooned two globs of Hellmann's mayonnaise. Next generous drip-drops of soy sauce. Atop this mound of pure delight, he broke two fresh eggs and mixed the feast into a beige and yellow rippled blob. This was Yum. Want some?

He ate Yum every day from the time he put the broccoli into the useless icebox until the end of 1962, eleven happy months. He was very willing to share his meals of Yum with

181

any visitor arriving at dinner time. There was often shyness or hesitance on the part of the visitor who watched the editor prepare the wet, yellow, yum-mush, to share it with him.

The spirit of Yum pervaded his life. Once just after the lights went off, his blond love was due to arrive at night to sleep over. He went down to Houston Street to a wholesaler and purchased a twenty-five pound bag of raw oats.

That night they poured the entire sack of oats into the bathtub and added generous amounts of corn oil and hot milk she had brought in a thermos. Then they celebrated their first stay together in months by an immediate act of love in the hot bath of oat-mush. They rubbed each other with fistfuls of oily oats and playfully poked the milky grain here and there, mound and entrance. Her breasts shone with swabbings of shiny oat-lint. They emerged from the tub looking like The Bark People and rolled upon the bamboo mat kissing and licking away the kernels of Demeter.

As soon as the apartment was painted and furnished, he turned his energies to the new issue of *The Shriek of Revolution*. Through extensive correspondence, he had received enough good poetry from the peripatetic writers of his generation to print the fourth issue.

He typed the mimeograph stencils, always a tedious chore requiring slow correction of mistakes with an erasing device and rubbery correction fluid which was brushed on the typo, blown dry with a breath-huff, and then the word was retyped. Sometimes he typed far past midnight by candlelight until the man next door began to pound the wall with a broom.

He wrote several editorials, one calling for everybody in the Lower East Side to mail the sooty contents of their noses every day to the Con Ed company in protest against their volcanic smokestacks. He wrote another "editorial" in which he described a mythical meeting of the "editorial board" of *The Shriek of Revolution*, using the real names of five or six of his friends.

As he described it, the editorial board meeting quickly abandoned crucial judgments regarding the business of publishing *The Shriek of Revolution* and assumed the form of a bunch-punch. Prominently mentioned in the description was a poet named Cynthia Pruitt, known as Cynito to her friends at Stanley's Bar. Cynthia was a wonderful person who roamed the halls of the peace movement and the pads of the Lower East Side for several years in the early sixties. She was an outstanding poet. He had printed some of her work in *The Shriek*. He wrote the "editorial" never thinking for a minute that any of his friends, including love-loving Cynthia, would take exception to his very detailed description of uncompunctious conjugation.

After the stencils were typed he ordered a few boxes of blue mimeo paper. When it was delivered he began to print the new issue. He placed the small mimeograph upon the white metal bathtub-covering and brushed the ink upon the inside of the printing drum. He placed a stencil on the outside of the drum, smoothed it out, checked the inking, put paper in the feeding-tray, and began to turn the handle to print with a feeling of elation that was just about religious. Everything was deity. Galaxy was. Star-robes trailed the void. He adored his mimeograph machine. He kept it sparkling clean. He sometimes would sit meditating upon the bamboo mat looking for hours at the Speed-O-Print sitting up on top of his bathtub.

After all the pages had been printed, there remained the grim job of collating them. Since the magazine was usually around thirty pages in length, he could collate one whole issue at a time by the following method. He would sit cross-legged on the floor in the Bodhisattva position, man, and nearly surround himself with three concentric semicircular rows of page piles. He proceded to lean out and to collate, working left to right through the outer circle and then through the second half-circle and finishing with the last page by sweeping across the innermost row that surrounded much of his cross-legged body. He tamped each completed issue on the floor along the top and side edges to align the pages for later stapling. Slowly the pile of completed issues grew until he finally finished all five hundred.

The next and last tiresome task was when clunk! clunk! clunk! he stapled each copy three times along the left edge. Whew. Then he addressed, stamped, and mailed out as many magazines as he could afford postage for, to his poet friends, to other editors, to his former literature professors, to his easily shocked aunts and uncles.

It was 12:30 A.M. and he was reading by candlelight when there was a knock at the door and the high whines and growls and huffs of what sounded like a dog pack out in the hall. He opened the door and in trotted two unleashed German Shepherds who ran about the bedroom-kitchen-workroom sniffing and salivating. With them was a person whom the editor had met only once, a very nervous man named John Carlin, slight and five-foot-ten, with carefully combed hair that was almost crewcut short at the nape of his neck, but was long on the top, whence it was brushed forward down over his forehead obscuring his eyebrows, just below which the remaining hair veered sharply toward his right temple. His beard was short and most precisely trimmed. He was a speech instructor at N.Y.U. who lived in a small three-story house on East 7th, near Tompkins Square.

184

He announced that he was very very disturbed about the description of the editorial board meeting in the new issue of *The Shriek of Revolution*—especially the portion depicting Cynthia Pruitt uttering suction with respect to the editor and the editorial board. He was so mad, in fact, that he had come to beat and to pummel. A quick glance at the person's face and at the large canines, who knows—perhaps trained to eat larynxes, convinced the editor of his certain plight.

The passage of the editorial in question was this: "And Cynthia rolled upon the floor filling her mouth with the carnal cob of Nelson Saite, drama editor, as he lined her ravening buttocks up against the steam-valve of the radiator and completed the metal node within her."

Now, the editor knew that Cynthia had been staying down at John Carlin's house for a few weeks but he had not heard from anyone—and such gossip spread quickly on the East Side, any indication that Cynthia and John were setting up an exclusive relationship—that is, a pact of mono-grope relative to groin-clink. He had also to consider whether or not Cynthia herself may have urged Carlin to come over to confront him. He decided she had not done so. First of all, if the editor had actually wanted to describe a *real* event, he certainly had observed Cynthia, Charlotte, Nelson, Claudia Pred, and other friends of his participating in strenuous intergroin group-grapples, so that what he had reported in his editorial board meeting had not been so far removed from fact.

On the other hand, he did feel upset that someone was unhappy over what he had printed with the intention of creating pleasure. And he well understood the possible jealousy that could be involved. So he apologized and said that most of the magazine had already been mailed out but had

185

he known of John's concern he certainly would have not printed the description.

After a few more minutes the man with the dogs left, with a parting statement to the effect that if the editor had not at least expressed some sort of apology, he would have beat him up. The episode caused the editor to retire to Stanley's Bar where he handed out a few copies of the new issue to his friends. He drank till four and returned home slouchy drunk, singing and stumbling against the sides of the narrow halls climbing to his third-floor bamboo lair.

The Filmmaker

IN LATE WINTER of 1961–62, just before spring, the Jonas Mekas columns in the *Village Voice* on underground films and filmmakers stirred Sam Thomas to make the leap into the 16-mm universe. Week after week the information swept him forward until that wintery night, fraught with brrrr, in a year when it still snowed deeply in New York City, he was sitting in the Total Assault Cantina on Avenue A.

A bunch of them had been popping cylinders of amyl nitrite into their innocent noses in the bathroom for that instant heart attack rush-flood. He was afterward clearing his senses with tea from the big Total Assault crock by the window when he decided. Not that he considered it a moment of history or anything. It was just that at that moment all obstacles melted.

He walked over to his friend Nelson, who was lying upon a bench in a far corner of the cantina. "Hey, Nelson, I just decided to make a film, but I don't exactly know where to start."

187

"You have to remember the three A's, man: action, arrogance, and aggression!"—was Nelson's advice. "If you want to make a film, don't wait around the lobby of the Bleecker Street Cinema looking for ideas. Buy a camera and commence!"

And that was the way it was. For about two years, he had worked steadily at two part-time jobs—one in the afternoons for a messenger service on 47th Street near the Gotham Book Mart, running the toothpaste slogans back and forth among the midtown ad agencies. The other job was on the weekends when he swept and washed glasses at the Jazz Gallery on St. Marks Place. Slowly the moolah had accrued. And now his brain was moiling like wax paper afire to jump into the abyss of Absolute Joy he felt making a film would be.

His mind flipped through an assortment of problems: film cost, development, his lack of knowledge regarding lenses and lighting and lens-settings, what kind of camera to get, shooting techniques. To solve the problem of the camera, the next day he called Harry Jarvis, a brilliant filmmaker whom he had met one memorable night at Stanley's Bar during a time Harry was quickly cognac-ing his way through a seventy-five-thousand-dollar Rockefeller grant to make a film version of Maspero's translation of the Egyptian *Tale of Two Brothers*. Harry urged him to purchase a so-called "battle camera, like, the kind they used filming the war." He specifically recommended a used Bell & Howell model 70-DE, which would be sturdy enough to withstand a few drops and bangs.

Sam lived near Stanley's Bar at 12th and Avenue B. Stanley's place was *the* bar of the time; as through its doors passed a steady stream of artists, poets, filmmakers, musi-

188

cians, and every type of radical publisher and nuclear-disarmament peaceworker.

Avenue B between 10th and 12th, in those days, was a sacred road. In addition to Stanley's, there were several other artists' bars there, and above the bars the cheap pads, and there was the Charles Theater where there were regular showings of underground films. The filmmakers met at Stanley's after the screenings and there was a great sense of energy and excitement.

Sam had met a number of the filmmakers in Stanley's, including the legendary Ron Rice walking around in green shoes with his sad Chaplin face; and Taylor Mead, the poet and star of Rice's seminal film, *The Flower Thief*.

There was Tuli Kupferberg, standing outside the Charles Theater selling his inimitable magazines. There was Harry Jarvis urinating on rare magic texts in the porcelain egressatory in Stanley's, novelists raving about form, poets looking for Shelley in the crowd waiting to get into the Charles for the Mekas brothers movie *Guns of The Trees*. It was a thrilling era. And Sam Thomas hungered to leap into its frenzy.

As he sat in the Total Assault Cantina, vowing to become a filmmaker, the two main influences in his life were Mekas and Samuel Beckett. The Mekas influence was this: that the obstacles standing in front of making a film were hallucinations. There were no obstacles. Or rather, piss on obstacles.

That was where Beckett came in. He thought, I'll treat them like walls at whose foundation I will fall and scrape, looking for chinks through which to chew and to chip till completion at the other side.

He was greatly moved by such Beckett characters as Molloy and Watt, often modeling his speech and mannerisms after "Beckett-folk"—as he called them, as if they were a colony of the living. Scrape scrape, chew chew, persist

189

persist; to the neophyte filmer, this was tough Sam B.'s message to the citizens of earth.

He searched and priced equipment throughout the city. At Willoughby's on 32nd Street he finally located what he wanted at a reasonable price. The 16-mm "battle camera" had a rotating lens stage with threes lenses: telescopic, wide-angle, and so-called normal. He called up Bell & Howell after the purchase and obtained an operating manual for that model. He sat up all night slurping tea at Total Assault memorizing the data.

Sam met a filmmaker from Colorado at a reading and received from him a wonderful lecture on the "Yoga of the lens." His friend told him to take the camera with him wherever he went, to forget about loading it with film for awhile, and to practice ten hours a day for a few weeks "filming" things he observed, especially heavy action, like fights, crowds forming in the park, angry truck drivers, police raids. The point was to be able to stay cool. His friend advised Sam to undertake a rigorous program of physical exercise. "A moviemaker should be in as good a shape as any other athlete," he said.

He should be able to twist, contort, lean slowly forward while sinking to the knees, bend backward, all while keeping the camera exactly on the imaginary line smoothly filming the action. A cameraperson should be able to walk through a scene of grisly riot, chaos, or site of snuff, the camera running, following the action in a smooth flowing riverine motion: you dig, muh fuh?

He also recommended that Sam purchase a device shaped like a large seven, called a Stedi-rest, which greatly aided hand-held camerawork. The Stedi-rest enabled the filmmaker to avoid spastic jerks and quakes during filming. The camera was screwed into the top of the "seven" and the

arms of the Stedi-rest pushed against the stomach and upon
the shoulder by means of curved cushioned supports which
were built on the ends of the large seven, perpendicular to
the ends. With the torso supporting the camera's weight, the
hands were relatively free to move about, the camera was
much less likely to be dropped and it was always more or
less in position ready to be used.

He rigged his apartment with film equipment and photo-
flood lighting. The photo-flood equipment was positioned to
beam full Ra-glare on the top surface of his madras-covered
mattress on the bedroom floor. He draped the walls with col-
orful cloths purchased on Orchard Street. And he began to
make short sample films to make certain he had fully memorized all necessary information about lighting and lens-settings. He corralled his friends for epic sessions of fornication
after poetry readings and concerts. Some of the outstanding
humans of the beatific era were filmed for posterity, all en-
gaging in various desperate frothings of skin. Sam looked
forward to that day in 1983, when he could show up at the
good junior senator from Tennessee's office down in D.C.
with a wonderful film shot when the senator was just a wee
young experimenting lad on Avenue A.

After a month of constant practice and experiment, he
was ready. By stroke of luck, he located a cheap film source,
a Mr. Joive who had an office on Ninth Avenue near 46th
Street. The rumor was that Mr. Joive had borrowed about a
million feet of film from the U.S. Air Force on huge reels
each containing thousands of feet of film. The same rumor
stated that the film had been destined, prior to Mr. Joive's
interception, for use in high-altitude aerial surveillance of
the Chi-coms. Mr. Joive had a lab out in Brooklyn where a
blind employee sat, in total darkness, peeling off hundred-
foot rolls from the big reels. Mr. Joive sold the rolls at a

191

wonderfully low price, in black unmarked cans—and was really responsible for a lot of the underground films being made in New York. For instance, Sam Thomas was able to purchase one hundred cans of Mr. Joive's Chi-com film, and to begin at once his first movie.

For a long time, the filmmaker had been aware of the A-heads. If you lived on the East Side, and spent much time mixing with the street culture, the A-heads were unavoidable. They roamed the streets, bistros, and pads compulsively shooting, snorting, or gobbling unearthly amounts of amphetamine, methedrine, dysoxin, bennies, cocaine, procaine—all of them burning for the flash that would lead to FLASH! It was almost neo-Platonic, as beneath the galactic FLASH! were subsumed the demi-flashes all urging toward FLASH!

Everybody from Washington Square to Tompkins Square called the streets "the set"—as "I've been looking for you all over the set, man. Where's my amphetamine?" With a generation readily present who viewed their life as on a set, there was no need to hunt afar for actors and actresses. What a cast of characters was roaming the village streets of 1962!

There was plenty of gossip at the time that the president used amphetamine and that his doctors injected him every morning. There were further speculations that the generals who met in the Pentagon War Room every day planning atomic snuffs were a bit A-bombed themselves.

In New York, the filmmaker was amazed observing the violence of the amphetamine-heads and the raw power-grabs that occurred in their glassy-eyed universe after a few months of sleeping just twice a week. If generals, corporation executives, presidents, premiers, and others were users of A, what were the implications? Shudders were the usual response to speculation that A-heads had taken over the governments of the world. As noted A-head artist Zack Thayer put it, "I *know* the president of the United States uses amphetamine. He *has* to. Otherwise how could the muh fuh play all the tunes, you dig?"

It was also commonly accepted on the set that the Germans had invented amphetamine and that the Nazis had shot up amphetamine during campaigns in North Africa in W.W. II, inspiring tales on the East Side of futuristic battles involving fierce-breathed amphetamine humanoids, babbling shrilly like rewinding tapes, in frays of total blood.

Another commonly accepted thesis was that amphetamine temporarily raised the intelligence of the user—"I am the genius of A! I am Rimbaud!"—yelled Zack Thayer, squirting purple ink from a hypodermic needle upon a canvas. They also seemed proud that A-use destroys brain cells. "I lose trillions of cells every day, man, grooo-VY!"

Amphetamine altered sex. Some under A's spell waxed unable in Eros or sublimated their desire beneath the frenzy of endless conversation or art projects. Others with strong natural sensual urges, experienced this: that the erogenous areas became extended under A to include every inch of bodily skin. "No piece of skin where you can't cop a riff of flash, man."

Men could not easily spew and women loved it forever. The image of amphetamine-driven Paolos and Francescas writhing twelve hours on a tattered mattress was humorous but true.

Gradually the filmmaker became aware of their actual art as opposed to their lifestyle. Some of them were extremely talented artists. One of the problems was the high snuff-ratio of their art. Most of it was abandoned or lost in the endless succession of evictions from apartments. When they first

193

occupied a new pad they immediately proceeded to turn every surface and every room into an "environment" of murals, painting, sculptured piles of furniture and debris brought in from the street. A landlord, once observing that the entire pad had been turned into Art, so to speak, would throw up his arms in alarm and head for eviction court or the local police precinct.

The filmmaker decided to make a film about power, using the world of the A-heads as Archetype. He taped a presidential press conference, intending to intermix sections of the conference with the river of tapes he was making of East Side A-babble. For a couple of weeks he scouted the scene, lugging along his Wollensak tape recorder into the apartments, and taped shoot-ups, fights, conversations, and room noise. He decided to title the film, *Amphetamine Head.*

For a while, he considered holding a mock A-head cabinet meeting with Zack Thayer in the role of president. He soon abandoned the idea because he could not afford the props, tables, chairs, and so forth, to make it real. During his research for the film, he had located a schoolteacher on the West Side who had been collecting the A-head drawings and paintings for a number of years. His house was packed with canvases and sheets of drawings—literally thousands of works. The teacher submitted to a filmed interview and a number of works by Zack Thayer, Manfred the Nut, Bill Klinger, and others were filmed. Inspired by the quality of this art collection, the filmmaker decided to make the film a straight documentary of the A-heads at work and play, and to forget about the president.

He began work on the sound track. For the film's introduction he woke up one morning with a flash. He covered himself completely with the blanket to make a sort of

194

deadening sound chamber, reached over to switch on the
Wollensak recorder, pulled the microphone under the covers
and then, in the best zombi voice he could muster, started
bellowing: "Am, am, am, am [very slowly]—phet, phet, phet,
phet [slightly faster]—ta, ta, ta, ta, [faster]—mine, mine,
mine, mine [fast]—Head, head, head, head"—and over again,
"Am, am, am, am, phet, phet, phet, phet, ta, ta, ta, ta, mine,
mine, mine, mine, Head, head head head." And so on, till it
grew so quick his voice tripped on the syllables.

Later, when he was actually filming, groups of ten to fifteen A-heads huddled on street corners would join the
chorus of "Am, am, am, am, phet, phet, phet, phet, ta, ta,
ta," et cetera.

As a film set, Sam decided to rent an apartment and stock
it with choice crystals of amphetamine; and to allow A-
heads to live and work there upon the condition that he be
allowed to film freely and to tape everything said. He located an apartment at 28 Allen Street, a few blocks south
of Houston. It was a typical two-room tub-in-the-kitchen
slum apartment painted dogtongue green. The human who
had previously lived there had somehow caused the walls to
become streaked with long lines of gray brown grease furry
to the touch because of the trapped soot. The plaster was
tumbling from the ceiling and the front window, opening on
Allen Street, had been bashed in and replaced with the
door of a cigarette vending machine. What a crummy apartment. But a Moorish palace for the purposes of the
filmmaker.

He enlisted the assistance of his friend Llazo, a poet and
"space cadet" who had written various poems about the A-
heads, coffee-house classics such as *Flutemaker's Hymn* and
a long sonnet sequence titled, *Two-Week Flash*. Llazo was
dispatched to wander all over the set telling people about

the apartment lurking with free amphetamine down on Allen Street. The result gave insight into the finding of gold in Sutter's creek. Within fifteen minutes, the A-heads began to flock, and the sound of the trilling flute was heard in the hallway of 28 Allen Street, 'phet-freaks banging most urgently upon the door.

The onslaught caught him off-guard, and when he refused to let them in the pad right away, he could hear them muttering, "Oh man!" as they clumped down the stairs. He wanted to film the pad in its "natural state," and then to film the metamorphosis as the artists enacted their painterly transformations. He knew he hadn't much time, so he rushed around; he swept the floors, washed the bathroom, dusted the windows, made up the floor-mattress with clean sheets and a cover. He even placed around the pad some paper towels, soap, tissue, and a bit of food.

He had brought with him about ten clip-on light fixtures and twenty three-hundred-watt photo-flood lamps, which he clipped all over the apartment so that any area could be lit up for filming. He quickly checked the illumination on the walls, feeling them to be most important for filming the construction of wall murals and collages. He surrounded the mattress with lights. And the bathroom. He switched on the lights and filmed the clean, neatly arranged apartment.

Llazo had returned by this time, and Sam left him in charge while he rushed out to cop a few ounces of amphetamine, trotting up the avenue to score in a hurry, lest Llazo be faced with a riotous congeries of pissed-off A-heads.

He located a dealer who traded exclusively in the finest crushed crystals of amphetamine sulphate. When the dealer became aware of the movie project he was excited. "Wow, a movie called *Amphetamine Head*! Here, let me give you

196

some extra. I can groove with a movie 'bout A, man. Be sure and invite me to the opening!"

The dealer at once began to regale the filmmaker with lengthy anecdotes about his life story, but the filmmaker had to leave in the midst of the torrent, which continued unabated even after the door had been shut. Sam felt the weight of the brown sack. The dealer must have given him about four ounces for the thirty dollars, an unbelievably good buy.

Returning to Allen Street, the filmmaker discovered seven humans inside: a girl named Diane sitting in the bedroom drawing in a notebook, Zack Thayer and Claudia: artists; Tom Four-a-day—a famed dopefreak; Sheilah the micro-swirl muralist; Llazo the poet, and, god knows how, a Norwegian sailor.

Diane was seventeen—and six months removed from the Bronx, sitting with the others on the mattress and floor of the bedroom, yakkety-yakking. Amphetamine had possessed her. She wore her long black tresses swept back into a vague tangled knot behind her. Her eyes were huge and dark—capable of fixing a baleful glazed gaze upon a partner of shoot-up, art, or grope. She wore a black short-sleeved scoop-neck bodystocking. Her shoes and other clothes were in a brown bag on the window ledge between the rooms. There was a hole in the stocking's toe. "See that abscess?"—wiggling her white toe which bore a pink sore on the outer tarsal—"Zack shot me up with methedrine. A foot flash!"—breaking into giggles.

Diane drew eyelashes with ink and brush above her lips so that her mouth babbling torrentially had the look of a convulsing cyclops. Next, her twitching Rapidograph pen began to work on her toe. She drew flower petals around her shoot-up sore. Then she ripped at the toe-hole and peeled the stocking up to her thigh and spent the next hour drawing a maze of stick-figures all over the leg. Soon she had cut a jagged circle out of the stomach of the bodystocking with a razor blade. She studied her stomach, craning her head down, and then began to shave each pale stomach hair with the blade. Sometimes a meth mini-spasm would occur and the steel would nick the skin, leaving a thin red slice. Ouch. She drew an ink-sun in the Mayan style rising from the top of her pubic hair. This done, she stood up and said, "Hey, somebody said you were going to bring some amphetamine."

This startled the filmmaker who had been watching her, not thinking to switch on the lights and to film it. He pointed to the paper bag he had brought, "There're four ounces in there."

"There is!?"—she almost shouted, and jumped along with the others toward the flash-source. She cooked a solution and shot herself up. "Flash! flash! flash!"—she shout/laughed, pirouetting upon her leg fair-covered with stick-figures. Then Diane sat back upon the mattress and grabbed a notebook, "I'm going to jot some thoughts."

She wrote for several minutes then picked up the single-edged razor blade again and started scraping her lips with it. The filmmaker was busy at this time filming other peoples' shoot-ups. He glanced into the bedroom and winced involuntarily, seeing Diane scraping her mouth with a razor. When little edges of lip-skin would be hooked up, she would pick the skin with pinching fingers and tear it off. Soon long blood-pink strips had been peeled from her lips. The filmmaker stood on a chair and adjusted the photo-floods. He found it hard to photograph the event, so unnerving was it to see and to hear the scritch-scratching of the razor.

He had been worried about the moment when he would

first switch on the floodlights and begin to film, that people would get uptight. But nothing happened, the group just accepted the extra light and the camera as another tidbit of grooviness. That is, the babblers kept babbling, the painters kept painting, and the flautists kept fluting. In fact, the walls were so fully lit that Sheilah was happy: "Hey man, that light is groovy on my wall"—as she stood drawing on it with extremely small swirls, dots, triangles, and faces, as was her style, "I'm going to paint the light-blobs."

For the next several hours, the filmmaker scurried from room to room, shutting lights on and off, shooting the shoots, changing the location of the microphone, changing tapes, changing film. For film-changes, he had sewn together two dark cloths into a large sack, inside which he could crouch in darkness to change film. He didn't want to take any chances with the "government-surplus" film with respect to accidental exposure of the photosensitive surfaces.

Sam was eager to catch Tom Four-a-day on film because Tom was very famous on the set as the dope-fiends' dope-fiend. To Four-a-day, drugs were God. He got his name from his ability to forge or cash at least four hot checks a day. No one was certain of his real name.

"I am the Gauguin of dope"—he would brag, always careful to mention that he had once been a wealthy insurance executive who had abandoned it all, boring job and family, to worship the teeming cornucopious saxophone spilling dope-tabs down upon the table.

All Four-a-day would talk about was drugs. Like, the first thing he said when the filmmaker entered the room, "Man, yesterday I smoked a whole dime of Acapulco gold, today I took a grain of morphine, man I'm still nodding, then some procaine for a tough edge, also two yellowjackets. An hour ago I bought some bennies over at Lou's. Just took six in the bathroom of Rienzi's. Man, the high is out there, out there!"—looking up toward the ceiling, eyes closed, skin wrinkling on the back of his neck, shaking his head. All this was filmed, and many minutes more—capturing forever the sad-voiced dope-fiend.

There was a knock at the door. "Who's there?"

"It's Manfred. Let me in."—the knocker adding a toodle-doodle-doop on his flute. The human at the door was known as Manfred the Nut, a far-famed A-head just possibly certifiably crazy. There was the matter of Manfred's Phantom, a nonexistent "spirit" which accompanied Manfred day and night and was his constant companion in conversation. The listener, of course, could only hear one side of the dialogue.

Sometimes Manfred and his Phantom held heated arguments. He discussed everything with Phantom and often asked its advice regarding a painting or sketch then being undertaken.

Sheilah opened up and there he was, Manfred, flute in his belt, an old blue tie with a horse painted on the front. Stacked on his head, perpendicular to his physique, were about fifteen large pieces of tan cardboard and a brown bag of pencils, his art supplies for the next several days. "Hello there everybody"—Manfred greeted them, his voice strained and loud.

He turned back upon the hallway and yelled, "Come on in with me, Phantom!" And then, "Hey, I hear there's some amphetamine here and that Sammy is making a movie about us. Oh, hello Sammy!"—walking toward the mound of amph' lying on a suitcase, rolling up his sleeve.

When freshly shot up, Manfred the Nut became a vortex of activity. And it was as if his Phantom had shot up also. Both of them talked back and forth squeakily. Manfred decided to make a metal flute but he had no pipe. He left the pad and returned minutes later with some wrenches, drills, and a crowbar. After a sweating hour of groans and clanks, Manfred unscrewed and removed the radiator. "It's not winter yet. They don't need this."

The purpose of removing the radiator was to secure a short piece of pipe with which to make a flute. He dropped the radiator with a thud! in the middle of the room and loosened off a length of pipe. Aha! He lifted it like a prize then fell to his knees cackling and blowing hoots through the un-holed piping. Next was the task of marking the holes and the tiresome drilling and the fashioning of a wooden mouthpiece. This project took all night—with numerous pauses for additional amphetamine and for a few heated exchanges with his Phantom. The filmmaker followed the radiator-flute construction with a fifteen-second shot every hour or so.

He also filmed a great sequence of Sheilah shooting up the Norwegian sailor, who was in uniform. Everyone laughed as she told of the language problem when she had first picked him up at The House of Nothingness, but the sentence, "want beatnik girls?" was very understandable to the sailor. Sheilah conned five out of him for groceries which they brought to the pad.

Around midnight Zeb arrived. "Hey man, help me up with this!"—he shouted up at the window, huffing. He was bearing a large metal-edged cardboard drum which was packed with long triangular scraps in the shape of school pennants, in violet, red, and orange cloth shot through with gold and silver threads. Zeb had lugged the barrel ten blocks tilting it on its edge and rolling it, driven by the A-bomb.

"Hey, wow, dig this!"—Zack exclaimed when they had hauled it up the steps, "This'll make a groovy tapestry." Zeb

201

and Zack were known as "The Two Zs" in the A crowd. More specifically, Zeb was known as Bad Z and Zack as Badder Z, because of his crueler reputation. They were always getting into fights; their faces were scarred from slapping each other with razor-blade fragments wedged between their fingers.

Zeb was wearing a grimy patch over his right eye. There was a greasy lock of hair lodged behind it. "What happened to your eye?"—Manfred asked.

Zeb lifted his eye-patch to show the assembly. "Disgusting!" Claudia turned her face away.

"Your eye looks like a hemorrhaging clam, man; what happened?"

"Well, I stopped by Ace's the other day to deal some art books I'd offed from Marlboro. Ace tried to give me an eye-pop. He had a real special spike he said some nurse at Bellevue gave him for draining swollen eye veins. Well, man, I figured if this fucking spike can suck it out why not use it to pop some A in my eye? I wanted to shoot it into my brain, dig, through the optic nerve. Can you *dig* those changes! A direct brain-flash! Wow, something else!!"

"What happened?"

"Well, dig it, he found a lot of raised veins in my eye; I hadn't been to bed in four days. So he got ready to hit and, of all the times to turn spastic—the fucker lunged into my eye! Man, it was a dartboard scene."

"You're a lucky mother, man, you could be blind."

There followed next a long discussion on various arcane methods and places, of shoot-up. Someone dragged out the ancient tale of nut-shoot. How flashy it was, supposedly, to shoot up genital veins. "But you got to watch tying up your balls, man, because like you can become a tenor with the Mormon Tabernacle Choir if you keep the tie on too long.

The best thing is to use a rubber band, you can get it off quick."

Zack, Zeb, Claudia, and Llazo began the tapestry. They took the bedspread and nailed it tightly to the kitchen wall to serve as the base of the work. Then they started gluing the triangular bright strips upon the spread until it was covered in a weird quiltlike manner. Claudia made plaster of Paris in the bathtub and they all hurled globs of it upon the "tapestry." On top of each glop, which was more or less round in shape, Sheilah drew an indented circle with her finger.

When the glops had dried she painted the dented circles with oil paints.

Zack filled three salad bowls with red, purple, and orange. He dipped his hand entirely in the purple bowl and advanced toward the tapestry, smearing a neat purple borderline around the entire work. Then Manfred, who claimed the idea was from his Phantom, suggested that Zack "smear handprints on the tapestry like those caves in France where the Cro-Magnons slapped five on the ceilings."

"Good idea, good idea"—Zack muttered and proceeded to place about fifty handprints on the tapestry in between the globs of plaster. This whole act of creation was immortalized on film.

To finish the tapestry, Sheilah wandered bug-eyed into the bedroom waving a thick silver spinal tap from her great-uncle Mitchell's medical kit. "Does anybody want the final flash?" she asked, jabbing the mattress with the thick two-inch silver needle.

Diane thought Sheilah was serious and offered her buttock for a zap. Sheilah laughed, "I can't shoot you with this; this is filled up with paint."

Sheilah walked into the kitchen and spurted several arabesque swirls of orange paint upon the tapestry. Next, in a surge of formalism, she squirted two rows of four large contiguous orange circles, for a total of eight, upon the cloth. This done, she stood back studying the work and announced, "Total beauty! This should be in the Louvre."

All through the night and through the next day the events oozed past. Some he filmed, others he missed. He did catch for history the construction and destruction of the Miniature Garden of Amphetamine Sand. They apparently got the idea from the white sand Zen garden in the courtyard of The House of Nothingness café, on 10th Street and Tompkins Square North.

Zeb grabbed a double fist of amphetamine and made the suggestion, "Let's make a Clear Crystal Garden of Perfect Thought-Form!"

"What do you mean?"

"Here, I'll show you." Zeb turned over the barrel that had contained the cloth scraps and placed an inverted rectangular baking tin on top. He mashed the dope crystals into fine grit with a spoon and evenly dispersed the granules, like sand, over the metal surface. For the rocks necessary to such a garden, he broke up a Baby Ruth candy bar into three pieces and placed them at the end of the metal plate. Zack took a fork and, with the tines, raked even lines in the A-strand, like the raked patterns in sand gardens.

"Now we can be like the Gods, man. Let's lick up the Zen plate!" The four artists stood on all sides of the white rectangle with the triad of Baby Ruth hunks, and lowered their faces upon it, slurping, licking, and slobbering as they devoured the granules. This was destined to become one of the most famous vignettes in amphetamine filmmaking.

At 3 A.M., two musicians, Bob Krowe and Stu Elgin, tap-tapped at the chamber door. "Hey, man, we heard there was a party here and that some cat had laid five pounds of methedrine on you."

"Nah, only four ounces, come on in."

Krowe was a well-known jazz bass player who pushed his stand-up bass around the East Side by means of a half–roller skate tied to the bottom. Stu Elgin was carrying a battered saxophone wrapped in a pillowcase and a guitar adorned with glued bits of glass, nuts, decals, stamps, and feathers. In years past, Stu and Krowe had organized a jazz quartet that had toured the East Coast club circuit, like Buffalo to Baltimore, but had given it up for the East Side dope circuit. They were good musicians and the whole pad joined them for a 3 A.M. jam.

Manfred was on flute, Elgin on sax and guitar, Krowe leading on bass, Four-a-day was percussive with some short sticks with bells nailed on them—and then there were the Astral Wallbeaters: Llazo, Zack, Claudia, Diane, and Zeb, not to mention Sheilah, who was jumping up and down in rhythm inside the ice compartment of the overturned refrigerator. The sailor was left in the bedroom giggling and babbling to himself in Norwegian.

The music arose with an enormous din of sax, bells, flute, bass, and scat-along yowls. The wallbeaters bashed and whacked till the plaster began to drop. "Hey man, you recording this!?"—Krowe yelled over at Sam.

"Yeah."

"Groovy. We'll just call this piece, *Suite A: White Jam on Allen Street*,"—Krowe laughed, as he slowly pushed the roller-skate bass around the room, pausing at the trunk on which the mound of A was dumped, to reach down for a pinch which he honked into his nose, and then resumed his contorting bent-over fingering.

There was a thud thud at the door. Everyone stopped.

205

Zeb walked over and put his head against the panel. "Who is it?"

"It's the police."

At just that moment there was a tug-of-war in the other room as Zack and Llazo were jostling for control of a black necktie used to tie the arm. Each was the owner, although it was difficult to see why anyone would want possession of such a greasy, skin-smirched specimen. 'C'mon motherfucker, it's mine, I'll cut your ass!"

"Hey man, I was *wearing* it this afternoon. Gimme!"—giving a mighty tug.

"Shit, you never did nothing with this but tie your arm, man; it's mine!"—and gave a yank so that Zeb fell across the table of ink, glasses of water with hypos resting in them, paint, towels—all which cracked to the floor.

"Shhhht! Will you shut the fuck up. The fuzz are here."

"Psssst,"—he motioned at Llazo to stash the A, and whispered, "Don't spill any." The pad was totally still. Only Diane hissed and whistled now and then as she scribbled onward in her yellow-paper spiral notebook, "I want to write about my first ice-cream cone. Let me tell you about it. It was at Glower's Drug Store twelve years ago . . . ."

They turned out all the lights so that the police couldn't see a thing inside the pad, a timeless beat maneuver. Zeb opened the door, with the chain still attached. He saw that it was really the fuzz, so he shut the door, zipped off the chain, and opened wide. "Good evening, officers. We were just having a party. Sorry, if we were disturbing anyone."

The officer: "There's someone lying on the sidewalk outside by the garbage cans who claims to have arrived on a spaceship. We heard the noise up here and we thought maybe he belonged to you."

"Gee, I wonder who it is. He's not one of us."

"It's not *me*"—Manfred the Nut piped up from the dark bedroom.

"However"—the officer continued, "it's three-fifteen in the morning and the neighbors are beginning to call in about the noise up here. We heard it all the way to Canal Street."

"Sure officer, the band was just playing some dance music for us. I'll tell them to stop." Whew. As the officers turned and clumped down the stairs.

Zack Thayer became very sadistic under 'phets. That's how he'd met his wife Claudia, when he was crashing into a bank of amphetamine runway lights, and he pulled a cave-man scene, cutting up the face of Claudia's boyfriend, and forced her to come away with him. Claudia wasn't exactly a masochist but there was plenty of violence in their relationship. Zack and Claudia were the premiere A-head husband-and-wife team, almost a caricature of that violent puppet act that children dig.

After the police split, Diane looked up at Zack and opened her stripped lips, "Hey, why don't *you* shoot me up. I could dig it. Make me go to heaven, Zack!"

Zack was all too eager to accommodate her, and leaped for the glass of needles. He filtered a solution of dope and filled an eyedropper with needle affixed, to the brim. With a flourish he stuck the needle into a blue gray vein on the underside of Diane's forearm. Jabbed would have been a better word. He slid the needle long inside the vein much farther than necessary. Then, as he injected the dope within it, he shoved the needle to the hilt inside her and began to twist slightly so that the needle tip pushed up against the top of the vein from inside. The viewers could see the skin rise from the jabbing needle, like a mole burrowing across a putting green. It had to be painful. Then Zack began to twist the needle in all directions. The girl was expressionless. Her eyes were closed and she was gasping and breathing heavily. "Go on, man go on!"—she whispered, eyes still closed.

The filmmaker switched off the camera and even the lights, because he wasn't certain that she and Zack were not going through a sadomasochist riff for the sake of the camera. After what Zack did to her arm, the filmmaker stopped filming altogether for about an hour, though Diane, once shot up, did not seem to feel much pain from the gouging, but continued filling up her notebook.

Sam began to film again during a fight which would later comprise a vignette dubbed "The Glue-Bottle Violence Scene." It started calmly enough while both Zeb and Zack were operating on a large piece of plywood with a mixed media of paint, plaster, hypo-ink, and raisins. Zeb was gluing abstract patterns of raisins upon the wood. Zack had just discovered under the kitchen sink an old jar of nuts and bolts which he proposed to begin gluing to the panel. The problem was that there was just one glue bottle and the bottle was just about empty. It was 4:50 A.M., hardly an hour for such a purchase. Surly waxed the two glue-needers as each tried to hook out some glue at the same time.

"Watch it, motherfucker!"—Zack growled.

At that, Zeb grabbed the glue bottle and smeared the entire contents upon the portion of the plywood on which he was laboring. This caused the freak-scene immortalized in the film.

Zeb wound up getting stabbed in the top of his head with a hypodermic needle. He fell down to the floor, holding his head, the spike dangling from the skin, and Zack stomped him in the stomach. It was sickening to hear, sort of like a stomped paper cup. "Zack!"—Zeb threatened from the floor, "I'm gonna peel a slice off your nose! Like Diane did to her lips!"

208

It could have gotten worse but Manfred and Claudia intervened and a cut-up was averted. Zack was always getting cut, and more particularly, always cutting. The following year, after the film had been finished, the filmmaker was scrounging early one morning in Washington Square Park—when word was flashed along the benches that Zack had been stabbed in the chest that very morning during an altercation arising from a methedrine burn.

Zack had been delivered, according to the tale, d.o.a. to the hospital. Just as he had been declared dead by the doctor in the emergency room and the sheet was ready for his face, a miracle had occurred. Zack's "body" suffered an amphetamine twitch-spasm and his life-line, like, was revived in his body. When the doctor noticed the dope-twitch, Zack was rushed into surgery and saved. This story was told and retold like some sort of religious parable.

"Amphetamine saved Zack's life, baby, you better believe it."

When the sun had just risen, Sam turned out the floodlights. His film supply had run low and he wanted to save enough to film the comedown, certain to occur in a day or so, when he knew there would be strife aplenty.

He decided to sleep since he was very tired and he had abstained himself from sucking the white. He was the only one copping z's in the entire pad as the others raved and painted onward. As he drifted toward sleep he overheard a conversation between Llazo and Diane. Llazo wanted to borrow her blade so he could cut a hatchway into her bodystocking in order for them to make it. "I'll sew it back in place myself after we're done, I promise."

"Okay"—the girl with the coal-dark eyes assented.

He apparently cut a successful passageway for soon the groans and sighs were floating above the babble in the dark room. Others joined them writhing in insatiable A-sex. At one point Zack walked up to Sam and woke him up with a rude nudge. Sam squinted his eyes, trying to focus in on Zack whose bent fighter's nose was smeared with a streak of red, maybe paint.

"Hey, man, you got a rubber band?"—Zack asked. Sam had none. Zack was naked except for a gray ink-stained T-shirt with the arms cut off. Zack removed the sealing strips from one of the film cans and proceeded to wrap it around the base of his erection, then strode back into the other room, apparently to pull a sodomy scene on the reluctant Claudia.

"Zack! Zack! No, No! Zack!"—followed by guttural growls from the dark, as Sam drifted back to sleep.

It was late in the afternoon when Sam woke up. Things had pretty well quieted down. It wasn't long after he awakened that the last of the four ounces was used up. After this it was all comedown. Forays were made into the streets looking for the white gold. They began to hit on the filmmaker for some more dope, "C'mon man! Buy some more A!"

"Or else get out!"—Zack snarled, giving Sam a shove.

In terms of power, Zack Thayer began to take over the pad. He ruled with the irrationality and violence of a textbook on dictatorship. He beat up Claudia so much that she had to move over to Mary Meth's pad. And the police started raiding the place though no arrests were made.

Police visits were made easier by the fact that someone had removed the front door of the pad—"I want to make a table with it, dig?"—and, in place of the door, had nailed up a shower curtain. As for ownership of the place, Llazo had actually signed the lease originally, but Zack forced him to sign a statement relinquishing the entire scene to Zack. Zack

210

nicked Llazo's finger with a spike and coerced a red finger-print on the document.

To make things worse, for reasons unknown there was a dope-panic in lower New York. The sudden amphetamine drought made the East Side a Sahara of violence. They held meetings to discuss raising funds, with occasional hock-shop glances at Sam's camera equipment.

Finally the filmmaker left, having used up all his film, and uneasy for his own well-being under the circumstances. He carried with him all the light fixtures, film, and, with fearful clutch, the camera.

Several days later he returned to the Allen Street pad to take some shots of the pad's "final state" since he had heard the landlord had thrown everybody out. The condition of the pad, as Sam encountered it in doorless dereliction, was that of bombed-out chaos. A large mound of debris had ac-cumulated in the middle of the kitchen, including the re-frigerator which lay on its back, the door open, its trays and grates removed.

The refrigerator was stuffed with old clothes, drawings, bags of garbage, and pieces of the bright triangular cloth used for the tapestry. There was an old TV set, guts dangling to the floor, sitting next to the refrigerator, with a headless mannequin protruding from the picture-tube hole and paint-ed with ornate configurations.

The sink was completely clogged and filled to the brim with dried plaster. The tapestry with the huge orange cir-cles on it was intact on the wall. Sam was tempted to take it with him except the landlord showed up and threatened a violence scene if Sam didn't stop filming and split.

He managed to film the final state of Sheilah's micro-swirl wall mural before he had to leave. The mural was in three sections, covering the upper half of the kitchen wall plus the

211

entire ceiling and the bathroom floor. She had poked holes in the plaster of the kitchen wall and inserted some of Manfred's abandoned flutes which gave the artwork a stubbled effect.

The bedroom was a tangle of wet clothing, shoes, and notebook pages featuring ornate eyeballs and melted faces. Someone had ripped the mattress completely apart, apparently to secure a piece of stuffing to use as a dope filter.

The panes of all the windows were each neatly x'd with crisscrosses of the black tape Sam used to seal the film cans.

"Why?"—Sam asked Zack.

"The Out doesn't exist"—he replied. "You dig, it's all *In*."

Sam spent the next few months shooting the A-heads, when he could afford it, in outdoor settings, mainly in Washington Square. He finally finished the sound track and edited the film. The credits were shot in the form of a moving hypodermic needle squirting letters upon a raw canvas.

In the succeeding years, the filmmaker turned his attention away from film and became a schoolteacher and printer in a Washington State mountain valley.

But his fifty-five-minute, black-and-white movie *Amphetamine Head—A Study of Power in America*, remains. A print may be ordered from the Total Assault Film Archives, Battle Creek, Michigan.

The AEC Sit-in

RUSSIA DROPPED A 100-megaton nuke-puke in November of '61 causing a spew of strontium 90, cesium 137 and other carcinogenic spores to float upon the wild winds. The Russian tests wreaked despair within the nuclear disarmament movement in New York City. To oppose the blast, a few pacifists decided to picket the Russian Mission to the United Nations located on Park Avenue at 67th. They were arrested outside the mission because of a New York City ordinance prohibiting picketing there, a law spawned of the fear of right-wing violence during the cold war.

Then, tooth for tooth, rumors began to float throughout the late winter of '61–'62 that the U.S. government itself might set off high-megaton nuke-puke. In New York, various nonviolent peace groups held meetings, including the Total Assault Ahimsa Squadron (the action arm of the Total Assault Cantina), Maniac Artists of The Abyss (MATA, a group of artists and painters 'gainst the nukes), and the two main peace-action groups of the era, the Catholic Workers and the Committee For Nonviolent Action.

213

After a lengthy stomp-dance upon the ahimsa threshing floor, the decision was made that immediately after any announcement of atmospheric testing by the U.S., the peace groups would sponsor a nonviolent sit-in at the front entrance of the New York office of the Atomic Energy Commission in order to prevent the entry of AEC employees.

On Friday, March 3, President Kennedy announced that if the Russians did not sign a permanent cheat-proof test-ban treaty before the end of April, he would resume testing of nuclear weapons in the air.

The sit-in was scheduled for Monday. The weekend was spent preparing and printing the leaflets and notifying demonstrators. Two leaflets were written—one as a fact sheet for those committing civil disobedience which recommended serving jail sentences rather than posting bail or paying fines. The other leaflet was to be handed out at the sit-in explaining the purpose, decrying atmospheric tests, urging the workers to quit their jobs at the AEC and not to pay taxes for nuke-puke. The peace groups pursued the doctrine of "openness and truth"—that is, of informing the police and AEC officials exactly what was going to take place. They sent out announcements to the press.

Monday morning was a bitter wind-swept day of foul septic blasts from the direction of New Jersey oil refineries. The New York Atomic Energy Commission was located at 376 Hudson Street on the lower west side of Greenwich Village near the piers. Before the demonstration, the police had erected a ring of gray barricades around the entrances.

That morning the poet awoke nervous. He washed himself slowly and did not eat, meditating about the impending confrontation. He washed with meticulous detail because he remembered all too well the shabby treatment afforded by a sheriff in Ohio who had once arrested him and had scoffed

214

at the condition of his body with respect to grunge. Ever thereafter, the poet had always spick-and-span'd himself prior to any demonstration.

As he left his apartment, he was scared in the pit of his stomach and walked down the street, often with his eyes closed, as imaginary clubs bashed his face. That very weekend there had been demonstrations in Times Square where club-wielding police on horses had ridden up on the curb into a large crowd packed upon Father Duffy's traffic island—and the blood had dripped from the whacked skulls.

When he arrived at the AEC, there was that strange electric aura which always seemed to occur just prior to civil disobedience. The bitter cold, the throngs of police, the pickets, the barricades, the weird intelligence agents with movie cameras, the traffic oozing extra-slowly by, the reporters, the nervous protest leaders—all combined both to thrill and to terrify. He spotted a few of his friends already sitting behind the barricades outside the front door. They waved and soon he too had slipped through the blocking legs of the police and under the gray boards, silently nodding to those already sitting.

He sat with his knees bunched up and his arms locked around them. He could see the supporting picket line move slowly in a large oval, their signs hoisted against Kennedy's nukes. They were warned by a police captain to move from the door or they'd be arrested. Then it began.

There was a quick engine roar as a paddy wagon backed up to the sit-in. Two detectives with food-bloated faces in thick dark blue overcoats and narrow-brimmed felt hats, double-nabbed the poet, one to a shoulder, sucking him out of the close hem-in of the barricades and hauled him toward the police van, half drag, half carry. Then it was a heave-ho scene and the poet plopped aboard.

215

Not all of the nineteen arrested "went limp"—as they termed a totally relaxed arrest posture, but some walked to the paddy wagon. The argument was that going limp created violence in that it tended to anger the gruff, huffing police haulers.

When the van was full, the back door was locked and it drove away to the New York Criminal Courts Building at 100 Centre Street. Those jammed aboard sang Numbers 1, 2, and 3 on the arrested-pacifist Hit Parade: "We Shall Overcome," "Down By the Riverside," with a little satiric "God Bless America," thrown in.

For the next five hours they were treated to the criminal justice stockyards, herded along with the hordes of sullen unfortunates arrested that day in New York City. Finally they were placed in a small "holding tank" packed with the accused, located just outside the courtroom. There was a parade back and forth of legal defense aides with scribbled clipboards trying to assist the poor.

After a seemingly endless chain of mumbling confrontations with the judge, many of which seemed to be drug related—the pacifists' docket numbers and names were moan-droned by the bailiff and they were herded into the room and the arresting officers lined them up in front of the judge, a dour scowler with curtains of chin blubber dangling.

The first thing to be noted in standing before de judge was that the big brown N in the motto, IN GOD WE TRUST, high on the wall behind him, had fallen off. The judge flashed some red onto his face when defendant Randy McDermott, lining up with the others in front of the bench, refused to face the judge, but rather insisted on facing the spectators. "I refuse to recognize the existence of these proceedings," he announced.

216

There were titters in the courtroom at this and the gavel-whacking judge admonished the supporters in the front row to shut up. The judge then launched into a cold-war lecture which culminated in the old "You'd never get to do this in Russia—you'd be sent to Siberia." Then he gave Randy, because of his noncooperation, notice of bail of five hundred dollars but the others he released on their own recognizance. All defendants were charged with discon, disorderly conduct. Those who had gone limp were given additional charges of resisting arrest. The august red-face set a date for pleading of March 23, 1962, 10 A.M. "And be on time!" the judge admonished.

On March 23, most of them pled guilty to disorderly conduct in exchange for the dropping of resisting-arrest charges. The poet and the others were sentenced to ten days at the Hart Island Workhouse. Thank you, Judge Wallach. Next they were escorted back into the colons of the Tombs to be fingerprinted.

The poet was opposed to the FBI fingerprint storage system and he knew that the New York City fuzz were going to flash his prints right down to D.C. for the big file. He notified the guards that he was not going to cooperate with fingerprinting, and was astounded at the commotion this seemed to cause.

His refusal convinced the jail officials that they might have some sort of Pretty Boy Floyd on their hands. Aha, they rubbed their hands, smilingly knowingly, aha, a criminal! They told him they were going to take the prints by force and still he refused.

Then they sent him to see a prison psychologist, the purpose presumably to determine if the poet would pull a wolverine scene while resisting the printing. He assured the

217

officer that he would be totally nonviolent but that they'd have to carry him to the print room.

When he was dragged into the room, the officer seemed to assume that he was going to cooperate, even when the poet fell several times from the chair into a limp heap upon the floor. The officer picked up the poet's limp right hand, the fingers dangling in desuetude. The officer rolled a smush of ink across the smooth desktop with a roller. Then he blacked the poet's fingers and placed them upon a fingerprint card. "Roll your fingers," he ordered.

"I'm sorry, I can't cooperate. I don't believe in fingerprinting."

The cop cursed. He grabbed a finger, and pressed it onto the card, trying to roll it himself. But it was too smudged to use. "C'mon, cooperate!" he hissed. The poet contemplated deliberately twitching his fingers with each attempt, but he didn't really want to get beaten up by a bunch of guards. He ruined four fingerprint cards before the set was finally complete, by which time a superior officer was waiting in the room, his carotid pulsing rapidly on a florid neck above a tight white collar bearing golden adornments. Mr. Florid Neck grabbed the finger card and raced away to run the prints. "Aha! Now we'll check *you* out right away!"

A few minutes later a gray school bus with barred windows drove the fresh prisoners up through the Bronx No Thonx and then to a ferry which slowly threshed into Long Island South to Hart Island. He told prison officials he was a journalist and poet and hinted that he was going to write an article about jail conditions. Apparently the prison staff assigned someone to check this out, because he was approached three times while on Hart Island and was asked things like, "How's the article coming along?" and "How are

218

they treating you? Be sure and send us a copy of the article."

They were processed into the citadel after which there was a nude stroll through a milky-hued footbath and a check for cooties. At the clothes bin, they were given some bent black shoes, loose jeans, blue shirt, towels, and a thick brown green overcoat. Never in his life had such a negative rush of immediate boredom stormed his soul.

They were assigned bunk-space in a large dormitory where there was a TV they were allowed to watch, staring from their double-tiered beds, in the evening. Newspapers were not allowed; something about people stuffing them down the toilets. In the cavernous chow halls the food was served on metal trays with workers glopping the slop into the compartments with defeated splats from griseous ladles. The bread was of punk quality, exuding uncooked flour and could have been used to make sod houses. They called them "rocks from The Rock," since they were baked at another jail out on Rikers Island, otherwise known as The Rock.

Everyone worked. The poet was herded to the clothes department (known as the "clothes bin") where he was assigned the job of keeper of the shoelaces. In later years, usually while drunk, he would rattle off exactly how many black, how many green; and then how many green long, how many green short, shoelaces there had been in March '62 in the Hart Island Prison. Ditto for the number of long and short black shoestrings. Each day it took him about thirty minutes to see that the jail shoes were all properly laced, after which there was nothing to do. He sorted the laces over and over. Whenever the guards were away he would stare out the back window upon the bay shore, and the listless waters, the gulls upon them, and in the distance the junkies burying bodies.

219

The prison assigned the heroin addicts, after they had gone cold-turkey of course, to dig the graves of all the New York City derelicts and unclaimed bodies. It was a grim scene, to see them march out each morn, shovels on shoulders, to the pits. The bodies apparently were buried in four layers, one atop another, with identity tags tied to their toes, so that later, should relatives want them, they could be claimed. After a couple of years, so the rumor went, the skeletons were dug up and thrown upon the crumbly beach, a bony roost for the gulls, and the same ground used for new burials.

The junkies who dug the graves were known as the "Garbage Squad," because of the voracious appetites of the freshly detoxified men. Late in the afternoon after the rest of the prison had eaten, the Garbage Squad was marched in from snuff-bury, to the chow hall where they proceded to eat every drip of protein remaining in the kitchen.

He felt such despair in the cold mornings lined up in a bent row on the sidewalk waiting for the first gobble-shift to eat their sausage and cornflakes and weak coffee. It was bitterly cold in the smelly island dawn breeze; their rough green brown coats were buttoned all the way. Where they lined up, the morning sun shone through the bushes on the left. The sidewalk lay several feet indented into the ground and the shrubs were planted at the top of a waist-high ledge so that the sun was only seen by gazing through the branches.

He heard the countless spits, like punctuations, of alcoholic men with colds. He fantasized a cloud of commas swarming across the sky. The alkies loved to spit into the shrubs, a thing once seen and never to be forgotten, the shiny hockers dangling from the branches, resplendent in the sun.

The single saving event in his stay at the island was encountering a dormitory full of poets, most of whom were there on long terms on drug offenses. Their quarters were in a small room reachable from his own dorm by a small corridor. To visit the poets was forbidden but he managed to sneak there about once a day.

The poets never wrote down their works, and they were unpublished. In the jailhouse evenings it was quite a thrill to hear them chant-sing literally for hours their memorized rhymed epics. The themes were the big-city tensions—the drugs, the arrests, the cops, the FBI, jazz, loves down the furtive gullet of no reproach. They memorized each other's poems, and there were numerous authorless rhymed tales passed down from the years. Readers may well have heard some of these poets reciting in Washington Square on Sunday afternoons.

When he told them he too was a poet, they invited him to recite some of his work, but he was very embarrassed to have to say that he had very little memorized, just a few flashes here and there. "Hey man," they said, "you should be like that cat Pushkin. That cat had *all* his poetry right in his head, you dig. That's where it belongs. He could close his eyes and recite for hours."

The night of his second day on Hart Island, 3-24-62, there was a televised fight for the welterweight world championship between Bennie "Kid" Paret and Emile Griffith. It was a grudge battle. Kid Paret, a former Cuban sugar-field worker brought to temporary riches via face-punch, had been the champion. Emile Griffith took away the crown in early 1961 by a knockout. Paret then recaptured the crown on July 30, 1961, in a hotly disputed decision. An angry feud developed. Rather than to retire, Paret was pressed

221

from all sides to continue his career and a further face-punch was arranged.

The jail dorm was totally silent and dark save for the tube. The dorm guard sat with his feet on the desk, watching the fight. The convicts sat upon their bunks and stared.

During the early rounds Griffith seemed the casual winner. In the twelfth round Paret was snuffed.

Griffith backed Paret into the corner ropes. Bash. Paret fell against the padded corner brace, his head and upper body jutting at an angle outside the ring. Then there were twenty quick bashes upon Paret's face and head: baf, baf, baf, baf, baf, baf, baf, baf, baf, baf, baf, baf, baf, baf, baf, baf, baf, baf, baf, baf, baf. The referee stood staring. The dormitory was staring. Everybody staring. In Miami the fighter's wife watching the battle on TV screamed, "Stop it! Stop it!"

The final scene for the TV-starers showed Paret bent back, eyes closed, loose light-colored trunks with wide stripes down the side, his kidneys pressed against the corner padding, his left arm hanging defenseless at his side, the right arm still cocked but skewered to the side. Griffith still bashing.

Finally, at 2:09 of the twelfth, the referee, Ruby Goldstein, yelled "Hold it!" and threw his arms around Griffith to prevent further hits. Griffith was loath to stop and made a lunge or so to continue—then subsided. And Paret slid down to a crouch, his knees askew. The lowest of the three parallel ring ropes was hooked under his right shoulder, his arm still jutting upward in a fighting posture.

He was in a coma. They removed his mouthpiece—and carried him away. In a few minutes the TV announcer mentioned that Paret had been given last rites. He was taken to

222

Roosevelt Hospital where a doctor gave him "chances of recovery one in ten thousand."

Shortly thereafter the guard switched off the TV. Lights out. No conversation. The poet lay stunned. He spat out the side of his bunk, as if a ptooey! could exorcise what he had just seen. He didn't know whether to pray for Paret or to fall into a frothing rage at the so-called art of boxing. He made a personal vow that if there ever were an actual revolution and if he were ever in an orb of power over the People's Bureau of Athletics, then he'd try to ban boxing.

On his bunk he tried to pray for the injured boxer. A few days later the poor man died. But he couldn't get the fight out of his mind. It echoed with the baf baf baf baf baf baf and the blood-lust roar, and the tense blood-stare silence of the dormitory.

The morning after the fight there was a radio news report announcing impending high-altitude nuke blasts out in the Pacific on Christmas Island. He immediately began to map plans for "indiscriminate sit-ins" against the tests. God, was he eager to hit the streets. He paced around the dormitory muttering and cursing. He was visited by fantasies of escaping, though he had heard no one *ever* escaped the island—something about marksmen who stand on shore and aim for the head, if swimming, and for the back, if rowing. "Two tried last year—got 'em right in the back."

He gnashed his teeth and thirsted to join his comrades roaming the streets. Instant! Instant! Though he knew that he had fifty more years to beat his head against the death machine.

Peace Walk

I

THE LIGHT BLUE GREEN Ford was at the top
of the hill two miles from town and started downgrade
when it came upon a straight line of walkers carrying some
sort of signs.

"Melvin, why are you slowing down?"—his wife wanted to
know. He didn't answer but pointed to the right at the
sign-bearing hikers.

"Melvin, why are you leaning down like that?" she
queried further.

Melvin was bent over the steering wheel, with his neck
craned up, trying to see. He read her a sign: " 'National Defense Through Nonviolent Resistance'—now what does that
mean?" The auto was now traveling about five miles per
hour. He could not see the pickup truck barreling up to
the hill crest behind them. There was a screech!/whomp!/
smash!, the wife-head punching a neat shattered concavity
in the safety glass. With the screech, the walkers scattered

into the ditch, signs plopping to the ground, leaflets fluttering upon the tarvia.

Mindful of cars careening snuffishly into the ditch, several walkers sprinted up the embankment not stopping till arrival at the edge of a cow pasture.

The woman was not seriously hurt; maybe it was the malletlike shape of her head which enabled her to punch out the windshield with impunity. An ambulance and several state police cars arrived and detained the walkers for questioning. They showed the troopers their cover letter provided by the American Civil Liberties Union outlining their rights.

"You all got anyplace to stay tonight?" a trooper asked them, as he cleared a pile of reports from the back seat of his patrol car, perhaps preparing to offer them the hospitality of the county jail.

"Yes, officer, we're staying tonight at the Shiloh Baptist Church." The marchers spoke in their most pleasant tones, seeking to nip at the earliest moment any thought of arrest for vagrancy.

After the fuzz departed, the walkers held a short meeting about their signs. The signs were large rectangular oilcloth envelopes fitted over light metal tubular frames which were affixed to lightweight aluminum poles with handles. The slogans were printed as large as possible on both sides of the oilcloth envelopes, and since they were so lightweight, they could easily be borne nearly perpendicularly by the marchers. After a discussion it was decided that not much more could be done by the walkers to ensure highway safety other than to hold the signs aright and not to engage drivers in conversations and to walk well away from the edge of the road. The marchers then picked up their fallen bundles of leaflets and their signs and walked on into the town.

For love of Peace, for a civilization of Ahimsa (nonviolence), for the end of nuclear fear, for guilt, for glory, for love of God, for sun-fun, for worship of Manes the Persian, for sensuality: a congeries of men and women, many from the Lower East Side of New York City, began a one-thousand-mile walk through Tennessee and Virginia to Washington, District of Columbia, in the spring of '62. They called themselves the Memphis to Washington Walk for Peace, and the project was sponsored by the New York–based National Committee for a Nonviolent Civilization.

The organizer of the walk was a brilliant Gandhian named Thomas Bartley, the architect of a series of peace marches in America, Europe, and the Soviet Union in the early part of the decade of napalm. Bartley was tremendously charismatic, the author of a book, *National Defense Through Nonviolent Resistance,* and had spent a number of years in India studying the Gandhian movement. Bartley did not accompany the Memphis walk but remained in New York helping maintain the all-important home office.

Bart was an expert at raising money, mainly through phone pleas and fund-appeal letters mailed to money-bursting citizens opposed to the arms race and to nuclear testing, a hot issue in the spring of 1962 when the United States H-bombed a couple of islands in the Pacific.

A lot of the money for the peace walks came from religious donors—from wealthy Quaker dairy farmers and supporters of the Fellowship of Reconciliation. And let us not forget the sudden largess of rich people in crisis, not to mention the secret checks of guilty liberals.

"Oh, another item that should be included in the main first-aid kit is a hemostat," Bartley added.

This created a couple of frowns around the room. "A hemostat?" someone asked.

A friend leaned to the questioner's ear. "It's that thing that looks like a jeweler's grip—Nelson uses one for a roach-clip. It's for spurt-stop in case the Klan operates on our arteries."

There was an atmosphere of fear which tinged the meetings held to plan the peace walk at the National Committee for a Nonviolent Civilization offices. For instance, there were reports that there were counties in the mountainous middle sections of Tennessee where the sunset-necks boasted that no black had ever slept for even a night. And everyone fully remembered the TV footage of that burning Greyhound bus. Still, the time seemed propitious for such a walk, and the danger seemed attractive, even thrillsome. An integrated peace-stroll through the rural South urging citizens not to pay taxes for war, to quit jobs at defense installations, and to renounce all forms of violence—such a project was a toke of paradise to the editorial board of *The Shriek of Revolution* magazine, most of whom signed up for the ahimsa saunter.

It was decided at the planning sessions that the walk would consist of a "core team" of ten to twenty members. Supporters would be invited to join for a few days, a natural phenomenon which occurred when the march passed through, say, a college town and netted the local dissidents and civil-rights activists.

There was no problem, in those innocent years, of violent provocateurs, shovers, jostlers, or FBI Cointelpro dissensionists who might have caused trouble. That was a situation which developed years later during the Vietnam War. There was, however, a sort of Ahimsa Security Clearance wherein potential walkers were required to submit short biographies and to explain their reasons for wishing to join.

After a hot debate, it was decided that although the march was to be fully integrated, there would be no inter-racial couples in the core group. A compromise was pushed through enabling such couples, "responsibly married," to join for a few days as supporters.

The walk was small enough not to have voting—it was talk talk talk, till there was consensus; and the next day, if some-one wanted to reconsider, the meeting was rebegun. In the event of impasse or trouble, there was a stratified decision-making system. When the so-called "core group" of march-ers was unable to reach a decision, there was a smaller steering committee who could decide. If the steering com-mittee was itself unable to agree in consensus, there were two walk coordinators who could finally decide. In the event of an emergency, there was a single project director. The Memphis-to-Washington director was William Storm, an outstanding black activist, poet, and French scholar who had moved into the peace movement after years of Free-dom Rides, voter-registration projects, and delicate flutter-tongued lectures on Symbolist verse at a Quaker college.

Many of the March preparations were a last-minute frenzy. Copies of the A.C.L.U. legal-rights letter and bro-chures describing the purpose and itinerary of the walk were sent to the police chiefs in every town along the walk route. Newspapers, TV, and radio stations were sent press kits. Ministers of churches along the route were sent exten-sive packets of literature, for it was extremely important to collect the sympathy of ministers. Indeed, without church basement floors for copping z's and without the use of church kitchens for communal meals, there would not have been the peace-walk movement of the early 1960s.

A team of advance workers drove along the entire walk route two weeks prior to commencement of the project, arranging hospitality at churches and setting up public meetings. They sketched maps of defense plants and military installations along the way to determine the best locations for picket lines and leafleting.

Just before departure, the executive committee presented each walker with a mimeographed document entitled "Memphis Walk Discipline," an item still interesting for its revelations regarding the mores of the era. Copies of the walk discipline were carried in abundance by the walk in order, for instance, to flash it to hesitant church wardens concerned that naked leftists might practice Tantrik Yoga on the sacristy carpet at 2 A.M. in a respectable one-hundred-year-old Methodist church. In the hallowed memory of Herodotus, the discipline is printed below:

MEMPHIS WALK DISCIPLINE

All participants in and supporters of
the Memphis to Washington Walk for Peace
are expected to accept the following discipline:

Discipline

1. Our attitude towards officials and others who may oppose us will be one of sympathetic understanding of the burdens and responsibilities they carry.
2. No matter what the circumstances or provocation, we will not respond with physical violence to acts directed against us.

229

3. We will not call names or make hostile remarks.
4. We will adhere as closely as we are able to the letter and spirit of truth in our spoken and written statements.
5. We will always try to speak to the best in all men, rather than seeking to exploit their weaknesses to what we may believe is our advantage.
6. All members of the Walk team will be sexually continent while members of the project.
7. Whether or not men and women sleep in the same or separate quarters will be up to the discretion of the Walk Steering Committee in consultation with hosts.
8. Any person using or under the influence of narcotics (taken for nonmedicinal purposes) will be asked to leave the Walk.
9. No alcoholic beverages will be taken on the Walk. No bars will be frequented. In other situations, the Steering Committee will decide on the appropriateness of taking alcoholic beverages.
10. All walkers will be as clean and neat as possible.
11. All women walkers are strongly recommended to wear skirts.
12. Hair and beards will be trimmed and neat.
13. Every member of the Walk team must be willing to perform any task necessary to the function of the project as long as it lies within his capabilities and does not violate his conscience.

Particularly difficult for bristling libidos to funnel down the gullet was Rule Number 6, humorously referred to by walkers as the Celibacy Oath.

Rule Number 9, no vodka and beer, was accepted by the editorial board of *The Shriek of Revolution* as an opportunity to dry out damaged kidneys and livers. As for Number

8, no dope, it was decided that cannabis was not actually a narcotic but more of a headache remedy and that therefore it was not within the purview of the regulation.

When the executive committee of the National Committee for a Nonviolent Civilization gained cognizance that key members of the editorial board of *The Shriek of Revolution* magazine were planning to join the march, the committee banned copies of *The Shriek* from being carried or, God forbid, distributed on the march. It was understandable, since *The Shriek of Revolution* advocated via editorial, story, song, cartoon, and poem many things opprobrious to Southern sensibilities such as immediate legalization of cannabis (a bold position in 1962). *The Shriek* also had once issued a rather famous manifesto urging civil-rights parades through Klanland featuring interracial fornication on flatbed trucks with accompanying loudspeakers blaring the lyrics to "Shenandoah."

The committee therefore dispatched walk coordinator Bill Storm to *Shiek of Revolution* headquarters, that is, to Sam Thomas' pad on East 11th where he slipped the following note under the door:

> *Chicken Little:*
> *The Sky has fallen in !!*
> *Do not REPEAT Do not*
> *bring any copies of*
> *The Shriek of Revolution*
> *with you ... I*
> *assume you didn't plan*
> *to anyhow.*
> *Explanations forthcoming*
> > *Storm.*

That note was the lead poem in the next issue of *The Shriek*.

In the days prior to their departure, the Congress of Racial Equality provided the walkers with several training sessions on how to deal with the violent, canine, often cattle-proddish extremes of Southern justice. This done, the backpacks, leaflets, sleeping bags, first-aid kits, and bags of powdered milk and food were packed up and the marchers converged on Memphis by bus, by thumb, and in the two walk-support vehicles. In Memphis they held a rally, picketed a local missile base, and headed east.

IV

An advance crew went out each morning in the station wagon to purchase food supplies, to do laundry for the march, to check on general-delivery mail at the next town, to deliver press kits to the local newspapers and radio stations, to call up the New York committee office, and to check in with the church or campground or house where marchers would sleep. Often housing was found at the last minute. Anywhere within a ten-mile circle of the final march-point of the day was suitable. On occasion a church would cancel out when an official would drive out to cop a visual on the arcane-looking peregrination and grow nervous. When this happened, the advance crew headed for the church section of the Yellow Pages or looked up the nearest state park on the map.

There was an old blue Chevrolet panel truck called the peacemobile bearing on its top a huge plywood food-storage box. The peacemobile always hovered close by the walk, for you could never know when you might need water, rain gear, first aid, extra leaflets, or safety. A decision was made not to decorate the peacemobile with any radical messages, or even with the peace symbol, because of the possibility that it might be pressed into service to escape marauding cattle-prodders or Klan types.

As the walk progressed, the number of core walkers hovered around twelve, half men, half women. They sang a lot. Several carried guitars and harmonicas and as the walk picked up local civil-rights activists and religious leaders along the way, the singing became a spirited combination of Gospel, Labor Struggle songs, and Bomb-ban. Like other intense peace projects (such as the San Francisco to Moscow March for Peace of 1960–61) the Memphis march developed its own special slang language, its own in-jokes, its own inner intimacies. When alone, they danced together and certain walkers resurrected twangs and Midwest accents suppressed for years. There was a bit of escapist guilt in some of them, almost a hedonist-Jansenist mix of fun and self-mortification.

But it was healthy. Who could deny the sudden body-rush of happiness each morning in belief that the day would have its sanctity. Today I shall give out five thousand leaflets! Today I shall enter the minds of the unaware with messages of peace! I will sleep upon your floors tonight, scary dark church, beneath a grand piano in your basement!

Some of the walkers cynically mimicked the Southern speech patterns they were hearing, especially the different types of Tennessee laughter. They noted the men waiting early in the morning by the roadside for their rides to work, attired in work shirts and overalls, thumbs often hooked through those tool loops at the side, standing in a slight slouch, one foot slightly forward, a striped billed cap usually associated with railroad employees; and the universal black lunch box with the curved thermos-bearing lid. They noted the worker-farmers, that is, families who ran a small farm and also worked at outside jobs. One failing of the

233

Memphis march was that it couldn't sow the seeds of alternate lifestyle, couldn't urge people to live, farm, share together, or to open up and dance dance dance. All they could offer was positions on peace and war and racism. Land-distribution and money-distribution issues were carefully avoided. The feeling was this: Who really wants to die in Tennessee?

Sam had not known Miriam Levy prior to the Memphis to Washington Walk, though both were from New York and both were partisans of Lower East Side culture. Both had spent numerous evenings at the Total Assault Cantina on Avenue A, and both knew the proprietors fairly well. Sam and Miriam found themselves walking side by side much of the time. They sang well together, and could lift up a two-part harmony version of "We Shall Overcome" that could make you cry. Every night they called up the Total Assault Cantina and exchanged information. There was a map of Tennessee and Virginia on the cantina wall whereupon the progress of the march was being followed with map-flags.

Sam was the walk marshal, with responsibilities covering the overall onwardness of the march, to see that the correct highways were followed, to mark where they had ended the preceding day and to direct the march to the same spot the next day, to make sure that no one was left behind sleeping in a Unitarian Church closet, and to ensure that all premises were abandoned in a clean and pristine condition.

Miriam was the treasurer—collecting the donations from meetings and forwarding the money to committee headquarters in New York. She kept records of all walk expenditures and provided the walkers with their five-dollars-per-week expense money.

Both Miriam and Sam loved the universe of the roadsides—filled as they were with the detritus of America:

234

strange oblong slabs of tire, bolts, flattened tins, squashed turtles, and an atomic amount of bottles and caps. Sam collected 1,763 Hav•a•Tampa cigar wrappers in Tennessee alone, not to mention Virginia where King Edward Imperial cigar packs seemed to prevail. The roadsides had their individual odors also, a sort of sweet putridity that varied slightly mile by mile. At first the walkers were tempted to serve as janitors on the roads of degeneration—stuffing debris into bags—but it was futile; who had the spaceships needed to clear the American ways?

Miriam was an ace bottle collector, dragging a brown gunnysack which she filled with muddy returnable bottles to sell to less-than-eager country stores in exchange for aspirin, foot salve, and Bull Durham tobacco.

About the time their romance was aureate and roseate, Sam was embarrassed by the hot Tennessee sun which barbecued him in tender parts necessitating the immediate purchase of underwear. Sex was out of the question, so punished was he by the cruel focus of Ra-rays. His arms also became severely burned and he was forced to treat the lesions with wrappings of gauze and bandages.

Sam slept one night inside a huge kitchen cabinet at a Methodist church. He shut the door upon himself and lay upon his sleeping bag. All night long on the cabinet shelf he dreamt of Miriam and her campfire eyes. When he awoke he knew it was love. He looked for her and found her by the powdered milk and vat of oatmeal in the recreation room of the fane. He stayed by her side through the day, stomach shivering with love-angst. The walk was proceeding through a particularly racist series of counties and every day local yokels shouted hatefully from passing autos; the sheriffs stopped the march for lame reasons; even school buses put-

235

ting past were a source of thrown sandwiches and fruity missiles.

The fear from such events intensified Sam's and Miriam's friendship, although it took a week of walking together before they summoned nerve enough to hold hands on the way to a nighttime rally.

After the meeting Miriam suggested, "Let's take a drive in the station wagon," but Sam was far too uptight to accept the possibilities. Instead he became irate and demanded that they return immediately to the church.

One thing he didn't like about Miriam was her extreme knowledge of the details of peace-movement gossip. She knew everything. Another was her frequent allusions to the extraordinary sexual abilities of her former boyfriend. She was reduced, she hinted, because of the austere walk discipline, to kicking sex at the age of twenty-two after four years of making love three times a day three hundred and sixty days a year.

As for Miriam, she did not admire Sam's seeming inability to bathe. Sam was weird, with his shouted Greek poetry, his arms wrapped like a mummy, his shyness combined with the filthiest language she had ever heard. But she liked his intensity and also his writing, a fact which, when stated by her, flipped him into a temporary Nirvana.

Certain frozen moments were glyph'd in his mind: Miriam in a corona of brilliance: Miriam of Eternity dancing like a backbending Egyptian sistrum-shaker painted on a potsherd: Miriam the Rebel, who declared she was going to organize for liberation even in heaven.

She often wore a brown and tan striped dress with ruffles of the same material upon the bodice. Around her neck, stagecoach-robber style, she wore a triangl'd red kerchief tucked down into her bosom. Sam trembled to look at her.

They told each other how the thrills coursed through their soul, how happy they were to be together. Both, however, were inclined to scoff at a "peace-project love affair," a common phenomenon inflamed by project intensities, and which usually failed miserably. Accordingly, they tried to stay aloof, with rare public shows of affection, and in private there were only caresses and half-hour kissing sessions.

v

There wasn't much chatter after the accident. Trudge trudge, then a pause to talk with a local neophyte newsman from the radio station, then trudge trudge trudge. Miriam was specially ablaze that afternoon, running this way and that in a gray skirt and heavy brown clodhoppers, leafleting distant farmers and children in yards. She was the finest leafleteer. An obscure plowing machine moving on a distant hill would send her into a sprint; she had a strange custom of holding a clutch of leaflets at arm's length in front of her as she trotted across a field to hand a leaf of peace to a startled farmer. Every mailbox passed by the march received a Miriam leaflet.

At the end of the long day the walkers were very tired. In the words of Sam, they were "skincovered onto-burgers trudging through dust." For the editor of *The Shriek of Revolution* suffered sorely from foot chop-up. Why he should have chosen to walk Tennessee hills wearing tight, frictional-to-calf-muscle, knee-high riding boots had its origin perhaps in his well-known lickerish foot worship and hangups regarding toe bondage. The riding-boot heels had quickly worn down so that as he walked toward the Shiloh Baptist Church, the nails ground hamburgerly into his feet. Later he limped into the only cobbler's stall in the town where he ordered new heels covered with horseshoe-shaped metal taps, to be ready by trudge-time in the morn.

Sam carried several items in his baggage he figured would aid any unforeseen boredom. One was a clandestine packet of plans for the forthcoming issue of *The Shriek of Revolution*. He also carried a book on birdwatching, a small telescope (gaze, oh voyeur, gaze), and a copy of Hesiod's *Theogony* which he was in the process of translating into a pornolaliac epic of New York slang. Sam loved Hesiod—and would drive fellow walkers nuts with his howling renditions of the "Hymn to Hecate" section of *The Theogony*. He scoured the poem for clues to the course of Western civilization, shouting "aha! aha!" as he sang the clue-ridden dactyls of god-birth.

Like most of the walkers, Sam kept a journal in a notebook. He called his entries "Tennessee eclogues" as if the South were Boeotia. It was during this period that Sam began translating Sam Beckett's poetry (especially the poem *Enueg I*) into Attic Greek, endeavors rejected by every modern periodical from *Atlantic Monthly* to the *Kenyon Review*. Upon his trapezoidal-faced backpack were painted the wonderful words from *Oedipus at Colonus*, μὴ Φῦναι Τὸν ἅπαντα νικᾷ λόγον—i.e., better and groovier ne'er to have been born.

In his heart the strains of compulsive hedonism mixed with the bitter Manichean Nicht Nicht Nicht. He suffered from the malady of coldness. His demeanor was often a tundra of dryness, and never had he allowed anyone to look beneath the locks of his sullen heart where the grief coursed oceanic. And in back of it all was this personal belief: I am going to flip out. A chattering filthy mouth and weird intense scholarship were means he used to cushion his belief. "I am a depressed Buddhist," he told himself, "and this will save me from being flapjacked into a hell of mens insana in corpore delendo."

His position on the manic-depressive scale depended—not necessarily on the quality of, but rather on the quantity of, his breakfast. Throughout the walk, he continued his Lower East Side practice of compiling a gorging morning shovelful of Yum to gobble. Yum, you will remember, was Sam's steady diet during those months, and consisted of a foundation of about a pound of uncooked oatmeal poured into his brown wood Zen Yum Bowl, as he called it. Into the oats were folded several raw eggs, a glop of Hellmann's mayonnaise, soy sauce, and very occasionally a splash of vodka. Sam attacked the Yum Bowl like a starved canine, filling the air with expressions of joy, slurps, slurgles, and urgings for his sisters and brothers to share the delight. He revered his mode of breakfast, and rightly so—for sleepless drunken nights, ennui, fear, pain, metaphysical distress; all were conquered by morning Yum.

On the other hand, a shiny ovalness of Yum, garishly lit in the often fluorescent light of a church-basement morning congeries of sleepy peace walkers, was a less-than-mouthwatering, even repugnant, sight to the circle of eyeballs. It was the taste of Yum which was its thrill, however, and my mouth as I write these words, waters more lustfully for a Chinese porcelain spoon packed with Yum, than does my Faber-Castell pen ooze blackness. Ahh those days of Yum, eh Nelson?

At one time Sam had been a careless methedrine-shooting A-head. He had lived for the Flash, but threw his spike and dropper away during a demonstration outside the Bacteriological Warfare Center at Fort Detrick, Maryland—and ever since had been an enemy of the messengers of meth.

The Shiloh Baptist Church was located on the far outskirts of the village. It was a one-room wooden structure built up off the ground on posts. There was enough room under the church to crawl freely. The posts looked like legs and gave the church the appearance of a large walking box. There was farmland on one side of the church, a steep hill to the rear, and in front, between it and the roadway, the Crazy Bend River, actually more of a rivulet, sniveled through rocks on down past the gas station and the creamery.

That night there was a pot-luck supper sponsored by the local NAACP chapter, after which there was a fiery pacifist gospel meeting at the Shiloh Church. The meeting was more of a unity rally on the subject of civil rights than a debate on the nuances of unilateral disarmament. The minister was a woman with a great booming voice that could scare you into looking for ghosts and she could sing with such fervor that the dim-lit church pulsed with Jesus-vectors. Even the atheists among the walkers were swaying and clapping, pretending for a few minutes that there could be such a thing as a graceful eternity.

Walk leader Bill Storm rose to address the crowd, delivering his "Fool for the Lord, Fool for Peace, Fool for Liberty" speech he had developed for such occasions, with an immense intensity. Who would have known that the suave French scholar could have moved even his fellow marchers so much, exposed as they had been to various versions of the speech in church after church.

There was an hour of singing, with everybody, walkers and congregationists, standing in a swaying circle holding hands while singing that Civil-Rights/Gospel mixture that was so compelling. Spines shivered when they all hummed together while the minister sang "Were you there when they crucified my Lord," to a fantastic floating jazz piano background. Some order of Transcendence was achieved when the swaying circle sang "We Shall Overcome," especially the verse beginning "Hands around the world." At the meeting's end the circle hummed again, continuing the melody of "We Shall Overcome" while the minister uttered a searing prayer-chant-threnody to Jaweh God. "Deeper down than hell, wider than all heaven," was the Lord of whom she sang-spoke. It was the sort of experience the walkers would never cease to summon.

After the meeting was two hours over, Carole, Nelson, Sam, and Miriam walked out of the church, prior to bed, holding in mind a possible violation of Rules Number 6 and 8 of the walk discipline. They strolled down to the creek and along its bank until they found a spot downstream completely hidden by thick tree-growth and concealing boulders. They sat at the water edge and unstashed a super-secret pouch of cannabis which Sam quickly rolled by flashlight. They were talking and quietly peace-puffing when "splomp!" the water splashed up over the foursome.

"Jesus, what kind of frog could make a splash like that?" Miriam wanted to know. The splashes continued, then Sam got bonked by a loam-hunk on his sunburned arm. "Someone's throwing at us," he said, and scrambled to his feet, swallowing the roach.

"Yeah, let's get back inside. I believe we are being given a lecture by the rubicund necks."

Back in the church, they dismissed the event as just another item of weirdness. Soon the entire march was zipped up in its array of army-surplus sleeping bag cocoons. Sam and Miriam lay near each other, each on top of a cushioned open-back pew. They were holding hands in the darkness, pew to pew, until one of them fell asleep and the arms dropped away.

Suddenly it was as if Santa Claus and the reindeer were making an emergency landing on the metal church roof. Everyone awakened with a start. Several windows were smashed. The clod-ballers were at it again. They were throwing from the steep hill in back of the church so most clods were raining on the roof. After a whispered conference it was decided that a volunteer squad would take flashlights and approach the throwers for a nonviolent confrontation.

"Hey! Why are you throwing things at us? We are coming up to talk with you. We are completely unarmed! Do you hear us? We are a peace march on the way to Washington! Do you . . ."

Thunk, thunk, thunk, thunk, the hard clods fell. One marcher, a famous accident-prone organizer, felt his forehead split open as he advanced toward the barn whence the hurlers were hurling. Finally their flashlights located the culprits: a farmer and his two sons whose property was contiguous to the church's land.

The essence of the farmer's complaint, pried from him after a few minutes of hostile shouting, was this: "We don' mind you walking for peace and stuff lawk thet; whut we don' like to see is white girls and neegras sleeping in the same church."

The walkers explained as soothingly as possible that what they were doing was protected by the U.S. Constitution. The sons brandished their clods in reply. Besides, the walkers continued, they were leaving almost at sunrise, for they had a tough twenty-five-mile day ahead. Actually coming into contact with his enemy seemed to quell the farmer's anger. When they saw the farmer place a hand over a yawn, the walk realized the worst was over. Sensing a lull in the violence, Miriam did not want to lose an opportunity to leaflet the farmer and sons, so she raced back into the church and brought back leaflets and a copy of a pamphlet recounting Danish resistance to the Nazis called *Tyranny Could Not Quell Them*.

They invited the farmer inside to check on sleeping arrangements and were rather surprised when magenta-neck and his loamy sons accepted and toured the church. As he paused at the door, his sons already returning up the pasture to their farmhouse, the farmer delivered rather chilly parting remarks. "You folks are gonna have trouble tomorrow. They had a Klan rally over in Toupou tonight. Ain' no neegras ever slept over that way ever. You in trouble. They gon' git ya, hyuf hyuf!"—the farmer breaking into cackles.

Sam was worried that Farmer John and company might try to set fire to the church so he resolved to sleep out in back upon the woody hill as a sentry. He thought he had lodged a hint to Miriam that she might join him there in the paradise of a shared sleeping bag—but his hint, so-called, was so vague as not to be a hint at all. What he had said to her was, "I'm going out back to sleep on the hill. See you in the morning." That was a hint?

VI

Early the next day the walk passed the dreaded line into Toupou County, Tennessee, where blacks weren't and asskick was. The advance crew quickly reported back that the church where they were supposed to crash that night had canceled. A public meeting at the town library had been nixon'd also when several gruff voices phoned in threatening a big book-burn. A search among religious institutions revealed a lack of Christ-like charity, and the walk was faced

243

with a camp-out among the yahoos or perhaps a forced march throughout the night to reach another county.

There were dust-off attempts by the dozens—old roadsters swerving into the walk path. By the end of the day they were walking almost in the ditch. All along they were dogged by a reporter from the local radio station phoning in hostility reports every hour. The walk-support vehicle monitored the broadcasts on the radio. "Hello everybody, this is Vince Martinson, your Hound of Hillbilly Heaven, on Station JQLX, the Voice of the South, with a bulletin from our roving reporter out on Route Twenty-seven with the integrated Memphis to Washington Peace Walk. Come in, Wade Bixton:"

Hi, Vince, the group has just passed Gorder's Dairy Queen and is proceeding up the mountain. Sheriff's deputies arrested Clint Murt, the nephew of Mayor Jack Murt of Ellis City, for breaking the front window of one of the vehicles which accompany the walkers. One of the girls assures me that they walk every step of the way and that the vehicles are only used to carry their leaflets and other equipment. One of the walk leaders returned a few minutes ago from town with the news that they were turned down by the high-school athletic department for permission to sleep in the school gym. The Veterans of the Korean War offered to allow the marchers to camp out in their skeet-shoot range providing the lights are left on overnight; this was refused after a vote by the peace marchers.
And so, Vince, at this moment the pacifists have no place to stay tonight.

"Thanks Wade Bixton; now let's hear Lettie Hunt and her new cry-cry-cry sensation, *Tears on my Six-Pack* . . . ."

244

The march reached the top of Toupou Mountain by tortuous road and began the long steep twist down into the town
of Plinthane, Tennessee, the home of the State Champion
Plinthane Bulldogs and the county seat of Toupou County.
Cars of the curious were parked on both shoulders, teenag-
ers lounging and snickering on the fenders and hoods. Some
wonderful person rolled a ssss-ing cherry bomb toward the
walk line but Nelson sacrificed his tam-o'-shanter to the
gods by dropping it on top of the deadly firecracker, with
the result that it was shredded. Ha ha ha, went the
scoffers. "Where's the niggers?" someone yelled, squinting at
the line of sunburned peacelings.

By the time the walk had at wearily last reached the gas-
station edge of the town, they were singing defiantly at top
lung. This could have proved foolish for, in addition to "We
Shall Overcome," the editorial board of *The Shriek of Revolution* found itself in a splinter group singing "When is the
U.S.A. Gonna Have a Left-Wing Government?"—a tune of
no commercial potential from the liquid pen of Sam and
Miriam.

Standing directly in front of the city-limits sign the sheriff
was waiting. He had one question: "You people have a
place to stay?"—flashing an incarcerational smile. He
hitched up his trousers as if it were possible for the thick
brass-buckled belt to rise over the rotundity of his laundry-
bag-shaped tum tum, and received the A.C.L.U. cover letter.

"A.C.L.U. huh? That's a communist front organization,
isn't it. Don't mean a thing to me. You haven't got a place
to stay, that's what's important. I guess you ought to walk
straight through to the county line . . . ." He chuckled. "Ole
Bill Wintzer, he's the sheriff in the next county; I bet he'll

245

take you out to breakfast, you all wander into town about dawn. It's only sixteen miles."

Just about the time the sheriff was orating, Bill Storm arrived in the station wagon with the extremely helpful news that he'd found shelter for them in the only Unitarian Church for fifty miles. Overjoyed, the walkers piled into the vehicles and put kilometers between themselves and the hostile Tennies.

The minister was waiting for them outside his brand new brick church. His face was smooth and the color of flan. He wore clear plastic-framed glasses, and looked a bit like McGeorge Bundy. He was obviously nervous about the whole matter; his hand trembled clutching a copy of the walk discipline as he faced the tired end-of-the-day peacelings unloading their gear with a you-will-obey! stare.

He turned to Bill Storm. "We want to make certain, Mr. Storm, that no one uses the phone, that no one enters my office, that no one removes any foodstuffs, that no one enters the church proper, that men and women sleep in separate rooms."

"Certainly, Reverend Miller, certainly."

The good minister must have been moonlighting for some sort of intelligence agency because he was wearing a weighty photo shop of equipment around his neck, including a small Minox camera with the measuring chain for photographing documents.

It was a laugh. "What's he gonna photograph with that," Nelson wanted to know, "our grocery list?"

"Nah, our secret hoard of Polish money orders."

Whatever his purpose, the good Reverend Miller began to take pictures from all angles. He must have taken 250 snaps, with particular care to get front and side zaps of each walker.

Since it was Saturday night there was a virtual train of automobiles of the bored slowly circling the county courthouse bumper to bumper. Some of the walkers went to the courthouse to leaflet the old-timers sitting on the benches. At the church the walk steering committee was trying to hold an internal meeting to plan forthcoming demonstrations at defense plants. Beer cans were clunking regularly against the fane's front door as cars peeled by.

Soon there was the rrrrrrr of a siren and the sheriff screeched to a halt outside. He was flustered as he broke into the meeting room surrounded by a passel of his associates. "They gon' burn this church down if we don't get you out of here. You'll have to come with us."

The pacifists protested most vigorously, but the sheriff was firm. "Please, please, I don' want to hear anything about the A.C.L.U. We have the obligation to protect you. And the only place we know for sure where you'll be safe is in the armory."

"Oh, no!" four walkers groaned at once.

Just before their incarceration, Sam and Miriam managed to sneak a phone call to New York to the Total Assault Cantina. "John! John!" Miriam shouted. "They're going to lock us up in some sort of National Guard armory. They say—that is the sheriff says—that the Klan is out to do us in. Can you call the wire services and *The New York Times* for us? Ask them to call down here to inquire about our safety. It may keep us from getting hurt. We're really shaking in our shoes!"

They were transported in squad cars to the Toupou National Guard installation which, with its turrets, battlements, and long, thin vertical windows built of greasy, charred-looking brick, seemed more suitable for crossbow warfare than modern militaristics.

247

The walkers were herded rather roughly into a large basement classroom in the armory, and the door was locked behind them. They cleared away the chairs and lecture charts and the women rolled out their sleeping bags at one end, the men at the other. In the center of the room was a brass catafalque upon which was mounted a machine gun in cross-section, which apparently the Guard used for training purposes. No one seemed eager to sleep near the catafalque. There was a large mirror on the wall between two blackboards which reflected the weapon. There was a sign printed on the mirror's upper frame: DRESS NEAT! "This is hell," Miriam announced, and scrawled a red lipstick message on the glass above the reflected machine gun and beneath DRESS NEAT!

Welcome to Styx
Population 12

They had made no agreement to meet, but it was less than an hour after the lights were turned out that they crawled toward one another in the gloom and found each other's mouths at the base of the sawed-away machine gun. It was a suitable occasion for their first loving. Miriam lifted up a leg and rested it upon the machine gun and they padded a sleeping bag beneath them. There were the sounds of zippers unzipping and then the game of silence, as others listened, but could not see, to the silent caresses and stifled breathing of a peace-walk floor-fuck.

VII

The next morning was a beautiful Sunday in Tennessee.

They were ordered to leave the armory's premises as crudely as they had been ordered to enter. After breakfast back at the Unitarian Church, the walk decided to hold a short demonstration outside a church where it had been learned many of the town's outstanding citizens attended services.

The church was a beautiful specimen. It was built of large gray stones with rough convex faces. There were tall white fluted columns across the front of the church and upon the frieze above the architrave was a stained-glass window depicting a crook-bearing Jesus and a woolly lamb. There were fifteen white steps spreading like a fan from the columns down to the pot-holed boulevard. There the peace marchers slowly circled, holding their signs, handing out leaflets, waiting for church services to be ended so they could lay some peace data on the congregation.

From within the church they could hear an impassioned plea by the minister for sinners and I-see-the-Lighters to come forth to "be reborn again in the name of Jesus." The minister led his flock in a perfervid rendition of "Just as I am, O Lamb of God"—during which singing the sinners were supposed to come forward.

There was a final prayer and then the deacon opened the white perfect doors and the black robes of the minister swooshed upon the doorsteps to shake hands. Out moiled a Sears & Roebuck catalogue of spiffiness—seventy-five or so neat people gossiping on the steps, no one paying any attention at all to the leafleting pacifists.

There was one couple that lingered in conversation with the minister on the steps. The man wore a brown flannel suit and a flat-top haircut with just a hint of the ducktails he might have worn back in high school. The woman was attired in a very plain sacrifice-everything-for-the-children

249

dress and winter coat. Daughter A was dressed in white socks, white shoes, white bonnet, white sweater, white crinoline. Daughter B was dressed the same but all in yellow.

While Mom and Dad were encountering the minister, Daughter B wandered down the steps toward the marchers. Once within arm range, Miriam handed her a leaflet and bent down to talk with her. "Hi! Do you know why we're here?"

"No."

"We're passing through town on the way to Washington. We're going to walk all the way to tell people never to fight with one another, to throw away their guns, never to drop bombs . . . ."

Meanwhile Daddy Flat-top had spotted his daughter talking to Miriam and trotted down the steps, removing his coat, his face tone becoming borscht-like. The first thing he did was utter a strange sound, "Kwoakh!" which was a mouth action to garner saliva followed by a quick spit into Miriam's face.

He grabbed the leaflet from his stunned daughter and tore it up. And only minutes after reception of the wine and bread of Jesus, Flat-top went crazy. "I fought for my country, you little bitch!"—pointing to his Marine Corps tattoo (he had removed his shirt also) on his shoulder near where oft he rolled his Lucky Strike pack up into his T-shirt sleeve.

"We're sorry you're upset, sir," Sam butted in while Miriam mopped away the Eucharist-tinged spittle.

The man raised his fist at Sam. "The sheriff ought to round you all up and kill you in the town square. Machine-gun you. That's what happens to scum! You bums!" All around the raver the churchgoers were silent. Several approached

250

marchers and took leaflets, asking questions, one or two apologizing.

But the man foamed onward. Soon the sheriff arrived and the deputies dispersed the crowd, enabling the march to saunter away. Sam and Miriam paused to kiss, leaning up against the sheriff's vehicle. Miriam handed the officer a copy of Bartley's book, *National Defense Through Nonviolent Resistance.* "I hope you read it, Sheriff. We'll be seeing you"—waving goodbye and turning to stroll.

"Fuck him," Sam muttered, walking hand in hand with Miriam out of the Sunday village.

Raked Sand

"Thomas Jefferson, George Washington, Aristotle, Plotinus—all dead, all down on Uncle J's worm-farm, but we, we're *alive!*"—beating his chest, "We're alive!"

"Millard! Another round of 'arf and 'arf for Nelson and myself"—feeling in his pocket to make sure he had the fifty cents to pay for it. They were sitting in Stanley's Bar waiting for Kennedy's speech on the Cuban situation, for there was not only no TV set in their apartment, there was no electricity.

"If Kennedy zip-guns the Russians we *all* may be down at Uncle J's."

The Soviet build-up had first been publicized in September. Sam heard of it by word of bar-babble, since he had not read a newspaper in five years. "No time to dig everybody dying man. I have books to read." Jesus, he thought all this war puke had gone away. "So you say Cuba's got the big ones now?"—he asked, nervously writing

252

Lost lost
   lost
      lost
lost
   lost
      lost

in beer-ooze upon the oaken bar top.

Nelson tried to explain it to Sam: "Well, mu'f', because 'sixty-two is a congressional election year—you do know that, don't you, Sammy?"

Sammy did not know.

"The rocket-breaths in the Republican party—that is, the candidates and their ilk, were out there waving the flag whispering The Democrats are weak punks wanting the people in Kansas to hurry up and learn Russian, before the Big Parade.

"Russia began to ship bombers and rockets into Cuba. I'd be willing to bet it's shit for shat for U.S. rocket emplacements in Turkey. Anyway, Kennedy was out there last week campaigning for the Dems, when all of a sudden the CIA began to flash him some data about nuclear missile bunkers down in C. So he was called back to Washington. They said he had a head cold."

According to Nelson, the Kennedy brothers remained in the war room all the weekend of October 20 and 21. The code-scramblers were churning with messages back and forth between Kennedy and Khrushchev. The president announced he would address the nation on Monday night, October 22, 1962.

Wave after wave of fear spewed from the media. There was an extraordinary amount of Cuba-hate already present

253

in the country. Fear: Russians force U.S. out of naval base in Guantánamo. Fear: Russians zap access to Panama Canal. Fear: Russians brick out space and missile facilities at Cape Canaveral. Fear: Cuban-type governments in other Latin countries. Fear: Mafia never to get back its Havana casinos.

The Joint Chiefs of Staff were instructed to stick around D.C. Vice-President Johnson was called back early from a trip to Hawaii. Twenty-five commie ships were supposedly on the way to Cuba with chop-up parts. Soviet *Ilyushin-28* bombers capable of carrying nukes were being uncrated and assembled in Cuba.

Grovel, beatnik, grovel.

In response, the U.S. Navy and Marine Corps were beginning to stage a hostility scene in the Caribbean, with forty U.S. ships hanging out off the isle of Vieques near Puerto Rico. Twenty thousand servicemen, including six thousand marines, were ready to hit the bricks. The way Nelson was telling it to Sam, somewhat in the manner of someone telling a midnight ghost story in a graveyard, was making Sam twitch.

The Strategic Air Command was placed on alert world wide, meaning flight patterns with doom-nukes in the direction of Russian cities at all times. Even the American troops garrisoned in Berlin were alerted for imminent chop-up. God knows, Nelson said, what sort of instructions were given to the fleet of Polaris submarines with their rockets each coded to destroy a specific Russian city, sliding in the Russian seas.

Evacuation was ordered for dependents at Guantánamo Naval Base. *The New York Times*—Nelson handing him a clip—had printed high-altitude CIA photos of intermediate-range ballistic missile facilities being gouged into the Cuban

254

mountains, with a kill range of two thousand nautical miles. Shit in fear, beatnik punk.

That Saturday, the right-wing Cuban exile group Alpha-66, vowed publicly that its "naval units" would sink-snuff any British merchant vessels it discovered in Cuban territorial waters. When Sam heard that, he broke out into the song,

Cuba Si, Yankee No
Get the hell out of Guantánamo

lifting high his brown-black 'ark and 'arf.

"Shut up!" someone shouted. "The speech is about to begin."

Nelson adjusted his chair for total tube. He was wearing his kilt, a tam-o'-shanter, his Scottish colors, silver-buckled shoes, and rabbitskin sporran or waist pouch. "If we go, I want to go in my colors," he said.

Kennedy spoke for eighteen minutes. The tone, the somber convoluted doom-tinged eloquence, something gave the president's speech a fearful Poe-like quality. He announced that a total blockade of Cuba would begin at 10 A.M. on Wednesday morning, just thirty-some hours away. Not a slurp was slurped along the bar counter.

Kennedy banned all surface-to-air missiles, bomber aircraft, bombs, air-to-surface rockets, warheads, guided missiles, and rocket-support matériels. All ships entering Cuban waters would be inspected. He announced that the missiles in Cuba could strike as far North as the Hudson Bay and as far South as Lima, Peru.

"We're in trouble, Sam." Sam was sweating. The consensus in the bar was that there was going to be a war. "We'll

255

all die of leuk, that is, if our eyes don't melt"—Nelson shuddered.

"Shhh!"—they shouted along the bar.

"Seventh, and finally, I call upon Chairman Khrushchev to halt and eliminate the clandestine, reckless, and provocative threat to world peace and to stable relations between our two nations.

"I call upon him further to abandon this course of world domination and to join in an historic effort to end the perilous arms race and to transform the history of man.

"He has an opportunity now to move the world back from the abyss of destruction. We have no wish to war with the Soviet Union, for we are a peaceful people who desire to live in peace with all other people . . . ." Nelson began to hiss at this point, but the barkeep reached over and jostled his arm to silence.

"Any hostile move anywhere in the world against the safety and freedom of peoples to whom we are committed including in particular the brave people of West Berlin will be met by whatever action is needed."

After the speech, Nelson looked at his friend Sam and in his deepest voice said, "I'm going to get fuuuuuuuuuuuucked up!"

As of frig-up, they sat drinking tequila with clam juice till 4 A.M. closing time when the wet, staggering, skin-covered meat phantoms walked home.

All during the next day the tension grew, mostly in silence. There were no street riots, no shouts from any outraged opposition. There were a lot of sullen humans herding sullenly. The Liberal Party of New York busted its chops to send off a telegram of support to the president. Only a sliver of the population shook its fist. In office buildings, it was like the World Series all over again as the typing pool sneaked quick listens to radios in desks.

The stock market was unhappy. A day or so later when Premier Khrushchev wrote Bertrand Russell to state that he would not go nuke-batty or take rash action in the crisis, the stock prices rose in a brisk rally, thus enabling Soviet NKVD stock-market operatives, disguised as Wallstreeters, to reap a wheaty bundle.

There was another night before the impending doomsday blockade which Nelson and Sam again spent mugging their livers with tequila and clam juice.

The morning of the imposition of the blockade was awful. A dilapidated airplane hangar full of old shoes blew up in his stomach every time Sam tried to move. He dragged his crushed-turtle-on-highway body to work, an hour late. Mr. Ironheart, the head of the purchasing department, was upset.

"Piss on you"—Sam muttered, pulling his neck low into his old Navy highneck sweater so that his boss could not cop a visual on the grease-gray shirt Sam'd been wearing a week straight.

"What did you say?"

"I said, 'misty clue.' It's the last day of Pompeii, Mr. Ironheart."

"That's not what it sounded like."

During lunch Sam watched people on the street flag down passing cabs to get the latest on the blockade from the radio. There was a lot of Goodbye Cruel World chatter at the water cooler. Then it dawned on him that on today, of all days, he should probably be able to summon up courage to do something so outrageous as to get himself fired,

257

that he might suck up at last those sacred twenty-six weeks of unemployment checks.

When he should have been writing letters to expedite furniture deliveries, Sam typed idly. In a cloud of boredom, he typed Don't Care Don't Care Don't Care for fifteen pages, and mailed the "work"—at office expense—to *Fuck You/A Magazine of the Arts*, which protested it would print anything.

He opened up his desk drawer to fondle his trusty ashtray full of morning glory seeds. He gnashed several between his incisors, swallowed, and waited fifteen minutes for that stomach-wall thickness-flash. His hangover blended marvelously with the morning glory effect: i.e., of having stomach walls six inches thick filled with unspeakable fermented micturitions. But the colors flashing before him as he typed, they were pleasant.

His problem: how to confront the despicable wolverine of the purchasing department. Sam, he told himself, it's the end of the world maybe, and you can't even climb on some puke-suck in order to get fired! Come on!

But he couldn't do it. His blessèd early life had endowed him with a single overriding principle: when in trouble, fawn. He wouldn't have seriously hassled his boss if the ashes from the volcano were raining in the window.

He was contemplating puking, his stomach walls feeling like some sort of three-ply wineskin, when Ironheart buzzed for him. Now is my chance! He shoved open Ironheart's door and pushed the papers askew grabbing open the ritzy box of H. Upmann cigars which had payola'd its way there on Christmas.

"Hey!"

"Hey what, Mr. Ironheart? These are Cuban cigars. It cannot be that you will continue to smoke these when our

258

country prepares to destroy Fidel! Shame on you!" Sam picked one out, bit off the tip, and tongue-flicked it upon the carpet, also a Christmas gift for granting the university carpeting contract to the correct company.

"Yes, Sam, you seem to be upset. And certainly, I believe you are right. I *will* throw these cigars away. They were not very legal to begin with." Sam could not believe it, watching those unemployment checks vanish.

"Mrs. Hutchinson, please show Sam out of the office. He is apparently not feeling well."—into his intercom. Sam walked out, forgetting to scrunch down to hide his filthy collar.

"I am a coward!"—Sam spoke out loud, chewing morning glory seed back at his desk, the office faces lifting toward the sentence. One of the Sipletto sisters was sneaking a listen to her radio. "Are there any battles?"—Sam yelled over, much too loudly for Miss Sipletto who frowned at him.

"They ought to blow up the whole island"—she replied.

Anger pushed him. "Cuba Si, Yankee No!"—he bellowed in the startled office. He waved the *Times* at them. "This is a fear scene, all of it. All these circles of destruction, bah! The Democrats just want to get reelected! And the Republicans are death breaths!"—hoping to get Ironheart's attention. "What about *our* Polaris subs with H-bomb missiles right at the mouth of the Volga, man!"

"I am not man. I am Lois Sipletto. Now lower your voice or I'll go right in to see Mr. Ironheart!"

"Please do,"—he replied, almost with a tone of supplication. "Maybe you can get me on unemployment.

After work, he treated himself to dinner at Total Assault Cantina. Nelson joined him. "Hey, Sam, this may be our last

259

meal on earth, baby. Next stop, Saint Peter's pizzeria."

"Well, last day or not, I'm never going back to my job. I'm never going to work again for the rest of my life."

"Did you hear that Louise Adams is throwing an End Of The World party tonight over at Mindscape Gallery?"

"She is!?"—Sam was excited. "Uh, is Barton the bonfire back in town?"

"Yes he is. Why don't you give up, Sam? They're in love."

"Bullshit! Bah! Barton just wants to make sure her paintings and superior skills never leave the Lower East Side. That guy is a ghoul. Who's paying for the party?"

"Louise. I talked with her on the phone. She said, 'I sold a painting so tonight we celebrate the death of the West.' "

"You see? What did I tell you! That fucker will be standing at the door like it was his scene, praying for an art collector to come."

They went back to the apartment to get ready for the party. Sam underwent his fortnightly prefornication ablutions in the kitchen tub. Tonight is the night, he told himself. Tonight I shall declare my, my, my . . . . What I'll do is get drunk and high, and ride in on her mind in a Byronic hurricane. To hell with Barton!

Prior to departure, they assembled their meager hoard of dope upon the kitchen table: two capsules of yohenbine (a vaunted aphrodisiac then in vogue among the poets and artists), three roaches salvaged from the ashtrays, one Asthmadoro cigarette ("Forget that!" Nelson exclaimed, remembering his friend who had eaten a teaspoon of one and was found standing on her head in the corner carrying on an imaginary conversation with Samuel Beckett; her heart stopped beating three times in the emergency room.), six buttons of peyote, four capsules of amyl nitrite, twenty-seven morning glory seeds, two caps of mescaline, one quart of vodka.

Nelson surveyed the pitiful thrill-pile. "What a poor inventory of pleasure with which to usher in The Fall." Nevertheless, in a fast flurry of indulgence they smoked the roaches, ate the peyote/mescaline/morning glory seeds, popped the amyl nitrite, chug-drank three glasses of vodka, then rushed out to the street toward Louise's party.

Sam chuckled to himself as he swallowed the spansule of bitter legendary yohenbine bark (supposedly an import from Africa used by veterinarians at stud farms) just as he danced down the metal steps into the Mindscape Gallery, glancing all directions for his favorite painter.

"Where is she! I love her, I love her! Louise!"

As befitting the world's end, Mindscape was packed. The jittery partisans of Beauty were there, talking too loudly, drinking and smoking too much.

Sam's position was this: Louise Adams just *thought* she was in love with Barton Macintyre. Macintyre was the type that was a compulsive framer, who, if after a hard day turning out major works, had not put at least ten in frames, signed and ready for the checkbook, was unhappy indeed. "He also frames women!" Sam snorted, looking up at the paintings Macintyre was storing at Mindscape.

Sam sometimes went up to Times Square where he bought old sheet music to popular 1950s songs, underlining key phrases of bliss, and mailed them to Louise, anonymously of course. He had mailed her lots of old 45s also, like "Hearts Made of Stone," "Heartbreak Hotel," and "Mood Indigo," again anonymously. He was hooked.

Sam was bold enough when drunk. But being drunk, and

stoned on yohenbine, while attending an End-of-the-Universe teleo-Bacchic dope-grope, this set him on fire. But how could he speak privately to Louise Adams in such a revel? He decided to lie in wait for her in the gloom (he had unscrewed the lightbulb) by her loftbed in the small back storage room, a spot all would have to pass to get to the toilet. He leaned with an arrogant shove against a tied-up packet of Barton's *oeuvres,* chugging down toward the dregs of a small demijohn of vintage Flatbush '62. It seemed like hours before Louise finally walked into the room and nobody else was there.

"Louise," Sam began, "I am tired of sending you phantom plastic!"—thinking this to comprise a firm enough hint that he was the one'd sent the old 45s. "I will confess, Louise, well, I want to touch your boooooooody!"—adding a bit of humor to ease the uncertainty, as he continued blocking the entrance to the bathroom.

"You, know, Louise. Barton has spoiled everything with the brutish imperium—it's really a blockade, you know—he has placed on your *soul,* Louise. Maybe if this wasn't the end of Western civilization, ha ha, I wouldn't say it, but, I, I, need you. I swoon, I fail, I . . . ." breaking off into a paraphrase of Sappho.

Suddenly she was against him. She kissed him and cured Sam's schizophrenia in an instant with her tenderness. "I promise," she replied, "if the world doesn't get blown up, I promise to come over one of these nights—and then we'll touch each other's boooooooodies!"—mimicking but smiling.

Sam melted with happiness. But meanwhile the yohenbine was working him up into a state of panting, bristling ardor. Sam's family curse (Thou shalt fail, O earth-punk, thou shalt fail) visited him once again as Macintyre had to return just at that moment from the liquor store, breaking

262

up Sam's furtive kiss-flash with the woman he felt possibly the reincarnation of Elizabeth Barrett Browning.

Sam hacked the mini-tented front of his trousers, feeling obliged to push down perforce the evidence of the apparently permanent hardness. Then he rejoined the party, now degenerating slowly into a doom-hoot. The drunken revelers waved back and forth in a circle singing, "Neow is the howr, when wee muss' say goodbeye. Soon we'ull be saaaayling . . . ."

All of a sudden Sam was nude, standing with an erection like an ectomorphic herm. He began to sing a Hank Williams song to which no one—not even Sam—knew the words. But nothing stopped the sex-maddened young human who twang-sang onward but found himself suddenly uttering chyme. Difficult 'twas to sing while the bitter fingers of barf crawled up the throat. He lunged to the dark pissoir, still singing—

I saw the light! I saw the light!
No more darkness, no more night
Then Jesus came like a stranger in the night
Praise the Lord, I saw the . . .

"Blooey!"—Sam tossed the omelet, the yohenbine, the vodka, the morning glory seeds, the peyote, into the porcelain vortex. Naked, voiding his stomach, membrum prepared on the nonce to spume scoriaceously, he fell down striking his matted head, heaving again again, holding the bowl, head passing out on the rim, suave and cool, Sam, suave and cool.

He slept there fully for about ten. Refreshed, Sam strode back into the party to claim his attire, which he rapidly donned, and spoke the classic line of a cookie-tossed drunk:

263

"I've got to get something on my stomach."

He caromed from building to building, pausing at the dark stoops, leaning against the railings, as if it were raining, toward The House of Nothingness café. Four cups of coffee and a sandwich later, Sam felt aglow, although the yohenbine and the vodka still had their electrodes in his hypothalamus.

He walked into the chilly courtyard back of Nothingness to sit by the rock garden. He had always loved the raked white sand, the parallel lines that undulated in the raked waves—the autumn moon through the haze. "White! White!"—he shouted. He sprawled down upon the sand, upsetting a section of the perfect raking, his arms spread wide, his legs too, trying to fill up the empty sand in a moment of drunken horror vacui.

He splashed cupped hands of sand upon himself. "Nobody. Nobody. No cause, no hope!"—he whispered. He threshed about wildly in the sand.

"No brain! No brain! I ain't got no brain! No brain." He crawled toward the boulders—three of them closely spaced on the far side, with the sand raked in a neat circle around the triad. The only boulders, the rest just sand. Triad in white. No brain. No brain.

Still on his knees, he began to batter the top of his head into the rocks. "No brain No brain No brain No brain. I ain't got no brain! No brain!" Shouting till he was hoarse and the blood, like wet-weather springs, bubbled beneath his locks. Matted his locks. His head dabbing rough red smudges on the triad. No brain no brain.

He rolled in the white, red blotch here, red splotch there. He grabbed a fistful and jammed it in his mouth, bitter from the chewings of the night, the admixture of smokestack grunge, the incinerators. He tried to spit it out but the granules coated his tongue, teeth, mouth-roof. Some rolled down his throat and he coughed severely. Then he lay still, cried softly.

Several beers had still not rinsed away the white granules. Nelson had joined him at Stanley's Bar. Conflicting reports were tossed along the counter: Russian ships were trying to run the blockade. Or Russian ships had turned back rather than submit to forcible boarding.

It wasn't long before Sam got himself into a near fistfight with some beer-necked philosopher who kept talking about Iwo Jima. "I was there. It's the same. Up and down are one. If we die, so will they. It's a perfect circle."

"The hell it is"—Sam blurted. "Don't give me any of your Iwo jive! You fought for a corpse. Cuba Si! Yankee No!"

The man rose off the stool and made a fist. Sam suddenly remembered the anecdote he'd read about Hemingway and James Joyce who were out drinking in some Paris dive. Joyce was nearly blind and got into a quarrel. The fists were ready to bash and Joyce reached up to try to adjust his glasses, staring into the bleariness, shouting, "Deal with him, Hemingway! Deal with him!"

"Deal with him, Nelson, deal with him!" Sam growled in his most affected voice, a combination of British prison movies and Midwest twang. "Cuba Si!"

That got him a fist in the mouth, hurting his teeth to the roots and splitting his lip-skin. Through an immediate calm-down and through earnest imprecation, Sam managed to avoid getting eighty-sixed from Stanley's. Nelson led him to a back table to sulk.

Nelson had some bad news. "Sam," he said, "I'm going

265

back to Chattanooga. Maybe I'll go to law school. Or perhaps I can get back in at Heidelberg. Something besides this chaos. I've got to get out of the Lower East Side or I'll go nuts"—looking at Sam patting his throbbing head, a curling of coagulated blood down upon his chin.

"What would Elizabeth Gurley Flynn and Emma Goldman say to you going to law school?"—Sam replied scornfully. That's all Nelson used to talk about, the exploits of those two. Goldman's autobiography was like the *I-Ching* or the *Bhagavad-Gita* to him.

"I should have gone on to Heidelberg," Nelson continued. "By now I'd have my doctorate in theology. And I can just see my book, *The Husserl/Aquinas/Goldman Synapse*, on the presses right now!"

Sam tried to interrupt him with a few atheistic sneers. But he remembered too well Nelson's arrival on the East Side, where he'd planned to visit the *Catholic Worker's* House of Hospitality for a few days, and then it was off to Europe to study. It was perhaps the wonderful lure of hemp, of anarcho-pacifist Catholicism, and the poetry scene, the beautiful bars, the sex, which caused him to cash in his steamer ticket for a pad deposit.

Nelson did soon leave the Lower East Side for law school. Not too long ago he ran as a left-wing Democrat for the Tennessee State Assembly. Little does he know of the syndicate formed by some of us former Eastsiders who hold in a safety deposit vault certain 16-mm films of Nelson and Cynthia Pruitt in a bathtub of kasha varnishkes, which may well make him the first movie-star president, should his cursus honorum carry him that far up the ziggurat of power.

"All out! All out!"—Millard shouted, piling the chairs atop the doomed wood. Sam watched Nelson leave with Cynthia, biting his lip.

266

"Hey Nelson!"—Sam yelled, running out into the street where he handed him the last spansule of yohenbine. Nelson smiled and uttered a silent cackle, and gave Sam a quick slap of five.

Back at the apartment, Sam rolled his final reefer. He counted his candles. There were twenty-four. He placed them in a semicircle around his couch. He crawled halfway into his sleeping bag which smelled like burnt goose feathers from an accident on a peace walk.

He crossed his arms upon his chest, looking pharaonically cool. "This may be the last night. Thank God."

If I die, he thought, I'm gonna continue the struggle. I ain't gonna take nothin' from nobody. He fantasized a hieroglyphic headline: BEATNIK REFUSES TO PICK GRAIN IN YARU FIELDS, OSIRIS UPSET.

Then he lit the circle of candles. He thought about his mother who used to walk him and his brother home after the movies past the graveyard, telling stories of the vengeance of King Tut. "Next galaxy! Next galaxy!"—he mocked.

He could hear the woman next door listening to the radio. He prayed to his mother. Forgive me mother that I closed the door. Tears in the young man's eyes beneath his throbbing fontanel.

A Book of Verse

A CARLOAD OF them drove a hundred and fifty miles to the state university for a fraternity weekend during the spring of 1957. They were all graduating seniors at a high school in a small town near the Missouri-Kansas border. Some of them were thinking about attending State U. so they thought, what the hell, why not let themselves be beered and fed free by obliging fraternities.

They left early in the morning in order to arrive in time for the afternoon beer and barbecue party. He wore his forty-five-dollar R. H. Macy flannel suit with the pink and blue flecks he and his mother had bought for the homecoming dance in 1956.

When they arrived at the state university they were early so they killed time by driving around the campus. He spotted the campus bookstore so he said, "Hey, let's stop and check it out." There was a bit of grumbling, but they whipped into the lot and went inside. It was the usual campus bookstore of the time, with heavy emphasis on thick expensive textbooks written by professors cleaning up on sales to captive students. There was a poetry section and a section dealing with what was called then "the paperback revolution."

They stayed about a half-hour before the urge to guzzle beer tugged them outward. He purchased C. M. Bowra's *Creative Experiment,* plus *Three Ways of Thought in Ancient China* by Arthur Waley, and *Howl* by Allen Ginsberg. That's about all he could afford. Buying *Howl* was a last-minute decision. He had read an article somewhere about a court case and obscenity charges, and he had liked, when glancing at it in the store, the last lines of the William Carlos Williams introduction. And it only cost seventy-five cents so he grabbed it.

The trip visiting the fraternity was otherwise uneventful except that he threw up into the waterfall of a local fancy restaurant when he was drunk. That guaranteed him an invitation to pledge the fraternity. Puking, the symbol of the fifties.

When he got back home he read *Howl* and was stunned. Here was a young man whose family had prepared a map of life for him that included two avenues, either a) law school (like his uncle Milton), or b) to work in his father's dry-goods store. *Howl* ripped into his mind like the tornado that had uprooted the cherry tree in his backyard when he was a child. He began to cry. He rolled all over the floor of his bathroom crying. He walked down the stairs in the middle of the night to wake his parents and read it to them. His mother threatened to call the state police. His father went to work an hour early the next morning.

He could not go to school that day, but walked into the field behind his house and strode back and forth all day along a barbed-wire fence shouting and moaning the book in front of a bunch of cows. Over and over he "howled" the

269

poem, till much of it was held in his mind and he'd close his eyes and grab the book, almost tearing it, and shriek passages, stamping the ground. "God! God!" he yelled, "God!" He fell and rolled in the dirt, laughing and shouting, scaring the wet-nosed cows who ran up the hill.

When he returned to school the next day he was a changed person. "Holy holy holy holy holy holy holy," he must have chanted that word, in long continuous singsong sentences, at least four or five thousand times a day. He felt great. Every care assumed before evaporated. He read the poem to anybody who would listen to him and he got into trouble almost immediately. First it was shop class.

In shop class he had been working for almost the entire school term on a walnut spice cabinet for his mother. It was just about finished after a tortuous slow-motion construction process common to every shop class of the time. In fact, he had finished the project too quickly and was caught having to sand the cabinet for about five straight class days. Then he brought *Howl* to shop class. That day the teacher was called away for a teachers' conference so the students were left on their own, their activities observed by the class snitch.

The bell had barely ended when he began to read the poem to his shopmates, who stood for it for several minutes, staring at him; then right before his eyes they began to go about their business of sawing, soldering, sanding, and gluing. He couldn't believe it. Then they started talking loudly as he read, perhaps as a hint. Finally one of them walked over to him and said, "I don't understand what you're howling about"—and poked a bony forearm into his ribs; "Howling, get it? Yar har har!" And a bunch of shopsters joined in to elevate yar har.

He kept on reading the poem, however, and when done,

270

he walked over to his spice cabinet. He pulled a woodburning tool out of the storage shelves and woodburned a quote upon the door of the spice cabinet:

*I saw the best minds
of my Generation
destroyed by madness*

which he left on the teacher's desk.

When he arrived in shop class the next day he found a note taped to the howl cabinet from Mr. Russell the teach: "Take this with you and please go at once to the principal's office. He is expecting you."

"Johnny," the principal paused—"about this spice cabinet"—picking it up. "Now, we know the source of this quote and we feel it inappropriate for a boy of your background to dabble in such filth."

"What do you mean filth?" he replied. "There's nothing filthy about that sentence."

"Let's not kid ourselves, Johnny. What you allude to in this woodburned"—pausing for words, "woodburned stupidity is immoral and suggestive. It's the despicable ravings of a homo. And we both know the implications of that."

The boy couldn't think of anything to match his indignation. "I think it's great. It's going to change the world. There'll be something new come out of this poem. Things will never be the same."

"Nothing new will ever come to *this* town from this obscene filth, believe you me." The principal tugged at the corner of the flag on his desk.

"You just wait," the boy replied.

"Get out of here!" the principal ordered and gave him a light shove. Tears welled in the boy's eyes. "And I'm going

271

to call up your parents. We can't have you polluting our school with filth. Now get on out of here. Do not—you hear me? Look at me! Do not *ever* recite any part of this poem again on school property, do you understand?"

"I'll recite anything I want any time!"

"Get out. You are expelled from school for three days. I'll just call your mother,"—reaching for an index file.

The boy paused at the door and taunted the principal: "I saw the best minds of my generation destroyed by madness starving hysterical *naked*!!" then ran out to the parking lot and drove home in his pickup truck.

He returned to school three days later wearing what he wanted and saying what he pleased. Gone were the days of shoe polish, clean shirts, and paste-on smiles. He began to spend almost all of his time writing poetry. Things went oddly but smoothly until his senior writing class was assigned to write some poems, which were to be read aloud in class. For days he worked on a howling masterpiece. He typed various versions and gradually the poem evolved into the rageful shape he desired. It was a rather lengthy twenty-seven pages and there was a language problem. He knew he could never get away with the word *fuck* or other similar words. For a while he thought he could get away with *screw* if he, say, mumbled it during the recitation. Finally he chose the word *planked*—good old Missouri locker-room lingo.

Friday arrived and the teacher made each student walk to the head of the class to read their poems. When it was his turn he shuffled forth, stood, eyed the teacher, and began: "This poem is titled *Springtime Shriek*." Right at that moment the nervousness overcame him, and there was a twitch of his hand, and half the poem fluttered to the floor. Gray dabs of floor-dirt covered his fingers, as he reached down frantically to grab up the sheets before the teacher could help him. Then he read:

They dragged their fingers through
their skulls and sang in ambrosia

They lay in the shanks of the night
and screamed for the morn
and dawn was planked atremble on the
couch of the hill

They pulled three aces straight
before they drew the black nine
in the void of cards

They cried for food without profit
They saw in a vision the wheat pour from the
bins enough for the roar of centuries
and drank the champagne of God's eye

They screwed . . . .

"Wait a minute young man!" the teacher roared. "No one's going to read any filth in *my* classroom! I won't and never will stand for it! Now you take that nonsense with you down to the principal's office right now. Scat!"

He didn't even bother to go to the office but instead drove downtown to play pool at Ernie's Tavern. There was fifty cents riding on the game near the end, and he leaned low over the green felt, mumbling "angelheaded hipsters burning for the ancient heavenly connection to the starry dynamo in the machinery of night . . ." Clack! The ball bounced back and forth and into the pocket. He grabbed the money

273

eagerly and coaxed Sonny Marsh, who was over twenty-one, into buying a couple of beers with it. He and Sonny chugged it down and then he headed home to write.

A month later he graduated from high school. He went on a last and final drunk with his best friend, the one with whom he'd bunked at scout camp, the one he learned how to get drunk with, sneaking over the Kansas state line to purchase 3.2 beer, the one with whom he had driven countless circles around the county courthouse with a six-pack, gossip, and rock-and-roll on the radio. His friend and he got really loaded and then said goodbye. "I'm going to New York to become a poet."

And his friend replied, "Don't do anything I wouldn't do."

PS
3569
A49
T3

Sanders, Ed.
        Tales of beatnik glory.

PS3569 A49 T3
  +Tales of beatnik+Sanders, Ed.

0 00 02 0210467 5
MIDDLEBURY COLLEGE